In Pieces

A FORBIDDEN, DOCTOR PATIENT ROMANCE

CLEO WHITE

Cover Art by Sonny Zuckerman, Dextrose.png

Cover Typography by Sarah, Sarah Anne Author Marketing

Edited by Stacey, Stacey's Bookcorner Editing Services

 Formatted with Vellum

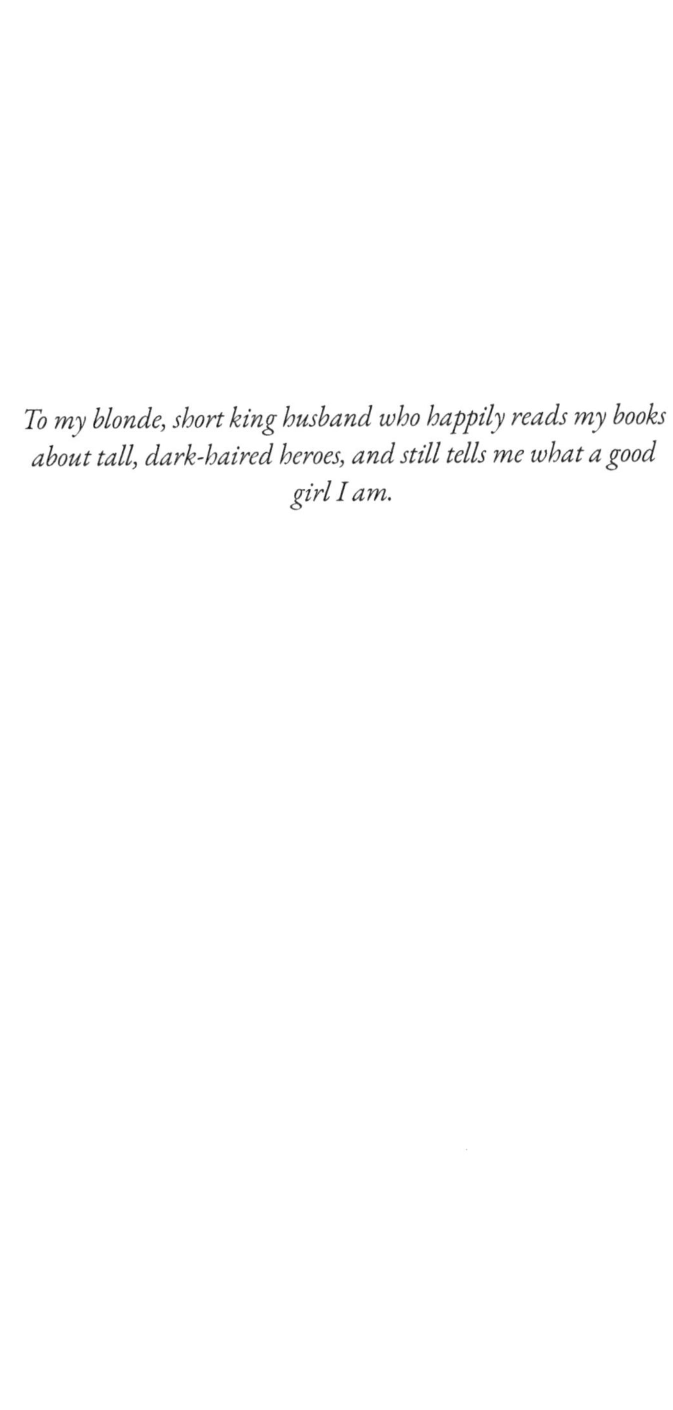

To my blonde, short king husband who happily reads my books about tall, dark-haired heroes, and still tells me what a good girl I am.

Authors Note

Warning:

This book contains mentions of prescription drug abuse, abuse of a child by a parent, manipulation by a parent, impact play, restraints, consensual BDSM scenes and might not be suitable to all readers. Please read with care.

3 YEARS AGO

"You're sure he said, Delta Jacobs? *That* Delta Jacobs?"

My receptionist, Courtney, glowers in response. I should probably be offended. I *am* her boss and a certain level of respect is generally called upon when interacting with the person who signs your paychecks. That being said, I can hardly blame her. It's the third time today that I've confirmed that the VIP consult coming in any minute is who I think she is.

It's not exactly a common name, but still—

"I don't have any information for you that I didn't tell you two hours ago, *the last time you asked.*" Done with me, Courtney turns her office chair to face the waiting room. The *empty* waiting room.

I wish I could say that it's been an abnormally light day, but in the months since I set up this practice with my friends from residency, Jenna and Caleb, business has been slow. At best. Most of our patients are overflow from the larger offices in the area, and while we're not completely financially fucked *yet*, business could certainly be better.

At the very least, it would be nice to cut myself a paycheck and move out of my brother's spare bedroom in the next decade. Believe it or not, there are only so many times a grown man with a supposedly high-powered job can tolerate being woken up in the middle of the night to the sounds of his younger sibling having sex through a wall before he loses his mind.

It was probably naïve, but going into this, I thought being an excellent surgeon was *enough*. After working my ass off through four years of medical school and five years of residency, I was offered a position at the largest hospital in my hometown of Denver. I built a reputation for myself in the three years I worked there, all while saving enough to afford my share of starting this practice.

We finally made the leap earlier this year, and things have yet to look up.

A high-profile patient would help.

I'm about to turn back toward my office when movement catches my eye and Courtney and I both freeze, craning our necks to see through the waiting room window as a black SUV enters the parking lot, circles once, and parks.

"Holy shit, is that them?" Caleb asks, appearing at the office door. We watch in silence as the driver's door opens, and a man steps out, looking around appraisingly. He's tall and blonde, with a short beard and eyes that seem intensely focused even from a distance. We've never met, but I'd know who he was even if I wasn't expecting him here tonight.

River Jacobs.

The passenger door opens as well, and a teenager hops out, pulling a bright pink hat low over her ears.

Delta Jacobs.

I back out of the office, swallowing the sudden tightness in my throat, and it's disconcerting to realize that I'm fucking *nervous*. I don't get nervous. Born into a family of big personalities and loud feelings, I've always been the odd man out. It was never difficult for me to set aside my shit and focus on the task at hand. I've been called cold, detached, a robot. Today, though... it's bizarre and completely illogical, but I'm more anxious than I have been at any other point in my career.

Then again, it's not every day that you meet two members of an Olympic dynasty.

River Jacobs is one of the founding fathers of snowboarding. He won about a dozen Olympic medals and countless international championships before retiring, marrying a famously beautiful bikini model, and having three kids who were probably flying down mountains before they could walk. Delta, the youngest, appears to be the only one who inherited her father's raw, natural talent. At only seventeen, she's fresh off her first Olympic games, bringing home a gold and two bronze medals for Team USA.

Last night in the grocery store, I almost bumped into a life-sized cardboard cutout of her holding a box of cereal in one hand and a snowboard in the other, grinning toothily from beneath a red, white, and blue knit hat. Delta is young, beautiful, a second-generation gold medalist, and one of the most gifted athletes of her generation. To say the media is obsessed with her would be the understatement of the century, and she's about to be my patient.

Maybe.

I linger in my office, drumming my fingers on the edge of my desk and straining to hear through the crack in the door. Our nurse's voice floats back to me, smoothly telling the Jacobs's that Doctor Harrison cleared his schedule and made sure the clinic was empty for their privacy.

He's getting a raise if this amounts to anything.

Though I obviously want to address her medical concerns,

today isn't really about Delta, it's about River. He isn't just a former Olympian and the father of another. He's also the head coach and owner of one of the top professional snowboarding clubs in the world. He and his team bring in talented kids from all over the nation and train them at a facility just down the road. River has been behind more Olympic team members than any other coach in the country, and becoming his go-to surgeon would be one hell of an opportunity.

Breaking into the closed circle of elite athletes that populate this corner of Colorado would be a game changer for my career, my practice, my business—the bottom line is that a lot is riding on this consult and when our nurse, Matt, pokes his head into my office to tell me they're waiting for me, I take an extra second alone to steady myself.

I haven't felt so self-conscious about my lack of interpersonal skills since I was a child. I'm excellent at what I do, but the last few months have proven that surgical prowess isn't enough. River Jacobs wouldn't have sought me out if my reputation wasn't impeccable. He doesn't need a friend, he needs someone who can treat his athletes. Still, it wouldn't hurt to appear friendly...

"Hi, I'm Doctor Harrison," I mutter to the empty room, holding out a hand to thin air. Do I always sound like that? Christ, I'm losing my shit. "Hi, River. I'm Doctor Harrison."

"Hello?" I jump, looking around wildly. When Matt left, he didn't close my office door and now a young woman is standing in the hall just outside, lips pressed together to stop herself from laughing, wide eyes glinting with amusement.

Delta Jacobs.

In person, she looks like any other seventeen-year-old girl. Dressed in jeans and an oversized, faded t-shirt, her hair is arranged in two long braids, and freckles are scattered over her golden brown skin. She's petite, probably barely clearing my chin, and there's nothing about her which suggests she's currently the best female snowboarder in the world.

"Uh—" I make a choking noise, taken aback.

The corners of her lips twitch. "I'm sorry to bother you. I was just looking for the bathroom. Your nurse said it was down here."

"Two doors down." I stand, edging past her into the hallway to point it out. Delta doesn't move, though. She's staring at me appraisingly, through eyes I can now see are an unusual shade of gray. There's something unsettling about the intensity of her gaze, as though she's seeing a lot more than I want her to. I clear my throat. "Well…"

"Don't kiss his ass." I still, shocked to silence as Delta blinks up at me. "My dad? He likes to pretend he's above the yes-men, so if you make a big deal over flattering him or me, it'll be game over. He was already rolling his eyes over what your nurse said about you canceling all your other appointments for us. He doesn't like too much pushback, though. So if he says something too off the wall, circle back to it later once he's had the chance to win a few points. He's heard you're no bullshit. He appreciates that."

She's giving me tips on how to deal with her father? On how to get her as a patient? "Why are you telling me all this?"

Delta shrugs and leans against the door frame, a lazy smile playing on her full lips. "I guess I like you."

"You don't know me. I might be an asshole," I point out, utterly bemused. I said all of three words to her before she gave me the inside scoop on River, and I *have* been described as a controlling dick on more than one occasion. Being *likable* isn't a priority for me, and I've never put much energy into it. In fact, I'm pretty sure Delta Jacobs is the first person in my entire life to so easily declare she *likes me*.

She cocks her head and the little smirk she's been wearing

blooms into a full smile. I don't understand why I feel almost defensive at the sight of it. "*Are you* an asshole?"

Sometimes. "Um—"

"Take it or leave it, Doc. I'm just trying to help. Plus, your office is right across the street from this place that makes the most *incredible* garlic bread. It'll change your life. Or *take* your life, considering there's a frankly unnecessary amount of bacon on it. Okay, I'm lying, all the bacon is necessary."

"Over there?" I nod distractedly toward the strip mall across the street. Because of a soul-sucking number of hours spent staring out the window the past few months, I know for a fact there is not an Italian restaurant in that plaza.

"Yup." She pushes off the door frame and moves past me to the bathroom. "Tell the ladies at the Chinese food restaurant that Delta sent you. They'll know what to do." She vanishes through the door with one last sly smile, and I'm so flustered by the whole interaction that I duck back into my office and close the door.

I don't know what to make of her.

In the days before this appointment, I'd gone down an internet wormhole, trying to pull together any scraps of information I could on River or Delta that might help me. I watched her gold medal run, the post-game interviews, and almost every significant event she competed in the last few years. The Delta Jacobs I saw on TV came off as hyper, bold, and more than a little cocky.

I was expecting a spoiled, snowboarding princess with a superiority complex.

I wasn't prepared for cheeky and kind.

Once I'm sure Delta has finished in the bathroom and safely returned to the exam room, I glance one more time at the notes my partners and I worked out for the consultation and throw them in the trash. They're riddled with not-so-subtle comments designed to flatter River's ego and googled snowboarding slang as if I could ever in a million years pass myself off as *cool*. Delta said River appreciated the fact I'm no bullshit, so I'll give him no bullshit.

It's probably stupid to blindly accept the advice of a teenage girl who may or may not be a spoiled brat, but my instincts are rarely wrong, and right now, they're telling me to trust Delta Jacobs.

Chapter One

DELTA

"**G**ood morning viewers! On today's 'Somebody' segment, we're sitting down with Delta Jacobs. For all our Winter Olympic fans, you'll remember Delta led the US women's snowboarding team to victory three years ago, at only seventeen years old. She is also the daughter of the legendary 'godfather' of snowboarding, River Jacobs. Delta, thank you for joining us! Tell me, with Olympic qualifiers about to begin for next year's games, how—"

"Turn that off!" I snatch the remote from Lake's hand and jab it at the TV just as the camera cuts to my smiling face. We're in the club lounge. It's early but anyone could walk in, and getting caught watching myself on the news isn't exactly the look I'm going for.

My brother just laughs and kicks his feet up on the coffee table. "I'm being supportive, DJ. I'll watch it later and send you the most unflattering screenshots. Don't worry."

I wasn't worried. If there's one thing in my life that can always be counted on, it's my brothers mercilessly teasing me at every possible opportunity. You'd think that as professional athletes, once—disturbingly—described as "hot enough to melt snow" by a popular teen gossip magazine, they would have better things to occupy their time with than tormenting me. Unfortunately, they've spent decades getting their daily dose of dopamine from making me wish I was an only child, and I doubt it will stop until I've died or killed them both.

"I'm blocking your number, don't bother," I bite back, chucking the remote at his head.

Regrettably, he catches it and tosses it to the cushion beside him with a leisurely stretch. "I don't know why you're so touchy about press shit."

"Because I hate it." Obviously. Media stuff has always been draining for me, but lately, it's felt so much worse. People like to put you into boxes they're comfortable with, and it's exhausting trying to mold myself into the Delta Jacobs that tests well with focus groups.

Lake rolls to his feet, stretching. He looks as exhausted as I feel, and we're only a few weeks into winter training. With the first Olympic qualifying event only a month out, everyone in Dad's club has been going hard. Unfortunately for Lake, Bay, and me, teammates with the last name Jacobs are blessed with private sessions with the head coach every morning.

Even people who've never picked up a snowboard in their life have heard of, and probably adore, my father. My ability to be "on" for the camera is nothing compared to his, and even if I spent all day, every day on this mountain trying to match his level of talent, it would never happen. Dad wasn't just a legendary snowboarder, he invented most of the tricks we practice every day and was part of the country's first-ever Olympic snowboarding team.

A deep, annoyed voice comes suddenly from behind us, making Lake and I jump. "Where's your brother?" We turn to face Dad, who is standing in the doorway frowning like it's our fault Bay is late. Again.

"No idea." Lake yawns, shuffling over toward the coffee machine. "He left when I did. We wanted to see DJ's interview."

Dad's mood shifts instantly. There's nothing he takes more seriously than training, but personal branding is a close second. Professional athletes only get a short window of time to compete, and sponsors don't want to invest in someone who doesn't show up and smile pretty for the camera.

"I didn't realize that was coming out today." He beams at me and walks into the room to pick up the remote Lake dropped.

I wince and begin to object, "Dad—" But it's too late. My enormous face has filled all fifty-five inches of the TV, smirking confidently out at the mostly empty lounge.

"I understand you sustained a hip injury several years ago. Are you concerned about that affecting your performance this season?" asks the reporter, and I wince. Shit. He had to turn it on at this part. My non-recovery is a touchy subject with Dad. I can never talk about it without making him either defensive or defiant.

Not mentioning it unless absolutely necessary is the safest course of action.

TV Delta smiles brightly, looking exactly like the optimistic, inspiring champion everyone wants her to be. *"Not at all! I've been incredibly fortunate. I have great coaches, including my Dad, behind me and was lucky enough to get Doctor Brooks Harrison as the primary on my case—"* The screen cuts to a picture of Doctor Harrison in scrubs, standing in an empty operating room with his arms crossed, and my heart kicks into overdrive at the sight of him.

The producers were smart to feature him in the segment. The man is hot. Like, *hot hot.* All tall and broad-shouldered with hazel eyes that make you feel warm all over and a square jaw that always seems to have exactly the right amount of stubble. Even in the picture I recognize from his practice's website, his dark curls are always a little untidy, the faintest traces of gray beginning to poke through at his temples.

The messy hair and obsessively ironed scrubs combo does things to me.

It's not just the hot, older surgeon thing either. I work with and see plenty of gorgeous, accomplished men, and none of them has made me feel even the tiniest fraction of what Doctor Harrison does. Last year, I did a sponsorship photo shoot with an Olympic swimmer. *In his uniform.* He flirted with me the entire time and invited me to a party at his house that night, but I couldn't muster up even the slightest interest.

I'll never admit it to anyone, but I haven't looked at another man since I saw Doctor Harrison psyching himself up in his office for my first-ever appointment with him.

According to an embarrassing amount of internet stalking, he's thirty-eight, which is a full eighteen years older than me. That alone should be enough to put an end to my ridiculous, annoyingly persistent crush, but even after three years of pining, I still can't shake it. Every time I just about convince myself I need to give it up, all the man has to do is laugh, or smile, or breathe, and I'm back to counting down the days until my next appointment.

My whole life is about snowboarding. I don't know how to do or be anything else, but with Doctor Harrison... he's my friend. My only friend, if I'm being honest with myself. Our relationship isn't contingent on how high I ranked at the last invitational or how hard I worked at practice. He couldn't give a damn whether I'm on the next Olympic team or if I never set foot on a mountain again. He just wants me to be happy.

How am I supposed to *not* catch feelings for someone who treats me like that?

I'm not an idiot. I know it's not going to happen. There will never be a day when Doctor Harrison walks into my exam room, sees my face, and falls madly in love with me. I might have been homeschooled, but I've watched enough dramatic teen tv to know how it works: he's the hot, smart senior and I'm the dumb jock freshman who once cried during an algebra test—true story.

Saying the man is out of my league would be the understatement of the century.

If it *did* happen though...

"Delta?" I realize I've been staring at the floor for far too long, and when I look up, both Dad and Lake are frowning at me.

"Sorry." I move around them to the table with fresh fruit and drinks on it and busy myself with selecting the least bruised banana from the bowl. The TV is still on in the background, blaring my bright, fake PR voice, talking about how lucky I am to have made such a great recovery.

It's bullshit, of course. All the medical talent and hotness in the world couldn't fix my hip.

Doctor Harrison has operated on me twice, clearing out scar tissue, and I get injections every six weeks to reduce inflammation. None of that's a cure though, and while I'm working through it for now, it's only a matter of time before it gets so bad I need a replacement.

Outside my family and medical team, nobody knows I'm having issues. The world of elite snowboarding is small, and rumors catch like wildfire. If even one person sees me limping or rubbing my hip, every competitor in the country would know within hours. The Olympic selection committee would put a big black X over my name, my sponsors would pull out, and it would be the end of my career.

Showing weakness isn't an option.

At the thought, I bite my lip, only half listening to the

interview still playing in the background. The start of winter training has been brutal, and I've been looking forward to today's appointment with Doctor Harrison for reasons other than the way his scrubs fit his butt—though that's *for sure* the pick-me-up I need right now. Just pulling myself out of bed this morning was terrible, and my stomach twists at the memory of how much pain I was in by the end of the day yesterday.

"I should see if Doctor Harrison can get me in earlier today, Dad," I tell him quietly, glancing over my shoulder to make sure no one else is arriving early. "Something's up with my hip. It's been hurting a lot more than usual."

Dad looks over at me, his expression tight. "Where are you at? From one to ten."

It's his standard question when we complain about pain, but I pause, my insides knotting. "Right this second? Like a three, but when I'm training—"

He turns off the TV before looking back at me, and the tired, exasperated look on his face makes me feel about a foot tall. "You have an injury, DJ. It's going to hurt sometimes. Do you want to pack it all in over a bit of pain? Is that what you think builds a winner?"

Shame wells inside me, and I shake my head. "You're right. I'll be fine. Sorry, Dad."

I'm standing here, talking to the man who competed *and medaled* at his last three Olympic games with a stress fracture in his ankle, complaining about some discomfort. Seriously?

To River Jacobs, pain only has as much power as you give it. He's a certified badass, and I don't know why I can't be like that. Why can't I push through this? I work so hard, do my very best every single day, and yet I can't seem to silence the ugly voice in the back of my mind, whispering that I'm never going to be good enough.

A voice that gets a little louder every time Dad gets that tired, exasperated look when I let slip just how weak I am.

I can tell he has more to say on the subject, but I'm saved by the arrival of Bay, who trumps into the room with his gym bag slung over his shoulder, mumbling something about a flat tire. Dad, Lake, and I watch as he pushes past us to get to the sink, pretending to be oblivious to the annoyance rolling off Dad in waves.

"Third time this week, Bay."

"Is it?" My eldest brother asks mildly, filling his bottle with water from the tap. Of the three of us, it's becoming pretty clear Bay is the least dedicated to this season. To be in the running for the Olympic team at all, you need to place among the top 30 in an international competition. I have a 2nd place medal under my belt, Lake's best performance was 10th, but Bay barely squeaked by, coming in 28th on a judging technicality.

He's twenty-seven now. Even if nobody says it out loud, his career is over.

As if all this wasn't bad enough for Bay, our father woke up today and chose violence. "Head to the gym. I'll text Tony to meet you early," he orders coldly. "You can join us on the mountain when you've done a full round."

I wince, but keep my mouth shut to avoid suffering the same fate. We had conditioning yesterday, and it says a lot that I would rather spend all day training on a hip that feels like it's stuffed with shards of glass than do one more burpee. If Bay is annoyed, he doesn't show it, just screws the top back on his water bottle and walks out without another word.

Dad watches him go, his expression unreadable. "I think he's going through some stuff," I offer quietly, my throat tightening with pain for Bay. Neither Lake nor I ever loved snowboarding like he does. We've never gotten that feverish, obsessive glint in our eyes when we talk about it or miss it on our days off. Our eldest brother is more innovative than we are, pushes boundaries harder, and does it all with a smile.

It seems like a cruel twist of fate that he was never quite good enough to make the Olympic team. He deserves it more than I do. He wants it more than Lake. Yet he didn't get the chance to stand on that podium and know he's the best in the world. If Bay's ever resented me for it, he never said, but sometimes I see the pain in his eyes when talk turns to the games.

"We're all going through stuff, DJ," Dad replies after a long moment, his voice gruff. "I don't see either of you slacking off when shit gets hard. That's not who I raised you to be. If Bay is ready to walk away, I won't stop him, but he's not going to stomp around here like a toddler, pouting that he didn't get his way. If he's here, he's working." He jerks his chin toward the hall, "Let's head out."

Lake and I follow Dad through the building, lost in our thoughts. None of us speak as we retrieve our gear from the rack by the door and step out into the frosty morning air. The mountain we train at, Blue Pike, has one side dedicated to recreational skiers and snowboarders, with a lodge, spa, and luxury hotel. The other side, where I've spent all the better part of my life, is set up for professional ski and snowboard training.

There are multiple clubs that rent space here, Dad's among them, and it's one of the best facilities in the country. I'm lucky to be here, but it's very *public*. Nearly every single person who trains at Blue Pike has ranked internationally. While I'm here, I'm DJ, Olympian, and daughter of River. There's no room for doubt, fear, or pain.

This entire mountain is littered with competition, coaches of competition, reporters, recruiters, sponsors, and sports photographers. Even now, with the sky pink, and formal training not beginning for another two hours, there are still a few members of the ski team by the chair lift and three guys from our junior club are just finishing a run.

"Morning Jacobs fam," Marty, the chairlift operator, calls merrily as we approach. "DJ, should I put money on you for the XT Games? My kid needs new skis."

My hip throbs, shooting white-hot pain up my spine, but I'm careful to keep my expression neutral as I call back to him, "Put your money on Lake! He's going to crush it."

Marty chuckles and salutes us as we line up and let the chair lift sweep us away from the ground.

"You're wincing when you walk," Dad mutters darkly, glancing over his shoulder as if he's worried Marty is gossiping about us to the next group getting on the lift. "Do you need to go home for the day?" His tone makes it clear this isn't so much an offer as a threat.

Yes. I need to go home.

I busy myself with wiping a smear from the lenses of my goggles to avoid looking at him as I reply, "No. I'm sorry. I just didn't sleep well."

Mostly because my hip made it impossible to get comfortable and the nightmares of being buried alive in snow weren't exactly restful. I woke up drenched in sweat and it took ages to calm down enough to sleep again. Just like pretty much every other night since winter training started back up.

Dad stares straight forward, his jaw tight, and I know what he's thinking. After all the resources and time dedicated to making me one of the best snowboarders in the world, am I going to let one stupid joint end my career? Injuries aren't uncommon in this sport. Half the members of Dad's club have had to take time off or see Doctor Harrison at some point or another, but they're still here, fighting to be the best.

What does it say about me that I spend most of my days fantasizing about how great it would be to go home and nap?

When we slide off the lift, I fall back, pretending to adjust my bindings while Dad and Lake head off toward the halfpipe. I wait until they're out of sight before swinging my backpack over my shoulder and pulling out my water and a bottle of prescription painkillers. They're leftovers from when I got my wisdom teeth out over the summer. There are only about ten left, but desperate times call for desperate measures.

Casting a look around to make sure I'm not being watched, I swallow a single pill and tuck the rest into my bag.

It's obviously against the rules, and I'd probably end up with a lifetime ban from competing if I had a positive drug test, but we're only ever checked before competitions. I'm not doing anything wrong. Your body takes a beating when you're training this intensely, especially with an existing injury. Sometimes you just need to make it through the day by whatever means necessary.

Doctor Harrison's injection tonight will help. It always does.

I won't need to do this again.

The phone hasn't stopped ringing all day.

My schedule, which was jam-packed already, is now pushed out six months for a simple consult. We're getting calls from athletes all over the world, all of them determined to be treated by me. I should be over the moon. This was my dream after all, but all I feel is guilty.

When Delta Jacobs first walked through the doors of Mountain View Orthopedic Surgery, it was only me, my two partners, and a few support staff. Now, on top of myself, Caleb, and Jenna, we employ three more surgeons, four physician assistants, twelve nurses, seven techs, and six admins. The practice grew so quickly that we had to take over the insurance office next door just to make more room, and we're looking at purchasing a larger property across the city to accommodate in-house physical therapy.

My name being mentioned on a national morning show won't just take us to the next level, it *is* the next level, and Delta did that for me without asking for a single thing in return.

As if I didn't feel like enough of a piece of shit to begin with.

I was never the type of physician to get emotionally invested in my patients. I give them the best care I can, advice on how to avoid further injury and send them on their way. Some of them listen, some of them don't, but it's *not on me*. I have a thriving practice and a handful of awards that say I'm an excellent surgeon *without* getting involved.

Delta Jacobs is the exception.

I didn't know it, but she had me from the very first time we met. Walking into that appointment, all I cared about was leveraging River's influence in the snowboarding community to save my business. Walking out, all I cared about was protecting Delta. We spent all of an hour together that day, but that's all it took. I couldn't help caring about her.

On the surface, she seems so strong, so capable, but I don't understand how I could be the only one to notice the cracks in that shiny, Olympian surface. She's struggling, and even after three years, I still can't tell how much of her perseverance is born from a love of the sport that dominates her life, and how much is a fear of disappointing River.

One look at her medical records is enough to see she was probably strapped onto a snowboard before she could walk. Broken wrists, concussions, dislocations, fractures, sprains, torn ligaments, the list goes on and on. Protective services would have taken her away from that family if she was any other child, but Delta *wasn't* just any child.

She was exceptional. A champion.

Nobody calls it abuse if the victim ends up on a podium and gets a gold medal for their suffering.

I felt protective of her. I wanted to see her happy and safe, and that was it... until it wasn't.

A few months ago I walked into that exam room, expecting to see a teenage girl, and the world as I knew it shifted beneath my feet. Delta wasn't a girl anymore, she was a woman, and all those things I've always loved about her were still there. I was struck by the same fierce, protective instincts she'd always brought out in me. Except now, I was feeling other things, too. Possessive things.

It hit me so hard and suddenly, I never had a hope of resisting, because this was so much more than ordinary physical attraction. I wanted her more than I knew it was possible to want another person. The kind of want that eclipses every other desire in your life. Obsession.

I stumbled my way through that appointment, avoiding looking at her and scrambling to think of any other cause for my raging erection other than the glimpse of her bare thigh beneath the paper drape. All the while, Delta sat smiling at me, talking about her life and asking about mine. She was normal and I—I'd become unhinged.

I still am.

I can pretend all day, every day, that it isn't happening. I can shove down my feelings for her until I can just about get through a single minute without thinking about her... it doesn't make a difference. Hours later, when I'm laying alone in bed, I can't deny it anymore.

In my fantasies, she doesn't just want the same twisted, depraved things I do. She begs for it.

It's her face I see, caught between pain and pleasure as I drive into her too hard.

It's her voice I hear crying my name.

It's her body I want to break and worship in equal measure.

The shit I've thought of doing to her—*to Delta*. Delta who trusts me and sees me as a friend. Delta who always gives but never takes... *Christ*. I'm going to hell.

I used to look forward to our appointments. Now, I'm desperate for them. Just seeing her on TV this morning was a shock to the system, and I've been pacing the office all day, snapping at everyone as I descend further into turmoil.

If I had a shred of integrity left, I would have sent her off to another doctor the moment I started having these feelings. There are days when I can just about convince myself to make the call, but even after months of this, I still haven't done it. Instead, I greedily hoard our moments together, finding any reason to draw them out, as if hanging out in a doctor's office is what she wants to do in her free time.

Self-control is a distant memory.

Even now, as the final hours before her appointment slip by, I can't pretend I'm not crawling out of my skin with the desire to be in the same room as her. She's thankfully the last patient on my schedule, and I spend the minutes before she arrives pacing my office and avoiding everyone. Finally, when the staff parking lot begins to empty outside my window, there's a quiet knock and the object of my obsession slips inside.

My chest feels like it's breaking open and being pulled back together all at once at the sight of her.

I missed her so much.

"Hey, Doc," Delta chirps, smiling at me as she moves around my desk to take her usual chair without invitation. She's wearing an oversized t-shirt and leggings, with chunky hiking boots laced up on her feet. Ordinary, casual, and she's still so beautiful I can barely breathe. I open my mouth and just as quickly, close it. I don't trust myself to speak right now.

It's always like this when I see her for the first time in a few weeks, as though I need to relearn how to function like a normal, stable human being in her presence. Today, the lust-drunk animal inside me is kept at bay only by how fucking exhausted she looks. Her face is thinner, bags color the skin beneath her eyes and she's too pale for someone who spends all day outside.

I swallow, willing myself to focus and not start demanding answers from her. "How are you? How's winter training going?"

"Good, busy." She leans back in the chair, picking at a hole in her t-shirt. "I hope I didn't overstep with the interview. By mentioning you, I mean. My agent didn't get the questions until the morning of."

Although the TV segment has been on my mind all day, I'm still so thrown off that it takes me a minute to remember what she's talking about. "Oh. That." My fingers drum mindlessly on the edge of the desk as I try to reorder my thoughts. "No, Delta. It's fine."

Her face falls. "I should have checked with you first, shouldn't I? I swear I tried to call the office the morning of the interview, but Courtney said you were in surgery and—"

"Delta." I hold up a hand to stop her rambling and attempt a grateful smile. "It's great. I'm sorry, it's been a long day."

She bites her lip, and it's all I can do to keep myself from groaning. Christ, if she could get through thirty seconds without making me hard as a rock, this would be a lot easier. "I overstepped, didn't I? I swear I was just trying to help. You've done so much for me and I wanted to return the favor, I guess."

I haven't done so much for her, though, not really. Delta's hip isn't a complicated case, and I treated her like any other patient who came in with the same diagnosis, albeit aggressively. I bought her a few extra years, but I can't save her career.

Meanwhile, if it weren't for Delta and her father, I'd probably have taken a job at the hospital or would still live in my brother's spare bedroom. My practice certainly wouldn't be the size it is today, and I highly doubt I'd have a six-month waiting list of elite athletes, all convinced I'm the man to fix the damage they've done to their bodies.

She's helped far more than I deserve, and all I can do is stab her in the hip with a needle and fantasize about fucking her.

"You didn't overstep," I offer a tight, reassuring smile. "Come on, let's get you that injection. We'll catch up while you ice it."

Delta trails after me as I lead the way into the hall and open the door to her usual exam room. Leaving her to get undressed, I go to grab the supplies I need, moving on autopilot as I try to steady myself in the few moments away from her. It's pointless. I know what's coming, and I have to wonder how long I'll be able to keep doing this when it would probably be less painful for me to put this needle in my own eye.

I fucking hate it, and her refusal to show she's in pain somehow makes the whole thing so much worse.

Delta is already perched on the edge of the table when I return, stormy eyes tracking the plastic-wrapped syringe in my hand as I close the door behind me.

"So, eat anything disgusting this week? Or has it all been kale salads and kombucha?" she asks a bit too casually, the paper beneath her crinkling a little as I fold back the sheet to examine her hip. There are yellowing bruises over most of her golden brown skin and a collection of small, slightly raised surgical scars I've imagined kissing a thousand times.

It's perverse, but the territorial, possessive monster she's reduced me to is satisfied I've left my mark on her body.

I tap the side of her thigh and Delta bends her leg automatically, allowing me to manipulate the joint while trying not to notice the cute-as-fuck hot pink, lace-trimmed panties she's wearing. "I had dinner with my brother last night. You'd like him. He ordered us bacon cheeseburgers with melted cheddar poured over them before I arrived. You?"

"Nope," Delta sighs, looking put upon. "Dad's got me on

this new high-protein diet, so I've been mostly good. Though I'll shamelessly exploit your legal obligation to keep my secrets and admit that I did sneak about six peanut butter brownies today. Somebody brought them in for a birthday and left them unattended in the locker room. I don't count the calories because they were shitty."

Pressing my lips into a flat line to stop myself from laughing out loud, I carefully keep my eyes trained on the small area of skin I have reason to be looking at. As opposed to the panties riding up her hip. "You ate someone's birthday brownies? Also, I feel qualified to inform you that caloric intake isn't dependent on your level of enjoyment."

"Shhh," Delta hisses conspiratorially and when I look up to meet her sparkling eyes, my breath catches. "You fold the corners of your book pages, which *at least* shows extremely questionable judgment. Let me have this, Doc."

My pulse skips.

I like her so much.

"Come on, would it kill you to use a folded-up receipt or a napkin or something? You're usually so civilized."

I choke out a laugh as my hands fall from her hip. She has no fucking clue how uncivilized she makes me. "I'll try."

Delta props herself up on her elbows and watches silently as I cross to the little metal tray table, my head spinning. I need to keep my shit together. I'm about to insert a hypodermic needle into her joint, for fuck's sake. We both need me to be focused on the medicine.

"Are you in more pain lately?" I ask, and I'm relieved to hear my voice is once again cool and professional.

"Some," Delta admits, her tone deceptively mild, and I glance over my shoulder at her, distracted. God damn it, why can't she just give me a straight answer?

"What does that mean, some?"

She wrinkles her nose. "I'm snowboarding four days a week and in the gym for two. Pain is normal, Doc."

Some pain is normal for athletes training at her level, but I have three years of experience in how terribly slanted Delta's pain scale is. River's brand of parenting seems to be more geared toward creating champions at any cost and less about raising well adjusted, healthy human beings. God only knows how old Delta and her brothers were when their father first taught them that showing pain is a sign of weakness. The only way I'm getting an accurate picture of her condition is if I see it for myself.

"We should do some scans..." I offer with no real hope she'll agree. Sure enough, I haven't even finished suggesting it before she's rolling her eyes.

"Is that going to tell you anything you don't already know? I'm listening to my trainers and therapists. When the Olympics are over, I promise you can cut me open and give me a bionic hip."

Yeah, she listens to the trainers and therapists whom *River* employs. I don't work for Delta's father directly, but after three years of treating his athletes, I've learned he rarely fails to get what he wants. The man is an ambitious, competitive animal willing to chew off his own leg to reach the finish line first. Would one of his staff stick their neck out to argue with him? Doubtful. Especially if Delta is feeding them the same crap she tries to tell me.

Her last surgeries were years ago now, long before I started feeling the way I do about her, and they were minimally invasive. A total hip replacement is different, it's brutal, and if I'm having this much trouble just giving her an injection of anti-inflammatories, there's no way in hell I'll be able to put a scalpel to her skin again. The thought alone makes me nauseous, and I'm not selfish enough to put Delta's long-term health at risk for the sake of my ego.

I don't bother correcting her. God knows she won't let me do the surgery anytime soon, anyway.

We're both quiet as I open the supplies and pull on my gloves, dread pooling heavily in my stomach. Delta is always so fucking stoic about this, so when I turn around to see the worried crease in her brow and the way her hands are twisting the hem of her t-shirt, it's like someone has dumped ice down my back.

"Hey." I hate how she instantly relaxes her expression when she realized I've seen, playing the part of brave for my sake.

I have no interest in the Delta Jacobs that River has polished for public consumption.

"I'm okay, Doc." She smiles bravely, and her voice is an octave too high. She's *not* fine, she's petrified, and who could blame her? We've done this so many times. She knows exactly how much it hurts. Has she been this scared every time, and I somehow failed to notice?

"Delta—"

"Can we please just do it?"

I want to argue with her, but it's not my fucking place. This course of treatment was my recommendation. Corticosteroids are standard for people with Delta's condition and really her only option if she wants to keep competing. It's the last line of defense before a total hip replacement.

My feelings for her are the only problem here.

My feelings and the fact that she's never given me a full, honest answer when we've talked about her pain.

Pulling on my gloves, 1 roll the metal procedure table to her side. Delta is lying back, her eyes locked on the ceiling, her chest rising and falling in determinately slow, measured breaths. On the surface, this seems like every other time I've done this to her, but it isn't. Something is going on, and I want to know what the fuck it is.

"Look at me." The words are out of my mouth before I can think to stop them. It's an order and my whole body floods with heat when she obeys it without pause. How many times have I thought about how good it would feel to boss this woman around?

This isn't a fantasy, though. It's a nightmare.

The moment her eyes meet mine, that stoic facade cracks. As I watch, a single tear runs over her cheek, and she makes no effort to hide it. The room is so quiet I hear the soft tap of it hitting the paper. I act without thinking. Ripping the glove off my left hand, I reach out, twining my fingers through hers together atop her warm stomach. It's not enough. I need to fix this, but all I can do is look on helplessly as her tears turn to sobs and her breaths come in gasping, greedy gulps.

It's agonizing to see her cry, but exhilarating too, because *this is real.*

Her tears are mine, her pain is mine, her honesty is mine. Only mine.

"That's it, let it out." My thumb draws back and forth over hers as my other hand reaches behind me, taking the antiseptic wipe off the procedure table and gently wiping it over the familiar patch of skin where I'm going to inject the drug. "Good girl."

Delta whimpers, gazing up at me with wide, fearful eyes. "I- I-" Her voice breaks and I shush her, shaking my head. We're so close I can see the dampness of her eyelashes and a fine white line, nearly invisible, just beneath her full bottom lip.

"How did you get that?" I ask, depositing the wipe on the corner of the tray without looking away. "The scar below your lip."

My fingers find the syringe.

She laughs breathlessly, tears still shining in her eyes. "It's my only non-snowboarding-related injury. I was five, my brothers used me to test the laundry basket elevator system to their treehouse. It didn't perform as well as they expected. Dad made them do whatever I wanted for weeks. I loved it."

Imagining a small, gap-toothed Delta bossing around her big brothers makes me grin too. "How many stitches?"

"Twelve."

"Holy shit." I pop the cap off of the hypodermic needle.

"I know, right?" Her eyes dart down, widening, "Oh—"

I wait to turn away until the very last second, and it's fast. She barely has time to squeak in surprise before I'm pushing the syringe's plunger forward, injecting anti-inflammatories and steroids directly into her joint, and pulling it back.

"Very good," I mutter, capping the needle and returning my hand to her hip to press a pad of gauze to the injection site. It's a miracle I keep my hands from shaking as adrenaline floods my body. I thought doing this was near-impossible when she was careful not to show pain or fear. Knowing how scared she is makes this so much worse.

Delta's eyes are squeezed shut, tears leaking down her cheeks all over again as I massage her poor hip. *Fuck.*

"Do you want me to get ice?" I need to do something damn it, but as I start to move away, Delta's hand closes around my wrist.

"Don't—" She shakes her head, taking a long, shaky breath, but still doesn't open her eyes.

My throat constricts and I carefully weave our fingers together again, giving her hand a reassuring squeeze. "I'm not going anywhere." Reaching into the pocket of my white coat with my free hand, I pull out a pen and a business card. Setting it on the edge of the table, I scrawl my number across the back.

I can't rationalize why I'm doing this. It's unprofessional. I've never offered my personal contact information to a patient before. Hell, even my partners email me unless it's an emergency. The only people who call or text me are my family. Yet, for what is quite possibly the first time in my life, the absence of a logical explanation for my behavior doesn't stop me.

She doesn't need to use it, but I can't stomach her wanting me, needing me, and having to get through my fucking phone answering system and receptionist, then waiting hours for an appointment.

"Here." Pressing it into her other hand, my heart flips at the sweet, surprised looks she gets when she realizes what I've written on the card. "If you need me. Even if it's just to talk. Use it, okay?" I plead, wishing I could excuse wiping those last few tears from her cheeks, too.

Delta nods, squeezing my hand a little tighter. "If you want me to."

My answering nod comes without hesitation. "I do."

I want her to do a lot more with that number, but calling me if she needs me is enough. It has to be.

Chapter Three

DELTA

octor Harrison gave me his phone number.

His *personal* phone number is on my phone. Right now.

He probably gives it out to a lot of patients, especially the pain-in-the-ass ones who sneak too much junk food and cry on his exam table because they're scared of getting a shot.

Okay, so it's a *big* shot, but still. Not my proudest moment.

The thing is, my appointment was over a week ago. I've played the whole thing over so many times in my head, and I keep coming to the same conclusion... Doctor Harrison wanted me to cry.

He looked like I'd slapped him when he turned around and saw how scared I was, but he seemed even angrier when I tried to pretend everything was fine. When he told me to look at him, it was like I was under a spell. He was in control. I trusted him, and I just... gave in to my emotions. I've had plenty of breakdowns in the privacy of my bedroom, but I don't remember crying in front of another person since I was very young.

The moment I did, though, it was as though the weight of the world had been lifted off my shoulders.

Of course, I walked out of the office half an hour later and immediately pulled out my phone to check if the witness protection program accepts victims of self-inflicted humiliation; they don't, but I did find a very nice commune in Central America which seemed like a pretty good alternative.

The logical side of me, the one who knows Doctor Harrison isn't even slightly interested, wants to shrivel up in embarrassment whenever I think about how awkward he must have felt with me crying my eyes out on his exam table. The other part, a tiny one that seems to be growing bigger and louder since my appointment, is convinced there was *something*. As crazy as it seems, at that moment, I felt closer to him than anyone else in my whole life.

I have no idea what to do, or think, and the only thing I know for sure is that I can't just text him to send him a picture of the cinnamon rolls I made or ask if he saw that new zombie movie. We might feel like friends, but that doesn't mean we are. He's my doctor, he's paid a *lot* of money to keep me in fighting shape, and I did him a pretty big solid by getting his practice national publicity for free.

Doctor Harrison has witnessed too many of my most embarrassing moments this season alone, and I refuse to become an obligation, too. Just the mental image of him picking up his phone and sighing tiredly when he sees it's me has been enough to keep me from sending any of the dozen texts I've composed over the past week.

Of course, if I had a *reason* to get in touch with him, that would be different.

The fact the injection hasn't helped yet is definitely the kind of thing he had in mind when he told me to call him. I took the day off after my appointment, icing my hip and staring at his name in my contact list. Normally, that's enough for me to return to training as usual, but not this time. Dad gave me one of his soul-withering stares when I vaguely mentioned *maybe* needing to take a second day off, so back to the mountain I went.

Unsurprisingly, it was one of the worst weeks of my entire career. Everything I've done has been *off*. Tricks I've been doing for years are getting fucked up, falling on my ass has become a bi-hourly occurrence and I've snapped at every single person who dared point it out.

All while the supply of pain pills has dwindled.

The resolution I'd only take them to make it through until my appointment went out the window on my first day back. As if I didn't feel like enough of an imposter to begin with.

Today is my day off, though. No training, no conditioning, and a blessedly empty house since Dad flew out to California to go to some A-List party with his latest girlfriend.

Lake and Bay moved out last year, getting an apartment downtown with a few of their friends. I've only been there once, and don't plan on repeating the experience any time soon. The sight of the mixing bowl full of condoms on the kitchen counter and the leaning tower of pizza boxes on top of the trash pretty much convinced me to make the place a no-fly zone.

My family isn't exactly quiet, and having a day to bum around by myself, no bras or pants allowed, is such a relief. The first thing I did after getting up way too late was order Chinese food and garlic bread, and my only plans are to melt into the couch, ice my entire body, and watch a full season of some reality celebrity dating show.

Maybe if I can manage to get over my orthopedic surgeon before I die, I'll ask my agent if she can get me on there. I'm technically famous-ish, and having twelve super hot, successful men desperately lusting after me, declaring their undying love before commercial breaks, would do wonders for my ego.

I'm researching if you have to be able to walk in five-inch heels to be cast on Famous Love—not a skill I foresee myself developing anytime soon—when a text comes in from the woman my dad has on staff to do PR.

> Brenda (PR lady who told me to go blonde): Hey DJ, Snowboarding Life Magazine reached out about an interview for their January issue. They're doing an article on sports medicine and wanted to feature you and Doctor Harrison. River gave me the OK, but I'm checking if you'd like to speak to the doctor or should I?

My cheeks warm. It says a lot about the depth of my obsession with the man that I'm suddenly tempted to agree to extra press just for an excuse to see him. Drawing attention to my hip is probably a bad idea right now, but I've been careful. Nobody has any reason to think I haven't made a full recovery. I'm being paranoid. Dad thinks it's a good idea, and it would mean seeing Doc outside the office...

> Delta: OK, sounds good. I'll talk to Doctor Harrison and get back to you.

Biting my lip, I open Doctor Harrison's contact and carefully type and retype my message.

> Delta: Hey, it's Delta. I hope it's ok I'm texting you, do you have a minute to talk?

I expect it to take a while for him to text me back. I even toss my phone onto the couch and start picking a piece of bacon off my garlic bread, but not even a minute later, there's a gentle chime beside me and my heart leaps into my throat.

Doc: Of course it's okay. Are you alright?
I'm walking into surgery, but if it's an
emergency, I can page someone else to
take over and meet you at the office in
twenty.

My stomach erupts with butterflies. He would do that for me?

Delta: I'm totally fine. It's business stuff,
actually.

Doc: Is it that snowboarding magazine?
They emailed me this morning, as well. Can
you come by at two? I'll pick up some of
that appalling garlic bread you love and we
can talk.

I look down at the precious, foil-wrapped bundle of heart disease in my lap and giggle.

Delta: Appalling, huh? So the next time I go
in there, they'll have no idea what I'm
talking about when I ask about the tall
doctor who orders extra cheese on his?

Doc: No comment.

Delta: See you at two.

* * *

I've spent so much time at Doctor Harrison's office over the past three years that his receptionist, Courtney, just glances at me over the shoulder of the patient she's checking in and waves me through to the back hallway.

When I started coming here, the waiting room was mostly

empty, but now it's rare to see an unoccupied seat amidst the tasteful modern furniture and big, leafy plants. Word spread fast after the Olympics that I was seeing a hotshot new doctor. My first surgery made such a huge difference in my range of motion that Dad sang Doctor Harrison's praises to anyone who would listen, and now every snowboarder in the country is trying to book in with him.

I try not to be too smug about the fact he always makes time for me, even though I'm pretty sure he has way more important patients.

Doctor Harrison's door is cracked and when I knock it pushes open enough for me to see the handsome doctor leaning back in his office chair, grinning up at a tall, thin blonde woman wearing the same kind of sky-high, deadly looking heels that the women on Famous Love wear. She's leaning against his desk, laughing at something he said. They both look around as I enter, and the warmth that usually spreads through me at the sight of my surgeon suddenly feels clammy and terrible.

She's beautiful. At least six inches taller than me, and curvy in all the ways I wish I was. Her hair looks professionally colored and her nails are painted the same sophisticated, pinkish tan color as her shoes.

Is she his girlfriend?

"Oh wow, you're Delta Jacobs!" I take a few seconds to realize the unknown woman is talking to me.

"Yes." My voice sounds... *off*.

She laughs delightedly and pushes off the desk, holding out a hand. "I'm Phoebe! *So* nice to meet you. I knew you were a patient of Brooks', but I didn't think we'd ever meet."

Not Doctor Harrison. Brooks. *She calls him Brooks, and I never have.*

Behind her, Doctor Harrison is silent, and though I don't dare look at him, I can feel the weight of his eyes on me. Can he see everything I'm feeling right now? Can he tell I'm so jealous and hurt that I want to run out of here as fast as I can and never come back? He's not mine, *I know he's not mine*, but the possibility that he's someone else's is so much more excruciating than the lightning-like pains currently shooting through my hip.

Phoebe is still staring at me expectantly with her hand outstretched, and when I take it, even my well-practiced media smile doesn't come easily. "Nice to meet you."

"I'll let you two talk. I'll see you tonight for dinner, Brooks," she says cheerfully, turning back to kiss Doctor Harrison's cheek, and I have to grit my teeth to stop myself from making a horrified noise. "Good luck with your season, Delta!"

I open my mouth to say something polite, but I can't quite manage it. Seconds later, she's gone, closing the door behind her like she doesn't have a single concern about leaving her boyfriend alone with another woman. Then again, why would she? I'm not tall, blonde, and leggy, I'm short, distinctly *uncurvy* and I'll probably need a walker just to get out of bed this time next month. I don't even own a pair of heels and can usually be found wearing t-shirts and leggings beneath puffy, technicolor snowboarding gear. I'm not a temptation for her *Brooks*.

Silence.

Awkward silence.

"I, ah, got this for you." Doctor Harrison gestures to a familiar, foil-wrapped package of garlic bread at the end of his desk.

"Thanks." I don't move, though, lingering uncomfortably beside the door. I've been in this room plenty of times, have sat across from him and made him laugh so hard he snorted, shared garlic bread, and fell harder and harder for this man who may or may not have a gorgeous, perfectly nice girlfriend.

Stupid, stupid, stupid. He knows everything about me, and even the most basic facts about his life are a mystery to me. Does he have a girlfriend? Where's his house? Does he like dogs or cats? I thought we were friends, that he cared about me, but I realize with a sick swoop of shame that it's all been completely one-sided.

This was always about his business.

I clear my throat, staring determinately at the wall just over his left ear. I don't trust myself not to make a fool of myself and cry my eyes out, and I'd like to leave this room with some scraps of my dignity intact. "I talked to our PR lady on the way over here, she says the article is going to focus on complimentary sports medicine. I guess they like you working with acupuncturists and stuff—"

"Delta—" He sounds concerned, and I'm so embarrassed. He's the only person in my life who *always* seems to know when I'm pretending to be okay, but I've never resented it before this moment.

"I really shouldn't have wasted your time with this. It totally could have been an email." My laugh is breathy and forced as I back toward the door. Closing my hand over the cool metal knob, I cling to it like a lifeline. "I'm in if you are, so we'll get it set up whenever you decide. Actually, I can just give you the PR contact so you don't have to go through me."

Doctor Harrison gets to his feet when I pull the door open, his eyebrows pulling together in concern. I'm acting crazy. He can totally tell something is up. "Delta." He tries again, but I don't want to hear it. I don't know this man, not really, and this was exactly the rude awakening I needed to make sure I never, ever forget that.

"I'll see you later." Ducking out of the room, I stride back down the hallway to the lobby, the pain in my hip overshadowed by the brand-new wound that seems to have opened up in the middle of my chest. I'm terrified he's going to come after me, but why would he? I'm his patient, not his friend, and certainly not his girlfriend. He's an amazing doctor. He cares about me because it's his job, and all his patients get that from him. I'm not special.

That moment we had at my last injection only meant something to me.

I'm in the icy cold parking lot, fumbling with the keys to my Jeep when I hear it. "Delta!"

Well, *shit.*

Turning reluctantly, I see Doctor Harrison jogging over to me, foil-wrapped garlic bread in hand. He stops beside my front tire, the winter wind ruffling his hair. "Are you okay? You left in a hurry." He holds out the bread, and when I make no move to take it, his hand falls slowly back to his side.

The fact I'm gripped with guilt for rejecting his garlic bread offering says a lot about the depth of my desire to please.

"Sorry." I smile tightly, my heart hamming against my ribcage. "Long week. You know how it is."

Doctor Harrison's eyes search my face, his frown deepening. "You don't look good, Delta."

My jaw drops. What the actual fuck? Did he really just say that? "Thanks," I snap, reaching blindly for the handle to my door and yank it open a touch too hard. God, do I look that bad? *I tried, damn it.* I wore makeup and everything. Though, of course, if he's used to looking at a tall, blonde, leggy model of womanly perfection—

"I didn't mean it like that." Furiously, I try to pull my door closed but it barely budges, and I don't need to look far for the cause. Brooks is holding the top, and he looks... well, mortified actually. He clears his throat. "You're, *uh,* fine?"

I let out an incredulous laugh. "Are you *kidding* me?" I try to yank the door shut, but Doctor Harrison growls in frustration, holding it firmly open.

"Would you *stop* that?" He steps into the space between

the car and the door and braces his forearm on the roof, glowering down at me. "I didn't mean that you're unattractive. You look exhausted, Delta."

"If you get out of the way, I'll go home and nap," I snap, gripping the steering wheel tightly.

He still doesn't move. "Do you want to tell me what that was about in there?"

Yeah, I would rather do conditioning for a week than tell Doctor Harrison I'm jealous of his girlfriend. I scowl, keeping my eyes resolutely forward to avoid looking at him. "*Nothing*."

"*Nothing*?" His tone drips incredulous disbelief. "Delta, come on, you know you can talk to me."

"Do I? Do I know that?" I round on him, glaring. I'm determined to stay angry as long as I can. Angry is good, angry is *productive*, whereas sad means crying into a pint of mint chocolate chip in the same sweatpants you've been wearing for a week. "Don't do the cool, relatable doctor thing to me anymore, okay? I don't want a fake friend."

His eyes widen in disbelief. "Cool? Relatable? Is that what you think? That I'm *faking* being your friend?"

"Are you my friend, *Doctor Harrison*? You know every single thing about me, and I know nothing about you. Do *you* call your real friends by their professional title?"

"Is that what you want? To call me Brooks? Fine, call me Brooks. I don't care." He's so genuinely confused, and just like that, all the fight drains out of me.

I want to kiss him. I want to fall in love with him *for real*. I want to cook for him and take care of him and be the person who knows what he's going to say before he says it. I want to know what he looks like naked, and the things that turn him on. *I want everything* and he doesn't care if I call him by his first name. *Whoopee*.

"Let me go." My voice is small, weak, and tired. "I promise I won't tell my dad I want a different doctor if that's what you're worried about. I just..." I trail off, shaking my head miserably. "I get it now that you treat all your patients like you treat me. I understand, but I'm feeling really, really stupid and embarrassed, so please could you just move? *Please.*"

The desperation in my voice must win me some sympathy points, because Doctor Harrison straightens up, finally stepping out of the way. "Delta, *you're not stupid.*"

I'm careful to not let myself look at him as I close it as quickly as possible, fumbling with my keys. The very last thing I want from this man is a pity pep talk. My stomach twists as I pull out of my parking spot, Doctor Harrison's tall frame lingering in the corner of my eye as he watches me go. In the space of a week, I've gone from his chill, easy-going patient to a crying, needy mess. *What is wrong with me?* Why am I suddenly incapable of keeping it together?

As I turn out of the parking lot, I finally find the courage to glance in my rearview mirror. Doctor Harrison is still standing by my parking spot, watching me go.

Chapter 4

BROOKS

Despite having treated half the skiers and snowboarders who train there, working down the street, and growing up just across town, I've never actually seen Blue Pike.

Even after bypassing the turnoff to work, calling Courtney to bump my morning appointments, and driving into the parking lot at the base of the mountain, I'm still trying to convince myself to turn the car around. I shouldn't be here. After months of struggling to keep Delta at arm's length, not even twenty-four hours of knowing she's upset has sent me right over yet another line I shouldn't.

Being closed off and professional is second nature to me. All those barriers I've been putting up between us come with a cost, and it was a cold, terrible shock to realize that I'm not the only one paying for it.

She believes I treat all my patients like I treat her, that she's nobody special to me, and the fucking wounded look on her face... I can't stomach it. I don't care if I'm throwing myself on the damn pyre. I'm not letting Delta walk around thinking any less of herself because of me, letting her *hurt* because of me.

Understanding the emotions of people in my life has never been easy for me. Facial expressions, gestures, and sarcasm often go right over my head. Even now, as an objectively successful adult, I spend most of my days wishing my interactions with friends, family, and patients came with subtitles. I hadn't needed help to realize Delta was upset, although I couldn't understand why until it was too late

I have no business being here, bothering her in the middle of her workday, but I can't leave this.

I've just gotten out of my car and wondering if I should get right back into it when a familiar voice calls my name and I'm reminded of yet another excellent reason for staying far away from Blue Pike.

River Jacobs. He's just leaving the building I parked beside, dressed in the same black jacket as Delta wears, a snowboard under one arm and a clipboard under the other. My tolerance for River has waned with each passing year we've worked together, and I'm almost positive he feels the same way about me. There was a time when I put a lot of effort into propping up his ego, but he uses his daughter for that. He doesn't need any extra help from me.

"Hi, River." I tighten my cheeks in something resembling a polite smile as I walk around my car toward him. "I thought I might find you here."

A lie, and a not a clever one. River might be an egomaniac, but he isn't stupid, and I need to watch myself. I haven't seen him in months, and I'm not sure if it's my imagination, but he looks more worn down than I remember him being the last time he came to one of Delta's appointments.

"How can I help you, Doctor?" he asks, shuffling his clipboard so he can grip my hand.

"The magazine reached out to me again this morning.

They wanted an answer by the end of the day, but I haven't been able to get ahold of Delta. Do you know where I can find her?"

River gestures to the chairlift, his expression unreadable, and despite myself, I'm a little rattled by his cool nonchalance. It's like being at an aquarium and staring into the eyes of a shark on the other side of the glass. "I've been having the kids leave their phones in the locker room to minimize distractions. I'll take you up. She's on one of the slopestyle courses."

I feel distinctly out of place in my wool coat and slacks as I follow River's lead. Among his people, he's like another person, good-natured and grinning. He waves to a few of the skiers and stops to introduce me to some of his assistant coaches. I'm not an expert, but the entire facility seems to be state-of-the-art. Not surprising, given Blue Pike churns out more champions than anywhere else in the country.

As we join the short line to the lift, I watch as a male snowboarder wearing the same black jacket as River executes what looks like a triple spin off a ramp of snow a little way up the mountain. He lands it so smoothly anyone would think it's effortless.

"My second son, Lake," River explains, following my gaze.

I knew Delta has two older brothers, though I've never met either of them. I've also never seen anyone do anything even close to that impressive in real life. It certainly looked fantastic, but despite having seen what must be hundreds of hours of Delta's snowboarding footage by now, I still couldn't tell what constitutes a "good run" apart from not falling on your ass.

River nods toward a place a little way up the platform where we're supposed to stand. I follow his lead and my stomach swoops when the chair hooks my legs out from under me, lifting us away from the ground. River pulls down a metal bar, locking us in, and we both watch as Lake takes the last jump on the course with just as much apparent ease.

"Is he another Olympic hopeful?"

I can't imagine being anything other than awed by my children if they grew up to be internationally ranked athletes, but River only sighs. "Lake is excellent, but his nerves have always been an issue. He never performs as well in competition as he does in practice."

"And Delta?" I hear myself ask. I hardly value this man's opinion, but I'm uncomfortable with how limited my knowledge of Delta's world is, especially given our last conversation. I grew up just across town from here, in the heart of ski and snowboard country, but while my classmates were skipping class to go to the mountain, I was getting elected president of the chemistry club. I was awkward, introverted, and obsessed with science, and I've fallen for the coolest woman on the face of the planet.

River chuckles, resting his arm over the back of the chair, his eyes on a group of snowboarders passing below us on the trail. "DJ performs best when there's something at stake. I get a lot of shit for how hard I push my team, but these kids *need it*. They don't get to this level without it. I take that natural determination and harness it. They wouldn't keep coming back if they didn't thrive under that kind of pressure."

I look away, my stomach churning. Is that what River tells himself? That Delta is *thriving under the pressure*? She's looked more worn down and stressed every time I've seen her this year, and I *know* she isn't giving me the full picture of how much pain she's in.

He offers nothing else, and I stare blankly out at the snow-covered trees, turning his words over in my mind. I want to rage at him, but I can't. She's never said anything to me. All I have are my suspicions, and gut feelings aren't empirical data.

The guys running the lift see that I'm not wearing snowboard or skis, so they stop the chairs to let me off. The top of the mountain is bitter cold despite the bright sunlight, and River points me toward the slopestyle course before heading off in the opposite direction.

I'm grateful for the lack of supervision. I haven't been in the same room as Delta and River since I realized my attraction to her, and I'd like to keep it that way until I get myself under control. I still haven't quite given up hope that this is all just a deeply unfortunate phase, an early mid-life crisis, and one day I'll wake up and this obsession will have vanished as instantaneously as it appeared.

It would be an ideal turn of events, but I'm not hopeful, considering where I am right now. I've never done anything this drastic for the sake of another person's feelings.

Especially when I emerge on the base of a massive hill, arranged with intimidating looking rails and ramps. My eyes catch on the top as a woman moves into view. She's dressed in the same black coat and a pair of tie-dye snow-pants, her face partially obscured by bright pink goggles, and she's far too far away. She could be anyone, but the familiar prickle of awareness I feel at the back of my neck tells me exactly who she is.

I watch as she talks to another woman in a coach's jacket, nodding seriously and, without warning, drops over the edge.

My stomach plummets with her, and I have to bite my tongue to keep myself from yelling out. I've seen videos of this, but they couldn't prepare me for the intensity of seeing it in person. A tiny cell phone video can't convey how fast she's going, or how gracefully her body seems to bend and sway with the board, gliding over snow that's so packed down it could be ice. Every time she breaks free from the ground, I hold my breath, fear twisting inside me, but she never falters.

She's so goddamn *good*. Perfect, even.

A shower of snow chunks flies through the air when she skids to a stop at the bottom of the hill. We're only a dozen yards apart, and I linger by the tree line as she snaps her goggles up, huffing in frustration.

"Damn it," Delta mutters to herself, panting. She must see movement because she does a double take, her eyes widening comically in surprise at the sight of me. "Doctor Harrison. What—what are you doing here?"

My stomach knots in apprehension as I step forward. How the hell did I get all the way up here without a plan of what I wanted to say to her? I'd been so focused on whether I should be here at all, I never stopped to consider how I'd go about this. "Do you have a minute?" I ask, glancing up toward where her coach was standing a few moments ago, but the top of the course is empty.

She hesitates, her face flat. "I guess." Not the enthusiasm I was hoping for, but better than an outright refusal. She leans forward to release her boots from her snowboard, carefully avoiding my eye as she tucks it beneath her arm and leads the way to the little spectator area. There's a shed, a few benches, and a highlighter yellow backpack which Delta yanks an insulated water bottle from, her expression stony.

She's obviously not going to make this easy on me or lead the conversation. Fair enough.

"I'm sorry to show up like this." I rub the back of my neck, which is burning from the cold despite my upturned collar. "I just wanted to tell you that we *are* friends. Our relationship isn't the same as I have with my other patients. I'm not the best at communicating, but it's not a reflection of you or what I think of you. It's just... me. I'll work on it. For you." It's such a rambling, disconnected speech that I have to force myself not to wince in embarrassment. The words feel unnatural in my mouth, but I can't think how else to say them.

This is so fucking embarrassing. She's never seen me like this, in my naturally awkward, socially stumbling form. Every interaction we've ever had has been on my turf, and now we're on hers.

Delta looks over her shoulder, and I'm relieved to see the guarded, cold look she wore moments ago is gone. Encouraged, I carry on, forcing myself to admit what I've never acknowledged to anyone outside my family. "I'm on the autism spectrum. I'm not ashamed of it, but it isn't something I'd like made public. There are negative connotations, ones that would affect my business and my partners. I don't tell people, but I think it's important that you're aware."

Delta turns slowly, her eyes searching my face. "Thank you for telling me. It does help me understand."

But she still doesn't look any happier, and the warmth that I usually feel from being around her still hasn't returned. "You're still upset."

Her lips press down into a flat, miserable line. "I don't have a right to be."

"Will you tell me why?" Fuck, if she won't let me fix this, I might go insane. I had a casual girlfriend in med school who would dangle her feelings over my head, making me guess and assume why she was upset, or get angry when I didn't care enough to beg. I would beg for Delta, but as it turns out, I don't need to.

"I—" she falters, her already flushed cheeks getting darker. "I'm hurt because you've never mentioned you have a girlfriend. It's just such a big, personal thing, and it made me realize how little I know you."

I choke. "Girlfriend? You mean *Phoebe*?"

Delta looks mortified. "The tall, gorgeous blonde woman in your office? Yeah. She... she *is* your girlfriend, right?"

Oh. *Oh. She thought*—"No." I assure her vehemently, shaking my head. "Phoebe is my older sister. She's married, has two feral children, and manages the spa on Taylor Street."

Is she fucking jealous?

Delta's face has gone completely pink and her eyes are wide with horror. *She's so goddamn cute.* "Your sister. Wow, I really am an idiot. I'm so sorry."

I don't realize I'm moving a step closer to her until I've already done it. "Don't be. It's my fault." In retrospect, I can imagine how it looked from Delta's perspective, coming into my office to see a woman she'd never met leaning against my desk, smiling at me. I would have thought the same if the situation were reversed, and my gut twists with jealousy at the possibility of some future man looking at her.

"So in the future, should I be more direct?" she clarifies hesitantly, her stormy eyes searching my face for signs of discomfort. "I'm sorry I ran off without explaining. That wasn't cool."

"There's nothing you need to apologize for," I assure her, but my whole body has warmed at her gentle offer. "But yes, direct is usually helpful. I'm sorry I didn't tell you that sooner." I'm not sure what I was expecting, for her pity maybe, or her discomfort, but if anything, Delta looks relieved.

She wants to know me.

The corner of her lips lift into a shy, crooked smile. "You came out here to tell me this?"

I snort. "I'm not exactly a social butterfly, Delta. I couldn't let one of my few friends walk around thinking she's just some ordinary patient." I nod back toward the slopestyle course. "I'm glad I came regardless, though. *That* is better in person."

She groans. "Of course, *that's* the run you saw. I was a mess."

"You were incredible." Granted, I'm probably ridiculously biased, but she *was* fucking amazing, and I won't be convinced otherwise. "I'll never forget that."

Things have been so intense lately that I'd nearly forgotten how easy it is to just *be with her*, to see her smile and hear her voice. I realize, with a dizzying burst of clarity, that the possessive, consuming attraction I feel for Delta Jacobs didn't come out of nowhere. We built it together in a hundred moments, just like this one.

"Want me to teach you?" she offers slyly. "I bet you'd be good."

"Absolutely not." I hold up my hands. "If I break a wrist, I won't be able to operate for months. I can't."

She laughs, backing toward the shed, her eyes sparkling with mischief. "You're not going to break a wrist."

"I'm an orthopedic surgeon, Delta. How many pins do you think I put into snowboarders' wrists every year?"

"Live a little, Doc." Now she's just being insolent. I watch, my retort on the tip of my tongue, as she turns to pull open the doors to the shed. I see over her shoulder that the inside is full of bindings, boards, and other supplies. "What size shoe are you?"

Christ, this is embarrassing. This woman is fucking *cool*, and I'm too chicken shit to take the responsible, pragmatic stick out of my ass for ten minutes? "Delta, I really shouldn't."

It doesn't escape my notice that I've gone from "can't" to "shouldn't" in under a minute. I thought there were only two women in my life who could demolish my resolution so easily, but it looks like a third has been added to that formidable list. My mother and Phoebe would be thrilled.

Delta must know she's closing in on victory because she cheerfully ignores my feeble objection. I watch, chest tight, as she pulls out a pair of battered snowboarding boots from the bottom shelf in the shed and traipses back to where I'm standing, her steps crunching over the packed-down snow.

It's all I can do to stop myself from groaning when she drops to her knees at my feet, fingers moving to the laces of my boots. "Come on." She smiles up at me, and that wicked little smile only a few inches from my cock must be enough to send all the blood rushing south from my brain because I nod jerkily.

Nobody is around, but I still feel shaky and self-conscious when Delta shows me how to step into the bindings on the board she found for me. I work out daily. I'm in objectively excellent shape for my age, but just standing upright on this thing is enough to make my thighs burn.

"This is hard," I huff, exasperated after my third attempt to stand on a flat section of the hill ends up with me on my ass. "Christ—"

Delta laughs, and she looks so carefree and happy it's worth the hit to my dignity. "Come on." She's been watching from a few feet away as I struggle, but now she moves forward to take my gloved hands in hers. I let her pull me to my feet and wobble unsteadily for a minute. "See? Easy." She steps to the side and pulls me along. I can't tell if the swooping sensation low in my stomach is from the sensation of the earth sliding beneath the snowboard, or being close enough to count the freckles on her nose.

I curse under my breath. "I can't believe you do backflips on this thing."

We're so close together that the mist from our breaths collides in the icy air and I can see the tiny flecks of blue in her eyes as she smiles up at me. "I can't believe you don't. Didn't you grow up here?"

"I've never told you that." I don't think so, anyway, and I've spent so much time obsessing over my interactions with Delta that I doubt I'd forget something like that.

Delta coughs, avoiding my gaze. "I probably read it somewhere."

"You Googled me?" I'm not sure why that's so surprising to me. If I was an athlete, I'd do my research into the doctor who had my career in their hands. The bashful look on her face raises a flicker of suspicion that maybe her internet sleuthing wasn't purely professional.

"I'm sure you looked *me* up," she retorts, keeping her eyes on the snow inching by beneath us as she pulls me along.

She's so much smaller than me, I don't want to lean on her, but when we hit a slight slope, my stomach plummets, and I cling to her forearms instinctively. "Do you remember your first time on a snowboard?" I ask quietly. In the distance, I can hear voices, but on this quiet stretch of trail, it's just me and Delta, suspended together in this moment.

She hums, her head tilting slightly as she considers. "I don't think so. I was young, obviously. I remember doing trampoline training on my fifth birthday and dislocating my shoulder. The nurses brought me one of those little ice cream cups with a candle in it. So, it must have been earlier than that."

Five? Christ. She says it so nonchalantly, like it's normal to begin professional athletic training before you've lost all your baby teeth.

I've wondered before how Delta's mother would have felt about how her children were raised. According to old internet gossip articles, she and River had a contentious relationship. There are paparazzi pictures of them fighting outside a restaurant, River's face contorted in anger as his two young sons stand to the side with tears in their eyes and his pregnant wife glowers right back. She died only a year later, drunk and driving at top speed through the mountains of Colorado, leaving River to raise champions rather than children.

"I think I've embarrassed myself enough." I smile tightly, and she lets me sit back on my ass.

Delta laughs quietly and plops down next to me, leaning forward to undo my bindings for me. Ahead, there's a spectacular view of snowcapped mountains and I ache with how badly I wish I could reach across the perfectly respectable distance between us and touch her again. "You were fine. I'm sure things would get ugly if you tried to teach me how to do your job."

I chuckle. "I can arrange a day for you to shadow me if you're interested in medical school."

"Pass." I turn to see her eyes fixed on the horizon, "Who knows what I'll do when I can't snowboard anymore, but it won't be anything that impressive."

"I doubt that."

We sit in silence for a long time, lost in our respective thoughts. Despite the icy wind biting at my cheeks and the snow probably soaking through the back of my jacket and slacks, it's a relief. I'm not worried that I'll say the wrong thing or give away my feelings for her. We're just together, and it might be the most peaceful moment of my life.

"Thanks for coming to check in." Delta finally tells me gently as we watch a pair of skiers pass by us on the main trail, moving so fast it seems almost inhuman. "And for telling me. About you, I mean. I promise I won't say anything, but for the record, I think you're amazing. You're my favorite person, and if someone believes that your being autistic is shameful or limiting, it says way more about them than it does about you."

I love her.

The certainty of it washes over me, flooding my body with heat and fear. This isn't an obsession, and I can't pretend otherwise anymore. I'm thirty-eight years old. I've had relationships. Some of them seemed good at the time, but none of those women made me feel as *seen* as Delta does. Looking at her now, it's heartbreaking to realize that fleeting moments like these are all we'll ever have.

She's my patient. My too-young, too good for me, patient, and *I'm fucking in love with her.*

I'm still numb with shock when she pushes back to her feet. Never before have I wished I could find a way to hold on to a moment forever. "Delta." My mouth is dry as she turns to face me, and I pull my phone out of my pocket. "Take a picture with me."

Her head tilts, a curious gleam in her eyes. Still, she holds out a hand to haul me back to my feet and we draw together with the snowy mountains behind us. There are so many reasons I shouldn't be doing this, why I shouldn't be here, why it's wrong for me to want her, but as our faces appear side by side on the screen of my phone, I don't remember any of them.

"We weren't smiling," Delta murmurs, turning to me just as I hit the button to take a second picture.

My throat tightens as I stare down at her, tucked under my arm with her own wrapped around my waist. "It doesn't matter."

Chapter 5

DELTA

"**G**et up."

I squeeze my eyes shut, trying to keep myself from screaming my frustration. We've been at this for hour, *hours*, and I still can't land it. The backside 900 is something I've been able to execute flawlessly since I was about fourteen, and now, only a few weeks away from the first Olympic team qualifying event of the season, I can't do it. Marianna, my usual one-on-one coach, not so subtly texted my father after my fifth straight failed run, and he arrived from the main office to order everyone but me off the halfpipe.

That was just before lunch.

Now, the pipe is lit by deep red light from the sun setting behind the trees as I lay on my back, panting, aching, and *done*.

So, so, done.

I took the last of my leftover pain pills yesterday afternoon, swearing to myself that I'd make do on ibuprofen and lots of ice baths from now on. Judging by my current inability to execute tricks I could once do in my sleep, that was just as much of a load of crap as telling myself I'd only need them once.

"DJ." Dad's footsteps crunch over the snow toward me, but I still don't open my eyes.

Pain is radiating out from my hip, cramping the muscles in my leg, back, and stomach. I'm tired, hungry and I hurt so bad that I can't think about anything except taking this fucking board off my feet and throwing it in the woods. I never want to touch it or set foot on this stupid, pretentious mountain ever again.

Dad exhales heavily as he sits beside me on the ground, his winter gear rustling. "You want to tell me why you went from fine yesterday to a mess today, kid?"

Nope. I feel shitty enough about my choices without seeing the judgment and disapproval in Dad's eyes, too. Then there's the fact that I'm still in pain two weeks after an injection. I should be fine, or *almost* fine, and the fact that I'm not means that all the warnings about this not being a permanent solution are finally coming to fruition. *They aren't working anymore.* Dad might not like Doctor Harrison's lack of ass-kissing, but he doesn't dispute that he's the absolute best. If he can't fix me, no one can, and the fate of my career now hangs on just how much pain I can take.

"Dad, I don't want to do this anymore." The number of times I've thought about saying those words are too many to count. Somehow, it never occurred to me that they would make my heart hurt just as badly as my body does. If I'm not good at this, I'm good at nothing at all.

When I finally find the courage to open my eyes, I see Dad staring toward the opening at the end of the pipe. "Do you know when I realized you were going to be exceptional, DJ?"

Wincing, I push myself up to sit beside him, my chest hollow. "No." Dad and I don't talk about stuff like that.

"You were about four. We were in New England, visiting

your grandparents for the weekend. I took you and your brothers snowboarding on the back hill," he chuckles and shakes his head. "It was cold as hell out. The boys were complaining the whole time, but you never asked to go in. Not once. My point is that winners are made, not born. You become the best when you show up every day and work for it, you *sacrifice* for it. You've never had trouble doing that, kid."

He doesn't know how wrong he is, how much *trouble* I've swallowed down and bottled up. "My hip is fucked, Dad. It hasn't been right since I started winter training, and I thought the injection would help, but it didn't. I want to keep going, I swear. It's just..." My eyes burn. "I feel like I'm falling apart."

Dad scrubs a hand over his face. "I'm going to take a shot in the dark here, and you don't have to tell me if I'm right, but I think you found *something* to help you get through it. And I'm guessing that something wasn't legal."

I don't respond, *I can't*, but Dad seems to understand anyway because he sighs.

"Call the doctor, tell him to give you another injection. He probably got the wrong spot, that happens, and in the meantime—" I sense the weight of his eyes on me, but don't turn to meet them. "There's plenty of shit in my bathroom cabinet. Take what you need. It'll get you through until we figure this out."

I should be relieved, happy even, but Dad's offer makes my stomach twist. "You don't... *you don't care?*"

He snorts. "You can't let yourself get hooked on that shit, so take it easy, but it's fine for now. I sure as hell did it from time to time."

Suddenly, the blood rushing in my ears is so much louder than the wind on the mountain or Dad's voice. He's told us the stories so many times, the ones about his beating the odds and working through pain to win it all. I should be relieved that he's not a superhero, to know he struggled just like I do now, but I just feel betrayed and alone.

I stare straight ahead at the towering wall of snow, every part of me hurting. "Why didn't you tell me before?"

"Do I want my kid using pills to get through training? Of course not." I don't reply and we sit side by side in silence for a long moment before he adds, "I didn't want to tell you until you were past this rough spot, but I got a call yesterday. Everwater is interested. They're sending their reps up on Monday to meet you."

I close my eyes, sucking in a shaky breath. He doesn't need to remind me that Everwater, a fancy energy drink company, is the dream sponsor for pretty much any athlete. Their contracts are worth millions of dollars and come with amazing perks, like traveling to industry events all over the world and seeing your face on billboards.

I should care, this is an enormous deal, and I don't understand why I can't muster up even a perfunctory level of excitement.

"Great," I croak, opening my eyes to offer Dad a shaky smile.

He stares at me for a long moment. "I'm proud of you, DJ. Crazy proud."

I can count on one hand the number of times I remember my father saying those words to me. They used to fill me up, make me whole, but I'm pretty sure that's impossible now.

This is the part where I'm supposed to glow with pride, and throw my arms around his neck, tearfully thanking him for making me who I am. Dad looks at me, waiting for it, and a shadow of worry crosses his face when it becomes clear I'm not going to bite. "Come on." He rolls to his feet and reaches down to pull me up, too. "Let's get you a good night's sleep. You can call the doctor in the morning."

I wince, pain flaring as I reach down to gingerly release my bindings. "He's not going to give me another injection. It's supposed to be every six weeks, and it's only been two." Doctor Harrison doesn't bend rules, and I can't imagine him overlooking medical best practices for anyone, even me.

"He will," Dad assures me, and looking up, my stomach drops at the hard set in his expression. "I built that man's practice, DJ. I can unbuild it, too."

* * *

It says a lot about my current state of mind that I haven't been using every free second to obsess over Doctor Harrison's unexpected visit to Blue Pike.

The last time we spoke was the night after, when he texted me to tell me he'd be too busy for the sports medicine interview, and he was sorry.

I'd spent half an hour trying to find the right words to tell him how much that hour together on the mountain had meant to me, but nothing felt right. Then it occurred to me that there was no way Doctor Harrison had spent so long composing that simple text, and I ended up sending a short *'No problem! I didn't want to do it, anyway!'*.

He never replied. It was ridiculous for me to be disappointed considering I hadn't offered anything worthy of responding to, but I still was. The only perk of the past brutal week of training that followed was not having spare time or energy to dwell on it.

Now, I'm lying in bed with my thumbs hovering over the keyboard on my screen, pulse throbbing. How the hell do I tell him I've been downplaying my pain? Or that Dad is about to put him in a really shitty position? Or that I wish I could text him without having a reason?

> Delta: Hey, hope your week's been good.
> Just wanted to give you a heads up that I'm
> going to call the office in the morning. I've
> been having some pain. Dad wants me to
> get another injection.

I curl deeper into my covers, not expecting him to respond tonight. It's nearly midnight, and he's mentioned before that he's usually an early riser like I am. My heart leaps when, not even a minute later, my phone vibrates, and I fumble to hold it up. Right on the screen is an incoming call from "Doc".

Holy shit.

My hands are clumsy and numb as I hit 'answer'.

"Hello?"

"Delta." I love it when he says my name like that, all growly and exasperated. Just the sound of it makes warmth spread through my whole body, and the muscles in my lower belly tighten.

I lean back in bed and close my eyes, relief flooding through me. "You didn't need to call."

Doctor Harrison scoffs. "You're admitting to having pain. Your leg must be damn near falling off."

"Not quite." I bend the leg in question. It's not so bad after the ice bath I took when I got home and laying still for the past few hours. "I just wanted to give you some warning. About Dad, I mean. I'll try talking to him in the morning, but you know what he's like."

"I can handle River, but you need to tell me right away when you're having pain." Through the phone, I can hear his footsteps and the sound of a door closing. "I can't give you another dose. It would be dangerous, but we can try another injection point at your next appointment. I can use ultrasound to guide the needle—" He doesn't get it, but then again, how could he? After all, I've covered this up until I physically can't take it anymore.

"That's not for a month." Somehow, I can't see Dad accepting that, and I won't make it that long, even with unlimited access to pain pills.

Doctor Harrison is silent, and I know he's probably doing that cute frowny face he makes when he's thinking hard about something. "There are other treatments we can try, but they all require surgery, which isn't an option for you right now. Delta, your cartilage is almost gone. There's not a lot I can do to treat that. We're reaching the end of the road here."

"I get it." We've had this talk before, with and without Dad in the room. My prognosis hasn't changed since the first time I walked into his office, but the end of my career always seemed like a far off, abstract possibility, not a looming inevitability. I never expected it to get so bad, so fast.

"I'm sorry." His voice sounds strained and low. "That was insensitive."

The hand not holding my phone fists the sheets beneath me. "It wasn't. It was honest. Is this a bad time? It's late."

"No. It's not a bad time. Are you going to sleep soon?"

"I'm in bed." It's a completely innocent thing to say, and the truth, but heat still crawls up my neck.

He's silent for so long, and I'm about to crack a joke about my insomnia to lighten the tension when Doctor Harrison clears his throat. "I am too."

Oh god. I press my thighs together, my skin prickling with awareness as heat twists below my bellybutton. How does the thought of this man just *lying in bed* make me horny? My whole body hurts, I'm physically and emotionally drained, and surely there's more pressing problems in my life than what my orthopedic surgeon wears to sleep in.

But I totally bet he's a boxers and t-shirt kind of guy.

"Do you normally go to bed so late?" I ask, shifting restlessly beneath my blankets.

He laughs quietly. "No, actually. It's my sister's birthday. I was conned into babysitting, so she and her husband could go to dinner. They came home a full two hours later than they promised. What could I do? Scold her on her birthday?"

"Wow. Shameless."

"I know. She's out of control." He clears his throat. "Do you, ah, like kids?" I can't put my finger on why the flat, politely nonchalant tone he uses to ask isn't quite convincing.

I bite my lip, considering. "Yeah, I do. A lot, actually. I'm sure you've heard my mom died when I was really young, so I have no idea if I'd be any good at it, but I think I'd like to be part of a real family. Mom, Dad, kids, dogs, cats, the whole deal. Someday." I don't remember my mother, but the few stories Bay has told me don't paint a picture of a wonderful maternal figure. Mara Ortiz-Jacobs might have been a beautiful woman, but she wasn't a happy one.

He clears his throat. "You would be. Good at it, I mean."

"You sound so sure." I roll over, staring out at the cloudy night sky beyond my bedroom window. We've lived in this house for as long as I can remember, but it's not exactly homey, and there's no comfort from the familiar view. It's in one of those gated neighborhoods that takes itself way too seriously and doesn't let you decorate for anything other than Christmas.

Through the phone, bedding rustles and I close my eyes, imagining he's doing the same thing I am. "I am sure."

Something seems to warm inside me. "What about you? Happy being a cool uncle for the rest of your days?"

"I'm hardly the cool uncle." Doctor Harrison chuckles darkly. "That title is reserved for my younger brother. He rides a motorcycle and brings them loud toys every time he visits."

I giggle. "Oh wow, that *is* cool. How are you supposed to compete with that?"

"Oh, I can't. I'm leaning into being the lame, responsible one. We did math homework tonight. They hate me."

Talking to him has always been so easy, but this? We're miles apart. I can't see him or touch him or smell him, but I'm positive I've never felt so whole just from hearing another person's voice. How am I supposed to go back to seeing him once every six weeks? How am I supposed to go through a single *day* without talking to him now?

I've always been a bit worried that I fell in love with the idea of Brooks Harrison rather than the actual person, but now I know that's wrong.

I love *him*.

Him, the man, not the surgeon.

Him, the friend, not the gorgeous, successful business owner.

Him.

"You didn't answer the question," I murmur, curling my free hand between my cheek and the pillow. I wish we were having this conversation in person, curled side by side in the same bed, peering at each other through the darkness. I've never wanted anything more.

It takes him a long time to respond. When he finally does, though, his voice is so quiet I strain to make out his voice over my own heartbeat. "I do, but I doubt I will."

The pain in his voice sends a sharp pang of sorrow through me. "Why?"

"I have a knack for being alone. Sometimes I think I sabotage myself so I can stay that way. Alone is comfortable, *easy*, I suppose." He's killing me right now. There's nothing I wouldn't do to make him see he could have that with another person, *with me*. I realize I've been quiet for too long when he asks, "Are you still there?"

I roll over again onto my back, staring up at the ceiling fan rotating slowly above my bed. "I'm here."

"Shouldn't you be asleep?" His tone is determinately light despite the intensity of the conversation.

I should, but I don't want this to end. It's not like I've had a full night's sleep for months anyway, and this is about a million times better than waking up drenched in sweat from yet another nightmare. "Probably. Shouldn't you?"

"Probably."

Neither of us hang up, and a tiny flame of hope kindles to life deep inside me as I lay listening to his breathing. Where for years there was once only me reaching out, wanting him, now there's something stretched tight between us. I'm young and inexperienced and he's so far out of my league it isn't even funny, but I'm not imagining this. *I'm not.*

"Did you always want to be a doctor?"

"Pretty much." I hear a smile in his voice. "Let's just say I wasn't exactly what you'd call popular. My parents used to beg me to go out and play with my siblings, but all I wanted to do was read. Orthopedic surgeon wasn't the plan, but I had a rotation during med school and fell in love." I smile to myself, thinking of what a cute kid he must have been with his floppy curls and serious face. "Did you always want to snowboard?"

"Pretty much," I echo, turning slightly so I can see the shelves of trophies and medals arranged along my bedroom wall. "I remember Dad putting me in a group class for little kids so he and my brothers could do the harder trails. They had to call him to come get me because I was faster than the instructors." Doctor Harrison chuckles, and I smile too. "I like snowboarding. It's everything else I could do without. The training and the competitions and *the press*—God, I hate the press stuff so much. Every time I get a news alert for my name, I feel sick."

"I know you do. Why do you think I turned down that interview? I'm not going to bring more of that shit into your life." He sounds disgruntled, and I feel my mouth fall open in surprise. He turned town a chance for free national publicity, because he knows I don't like doing press stuff?

I press a hand to my chest, trying to steady the wild pounding of my heart, to no avail. "But it would be really good for you!" I gasp. "You said you were too busy!"

He clears his throat, and I for the first time since we started talking, there's a shadow of tension. "It's not a big deal," he says at last, clearing this throat. "Listen, I don't want you to worry about tomorrow, okay? Call the office, I'll talk down River. I'll—I'll take care of it."

My eyes squeeze shut as the real world slips back in. "Okay." My voice sounds robotic, dead.

"Delta." His voice is laced with so much regret it makes my heart ache, and I can't bear to make him think he's said the wrong thing again. "I didn't mean to—"

"It's okay," I rush to reassure him. "Really, I'm just exhausted. Long day."

"Of course." He clears his throat. "I'll let you get some sleep. Goodnight, Delta."

I sink deeper into my bed, exhaustion making the edges of my vision blur and the arm holding my phone sags. "Goodnight, Doc."

Chapter 6

BROOKS

"She shouldn't be *walking*. Never mind flying down mountains. Delta needs to take this season off. We've run out of feasible treatment options, and giving her another injection so soon isn't possible—"

"Out of the question." River scowls at me, eyes flashing with the ever-present, unspoken threat that he can and will walk the hell out of here, taking his daughter and dozens of my other patients with him. "The cortisone injections are *working*. You clearly fucked up the last one, which is why she—"

I have to bite my tongue to keep myself from yelling. It wouldn't be productive. We've been going in circles since I walked into the exam room, River and I hashing it out while Delta sits silently on the table beside him. They came here at the end of a long day at the mountain, and I've felt cold with shock from the moment I laid eyes on her.

It's only been a week, and Delta has changed. She's lost weight, her expression is set and emotionless, and she's barely taken her eyes off the floor since I came in here. Anyone else might think she's tired or spaced out, but I know better.

She's in pain.

I watch River's mouth move, arguing his case, but I'm not hearing him. All I want is to throw him out of my office, gather up Delta in my arms, and beg her to *stop*.

"Enough." I cut sharply across River's rant, unable to listen to another word out of his mouth. I see his shoulders tense and know I've pissed him off, but I'm so far past giving a damn that I can't even see it anymore. How can he care about her career more than her? How can he look at her right now and not see the damage he's doing? "I'd like to speak with Delta. *Alone*."

River snaps back immediately, the vein in his forehead pulsing. "And let you convince her that she needs to sacrifice everything she's worked for? I don't think so." He turns to his daughter. "Mind over matter, DJ. If he won't do it, I spoke to a doctor in Denver who will. He says it's perfectly safe, but *some doctors*," he shoots me a filthy look, "are too scared of a lawsuit to do what's best for their patient."

Delta barely blinks. "Okay."

I think I'm going to be sick. "It *isn't* safe," I hiss for what must be the tenth time. "She'd be risking bone death, infection, or worse. Any physician who tells you otherwise is a hack, and I'll personally report them to the medical board if they do it." Murder also seems like an appropriate response, but one step at a time.

River, unsurprisingly, ignores this. "So you're telling me that her only option is a new hip? *At twenty years old*. Do you have any idea what's at stake, the opportunities she'll be sacrificing if she walks away now?"

"Delta." Slowly, like it takes an inordinate amount of energy just to lift her eyes, she looks up at me. "I'd like to take some blood to check for infection and any other issues, and we need to do an ultrasound to see what's going on. There are multiple complications you could be experiencing, and until we know if this is a result of the medication or your underlying condition, this conversation is moot."

A tear tracks down her cheek, and I would give up every single thing I have to cross the distance between us and wipe it away.

River opens his mouth to voice yet another protest, but Delta beats him to it. "It's okay, Dad."

"DJ—"

"Seriously, Dad. *Please.* Doctor Harrison is right. We don't know what's going on yet." She offers him a tight smile that isn't even a little convincing. "It'll just take a few minutes. I'll meet you at home and we can talk."

River stares at her, and for the first time since I've known him, I see a flicker of uncertainty behind those cold shark's eyes. *He's not sure,* and the fact he still isn't backing down is somehow more chilling than if he was utterly convinced he was right.

"Fine," he finally agrees, snatching his jacket off the chair in the corner. "Call me when you're done here, DJ." His eyes flash to me, an unspoken threat hanging in the air between us.

I nod tersely, the closest I can offer to an olive branch.

The moment the door closes behind him, Delta deflates. "You don't need to say it." Her fingers tear at the paper sheet covering the table beneath her. "I know."

"You're fucking up your body." I don't bother mincing words or being professional. Professionalism flew out the window a long time ago with this woman, and I'm too raw from walking into this room and coming face to face with a shadow of who she was a week ago. "Even *if* you manage to qualify for the games, and that's a big *if* Delta, there's no guarantee you'll be able to compete. Whereas if you take the year off and get this surgery, you *might* come back."

"In four years? With a hip replacement?" she scoffs, raising her eyebrows like she's daring me to say this is possible.

I don't reply, because I can't.

Four years is a long way off, and athletes who compete at her level rarely last until they're twenty-four, especially not with existing injuries like Delta's. To the best of my knowledge, there hasn't been a professional snowboarder with any kind of joint replacement, and not a world champion. I might despise the man, but River is right about this. Forcing her to stop now, asking her to get the surgery, means her career is almost certainly over.

"Let's just take a look, and we can go from there. I don't want to speculate, Delta."

We stare at each other, and finally, she nods, her bottom lip trembling. "Okay."

I swallow the lump in my throat, fighting the urge to cross the room and pull her into my arms. She's scared, *I'm scared*, and the lines between us have become so unbearably blurred I don't know if I should be comforting her or diagnosing her. I've let this go too far, and in my heart, I'm sure this is the last time she'll be here as my patient.

This is precisely why physicians aren't supposed to treat family members. It's impossible to think clearly when someone you love is in pain.

I turn away before I can do something I regret, crossing to the portable ultrasound machine we keep in the corner and unwind the cord to wheel it over to the table. When I look back at Delta, she's slipped down to the floor and is trying to shimmy out of her yoga pants, wincing even at that small movement.

Fuck.

In a trance, I move to her side, my mouth suddenly dry. "Here." I kneel, my thumbs slipping under the waistband to pull them over her hips and down her legs, all while fighting to not to let the sight of her bare skin or the tiny blue panties she's wearing affect me. This situation isn't supposed to be erotic. *She's in pain for fuck's sake*, and I hate my inability to separate myself from my attraction to her, even now.

When I straighten up, I realize too late that our bodies are only inches apart. We're so close I can feel the heat rolling off her skin and smell the coconut shampoo in her hair. The air in the room seems to have gone unnaturally still around us.

Her breath catches when my hands reach out, settling on her waist. "Let me help you back up." I have no control over how strained my voice sounds, or how her breathless little nod sends molten heat down my spine.

There are procedures for this, proper ways that medical professionals are supposed to lift a patient with limited mobility, and possessively digging your fingers into their waist isn't one of them. Delta's hands find my shoulders as I lift her back onto the exam table, and despite the fact I have no earthly excuse for it, I still don't let go.

Her inner thighs are pressed against my hips, and I don't dare look down, terrified at what the sight of myself standing between her bare legs will do to me. The alternative, though, staring into her wide-eyed face and seeing that she's just as affected by this as I am, might be worse. I can't pretend she doesn't want this too.

My cock throbs painfully.

"Do you—" I have no idea what I'm going to say. *"Do you like this?"*, *"Do you want me?"*, *"Do you need me as badly as I need you?"*.

Delta's hands slip from my shoulders down to my chest, her breathing ragged, and I know she must feel my heart hammering beneath my skin. Tension crackles like electricity between us, and there's no excuse for holding her this way, no justification, no way to call this anything other than what it is. We're suspended in time, hurdling toward the edge of something impossible, and all it would take is the slightest nudge to send us over into oblivion.

I thought I knew what desire was, thought I knew what it was to want another person, but those instances were nothing but feeble imitations of what I feel for her.

I'm drowning, and she's oxygen. Kissing her isn't a choice, it's instinct.

I'll never know who moved first, but it doesn't matter. I've imagined kissing this woman a thousand times. It's kept me up at night, picturing it slow and teasing, hot and desperate, but my imagination is obviously shit because all those fantasies pale in comparison to reality.

There's nothing hesitant or sweet in the way our lips crash together. It's frantic and all-consuming, an explosion of *want*. Within seconds, I'm dragging her into my arms, crushing her body against mine as I devour her. Delta moans into the kiss, her hands tangling into my hair, pulling. The pinch of pain sends my lust impossibly higher and my hips jolt forward, grinding the length of my erection into those cock-tease fucking panties, feeling the unmistakable slickness through the material.

She's wet.

She's fucking wet for me.

I'm out of control, drunk on how good this feels, and I need more. Without stopping to think, I hook my thumbs under the hem of her t-shirt and sports bra, shoving them up out of the way. Her tits are slightly more than a handful and perky as fuck, and she moans, arching forward for me to touch her. I rip my lips away from hers, ducking to draw one pebbled nipple into my mouth, teasing it with my teeth as she writhes against me, panting.

"*Oh!*" The breathy, shocked little noises she's making above my head send blood rushing to my already throbbing dick, and while I could happily spend hours kissing, licking, and biting every inch of her body, in the back of my mind I know we're acting on borrowed time.

Reality is coming. Any minute now, I'll have to face what I've done, and I need to take as much as she'll give me in whatever time we have left.

I drop to my knees, running my nose over the sexy-as-fuck damp spot on her panties. Delta's fingers tighten in my hair, and I can tell she's trying to keep quiet, holding back so nobody hears what her doctor is doing to her behind this door.

Getting caught with my head between my patient's legs seems like a fair trade-off for making her scream my name.

"Delta," I groan, nipping at the sensitive skin of her inner thigh, greedily inhaling the scent of her arousal. "I want to eat your pussy, baby. Say yes."

She doesn't hesitate, her lips parting in shock and desire. *"Yes—"*

Outside in the hall, a door to one of the neighboring exam rooms closes and we both freeze, the hot, heavy air that had filled the room so suddenly is gone in an instant. I lurch away, almost sprawling on the floor in my haste to put some distance between us, and the guilt churning inside me doubles when I see Delta's crestfallen expression.

"Doc," she whispers, her hands fumbling as she pulls her shirt and bra down over her chest, hiding herself from me.

"I'm sorry, I..." I don't have words, and I dare look at her as I get unsteadily to my feet. Turning, I fumble with the ultrasound machine, staring at the device without really seeing it as I try and fail to break free from the fog of lust that is still clinging to my every thought. "Lay back, Delta. Thank you." My voice is crisp, strained, and leaves no room for discussion.

"I want to eat your pussy, baby. Say yes."

I would have done it, too, would have ripped her panties aside and made her come on my face on my own fucking exam table with my staff and other patients walking the halls just outside.

My head spins, and I stare hard at the grainy black-and-white ultrasound screen as it flickers to life. *This makes sense to me. I'm good at this, and I know the answers.* Delta doesn't say a word, and I still can't bring myself to look at her directly. Wordlessly, I squirt a generous glob of jell onto her hip and press the wand to her skin.

Even the comforting familiarity of my job doesn't help quiet the turmoil twisting inside me.

Months of holding myself back, months of telling myself I'd never touch her, and I did it anyway. *What the fuck is wrong with me?*

When I get the angle I want and adjust the resolution, my already-battered heart plummets through the floor.

"Do you see that?" I turn the screen toward her and point to the area that alarmed me. "That's your joint, where the head of your femur is supposed to fit into your pelvis. The free space there? It means your cartilage has worn away, and this section here?" I point higher, willing my hand not to shake. "That's where we've been focusing the injections. It's inflamed, possibly infected. You'll need to come back for bloodwork on Monday morning when the lab is open."

I shove the ultrasound wand haphazardly into the holder on the machine and pace to the computer in the corner, panic and fear rising inside me. I can't let her keep training on that hip, *I just can't*. Her pain level has to be so much worse than I predicted, and the dangers of snowboarding with that kind of injury aren't the only factors at play here. If this goes on, she'll be doing permanent damage to the joint, damage that a hip replacement can't repair. She'll be in pain for the rest of her life.

I close my eyes, bracing myself for what I know I have to do. "I'm pulling your medical clearance."

Silence.

"You can't do that." Delta's voice shakes, and I feel sick. I would take every bit of this pain for her if I could. I would take a crowbar to my own hip if it meant hers was healthy again, *but I can't.* The closest I can get is protecting her from herself and River.

Now more than ever she needs me to be her physician, not her friend, and not the man who just rutted against her on the table where her entire world is now crashing down around her.

I can do my fucking job.

"Yes. I can." Turning, steeling myself against the effect she has on me. I can't allow my feelings to cloud my judgment anymore, not about this. "The US Snowboarding Association accredited me as a screening physician when I started working with River. Every six months, I sign off on your ability to compete, and I can revoke that at any time."

I'm being a bastard. I believe in what I'm doing and know it's the best thing for her, but it doesn't have to be like this. I'm being cold, *hurting her,* because I'm too much of a coward to face the consequences of my actions.

An almost savage pleasure fills me when it works.

Delta tilts her chin up, staring at me with her face ridged in cold fury, her lips still swollen from mine. "You don't care what I think?"

"No. I don't."

* * *

I find my brother waiting for me at the bar when I enter the Merry Monk, the pub halfway between his house and mine, where we've made a habit of meeting for drinks a few times a month.

Despite being two years younger than me, Elliot has always felt like my older brother. While I was busy with medical school, residency, and building my business, Elliot was living. He'd been married, divorced, traveled the world, and started the most well-respected motorcycle repair shop in the city before I was even a fully qualified surgeon. He gets people in a way that I don't, and he can read me like a book.

Coming here, I expected him to take one look at my face and know I had shit on my mind, and my brother doesn't disappoint.

"Oh no, did someone fuck with your supply organization system again?" he grins, nudging me with his elbow as I take the stool next to his. Elliot is wearing the same patched leather jacket he always does despite the freezing temperatures outside, and as I turn to look at him properly, I see there's a fresh tattoo on his neck.

"I never should have told you about that." I raise a hand to signal to the bartender. "Never mention it again, and I won't tell Mom about *that*." I jerk my chin toward the neck tattoo.

My easy going, amiable brother is unaffected by the threat. "Mom's given up on me. She has you and Phoebe to maintain the *esteemed* Harrison family reputation, and I'm free to be a degenerate. Thanks for that, by the way. So, are you going to tell me what's wrong?"

I hesitate, my stomach churning. I've never admitted the way I feel about Delta out loud before, *to anyone,* and I don't see how I could give my brother the entire story without breaching doctor-patient confidentiality as well. I can either say I have worries about a patient and leave it at that or admit I have feelings for a woman I can't have. Not both.

I drum my fingers on the bar, looking anywhere but at my brother, but my lack of response is enough for him to make some assumptions.

"Is this about *a lady*, Brooksie?"

"Don't call me that," I snap, feeling about ten years old the moment the words leave my mouth. "And yes, there's... someone. She's a complication. Nothing can happen." The bartender appears, dropping fresh coasters and beer in front of both of us. I wait until he's gone before elaborating. "She's too young for me."

Delta being too young for me is the least of my worries, but it's interesting enough to throw my brother off the chase.

Elliot's eyes widen gleefully, "Shit, there really is someone? You never date! Mom's going to be fucking overjoyed. Also, it would take some heat off me if you got married and had a few kids. Make that happen, would you?"

Unbidden, an image of Delta's hand resting on her pregnant stomach blooms in my imagination and I shove it away just as quickly. *No.* There will never be a time when it's okay for me to have her, no magic end date when all the barriers between us will fall, and I can freely want her. Not to mention that after tonight, I'll be lucky if she ever speaks to me again.

Wrong person, wrong time, *wrong everything.*

The sooner I accept it, the better.

"She's *too young for me,*" I remind him cooly, staring at the multicolored bottles lined up behind the bar. My reflection stares back at me from the mirror above them, stony-faced and unsmiling as ever. I take a sip of beer, just for something to do besides sit there like a fucking robot waiting for activation.

Elliot frowns. "She's eighteen, right?"

I almost choke on the beer and glare at him, my eyes streaming. "Of course she is! What the fuck!"

He holds up both hands placatingly. "I was just checking! Christ, I haven't seen you this bent out of shape in... ever. Your shirt is wrinkled, for fuck's sake. What did she do to you?"

Exist.

"I don't want to talk about this anymore." I drain the rest of my beer and set it back on the bar top with a dull thud. I'm hardly the type to overindulge. The last time I got drunk was over a year ago, but numbing the hell out of my emotions sounds ideal right now.

She wouldn't be stubborn enough to ignore that scan, would she? The cold, hard truth is that *I don't know*. She has to be in a tremendous amount of pain, and I have no idea how she's walking around, never mind training eight hours a day. If she's able to power through that, I'd be a fool to discount anything.

The only comfort I can offer myself is that no doctor could ever justify clearing her with a hip in that condition. Even risking the wrath of River Jacobs isn't worth losing your medical license.

"Can you drive me home?" I ask Elliot, my voice hoarse with exhaustion.

"Of course." His worried gaze burns into the side of my face as I stare down at my fists clenched on the glossy wooden bar. "Brooks—"

I shake my head. "Don't."

"I'm just going to say this once, and then I'll shut the fuck up until you ask for my opinion." His hand finds my shoulder, gripping it bracingly. "Some rules are worth breaking, big brother. I know you like doing everything the *right way,* but *right* isn't always black or white. Some of the best things in life are gray."

My heart wrenches as my mind wanders to the memory of Delta's wide, gray eyes, gazing into mine in the moments before I kissed her tonight.

I love her eyes.

Raising a hand to signal the bartender, I lean back on my stool. "You sound like you're speaking from experience."

My brother laughs. "My whole life is shades of gray. I'll let you know when I find my best things, though."

Chapter 7

DELTA

"How did your appointment go, DJ?"

Normally, when one of my brothers asks me a question that I'm not interested in answering, pretending I didn't hear them is a good way out. We spend most of our time together wearing helmets and ripping down Blue Pike at breakneck speeds, which lends itself well to a certain degree of plausible deniability.

Unfortunately, that strategy isn't effective when I'm sandwiched between them on a ski lift. It's even less effective when it feels like your heart has been crammed in a blender and congealed into one big, confusing, sloppy mess.

I stare forward, pretending to be interested in the group of skiers taking selfies in the chair ahead of ours. "It went fine."

Shit-show is more apt, considering I walked into Doctor Harrison's office on Friday night as a fully qualified professional snowboarder, and I walked out on suspension. *Fucking medical suspension.* We didn't talk about it. He didn't ask me a single question. He just took one look at my hip and decided he knew what was best for me, my body, and my career.

After an earth-shattering make-out session on the exam table, neither of us acknowledged.

A part of me knows he was just doing his job, that he was looking out for me, and, worst of all, that he was totally right to do what he did. I *shouldn't* be competing, but knowing how bad it is hasn't been able to silence that nasty voice in my head that says this is the only thing I'm good at. It doesn't stop the anger I'm feeling toward Doctor Harrison or the hurt that's burrowed deeper and deeper into my heart in the two days since I stormed—limped—out of his office.

He didn't even watch me leave, just crossed his arms and stared at the floor, the fingers of one hand tapping restlessly on his bicep as I struggled to put my pants back on. I knew he was freaking out, probably regretting kissing me and risking his medical license—as if I would ever tell a soul—but considering he'd just taken an axe to *my* career, his silence made the whole thing so much worse.

My level of pissed was nothing compared to Dad's when I told him, though. Hours later, when I finally went to bed, I could still hear him on the phone downstairs, raging at anyone with a pulse at the USSA who would take his call so late. It worked too, or partially, because on Saturday morning there were two emails waiting for me. The first was an automated message from Doctor Harrison's office, informing me that my records had been transferred as per my—*Dad's*—request. The second was a formal notice that my medical suspension was pending following an examination by another doctor.

The appointment is scheduled for Friday.

Dad only grunted when I told him, his hand pausing on the way to pick his cup of coffee off the breakfast table. "Make sure you don't have anything in your system."

Anything being the full bottle of pain pills he'd left on my bedside table the day after our talk in the halfpipe.

I looked it up. I'd need at least four days to make sure my

drug test doesn't turn up anything, and as I stood in the bathroom with the bottle in my hand this morning, something inside me broke. My hand trembling, I turned it over and let dozens of little pills fall into the toilet.

I want this, really I do, but not enough to do anything for it. If that makes me weak, or a loser, so be it.

Sensing the shift in my mood, Bay clears his throat, looking past me to Lake. Right at this moment, they're wondering if I have my period and if they should leave me alone for the next week or bring me chocolate cupcakes after training. "Are you nervous about Everwater?"

"Sure." I probably *should* be stressing about it, but I'm too emotionally drained to care. Physically, I felt good when I woke up this morning. Two days off made a world of difference to my hip, and I'm feeling confident I can fake my way through some fancy tricks to impress the reps. Most sponsorship contracts are performance-based, though, and me standing on any podiums this season isn't exactly what I'd call a sure thing.

Especially if I'm more worried about checking my phone for a text from Doctor Harrison than putting on my game face.

I mean, *really*, he couldn't have even texted me? Earth-shattering, panty-melting, life-altering kiss aside, we're friends. He told me we're friends. I thought he cared, but the complete lack of contact since Friday has firmly put that misconception to bed.

I've let myself get whiplash from this man's mixed signals, and I'm done with it. I'm not going to be the one to reach out. If he wants to apologize, he knows where to find me.

"Bay and I were talking," Lake says casually. "We're thinking about getting a new place in February when our lease is up, without the other guys, you know? Do you want to go in on it? We'll make sure you have your own bathroom." He nudges me with his elbow.

It sounds good on paper, to get some space from Dad, but looking at their current apartment as an indicator of how they'll keep the next one… They're trying to be nice, so I keep my shudder internal. "That's sweet of you guys, but I'm okay where I am. Thank you for asking, though." I drop my head on his shoulder, feeling the tiniest bit better.

Bay, unsurprisingly, isn't put off. "DJ, *I'm worried.* We both are. We never see you anymore. You're always on the mountain… Are your nightmares back?"

My nightmares never left. I just got better about shoving a towel along the bottom of my bedroom door so nobody walking in the hall could hear them. "No. They're not."

Groaning in frustration, my eldest brother glares at me. "Tell me the truth. Is there something wrong with your hip? Like, *really wrong,* because Dad isn't telling us shit, and he's trained you to keep your mouth shut too—"

"Dad hasn't *trained me* to do anything!" I snap, rounding on him. We're nearing the top of the mountain. The chair two ahead of ours is getting off, and we lift the safety bar in unison. "That is so patronizing, Bay."

"Bay. Stop," Lake mutters warningly. "If she says she's fine, then she's fine."

Bay snorts. "*Fine?* Seriously, Lake? She's lost a fuck load of weight, she looks like she hasn't slept in a month, and she's been snowboarding like shit. You said yourself you think something's up!"

My jaw drops in incredulous disbelief, looking between them. "I'm snowboarding like shit? Fuck you, Bay, and you know what? Fuck you too, Lake. You're probably saying the same thing behind my back."

"Dude, I'm trying to defend you!" Lake snarls, just as our snowboards hit the top of the ramp and we rise as one, sliding smoothly down to the long stretch of open space which branches off into different trails and courses.

I don't want to see either of them right now, but as soon as I make to board off toward the halfpipe where I'm meeting Dad and the Everwater reps, Bay snatches my wrist and I'm pulled to a stop. The unexpected jolt sending red-hot pain shooting through my hip and down my leg, and I yelp, ripping my arm away from him.

Shit.

Bay is staring at me with a look of grim satisfaction. "*Fine,* huh? Tell the fucking truth for once, DJ. How bad is it?"

Lake stands to the side, looking back and forth between us. "Guys," he mutters warningly under his breath, jerking his chin toward a group of girls who are stopped a little way off. They're all in our club, and while they're probably just here to flirt with my brothers, there's no way they'd fail to tell everyone on the mountain if they heard a word of this.

"I know what I'm doing," I grit out, turning so the girls can't see my face. "It's none of your business, Bay."

He stares at me, jaw tight. "I'm looking out for you. God knows you won't do it yourself."

Yeah, I'm getting a lot of that lately. I have no shortage of men in my life who want what's best for me, but I doubt any of them are going to take care of me when this all comes crumbling down.

"What exactly do you want me to do?" I ask Bay, my voice deathly quiet and calm. "I *barely* got my GED. If my hip is as bad as you seem to think it is, then I won't get recruited to any college teams. Every penny I earned from my endorsements before I turned eighteen, my winnings from the Olympics, almost everything I've made, went into a trust I can't touch for another *four years.* So you can sit there and think whatever you want about me, but *I'm doing what I have to do.*"

It's the truth... just not all of it.

Lake grips Bay's shoulder and mutters warningly, "Bay. Drop it."

Bay, predictably, ignores him. "So you'll... *what?* Snowboard until your fucking leg falls off? News flash, DJ, your days are numbered. Sooner or later, you won't be able to hide how bad this is from that hotshot doctor of yours, and he's going to put you on medical suspension. What then, huh? Going to have daddy make a call and fix it?"

"Fuck you, Bay," I snarl, my chest heaving. He has no idea what a fresh wound he's just poked at, but I don't care. "You want me to stop because *you're* stopping. You want me to be a failure because *you* are."

I wait for him to bite, to fight back, and I'm not disappointed. Bay's lip curls. "Tell yourself whatever you need to, little sister. I think you and I both know the truth. I might be the failure, but you're the fraud."

"Enough," Lake hisses, finally losing his cool. "Stop it, both of you! DJ, head to the pipe. *Now.* We'll follow."

Bay and I stare at each other, and though I'm sure I will be later, I don't let myself feel sorry. Like me, my brother knows how to go for the jugular in an argument, because his words cut me deeper than I'd ever willingly admit.

Without another word, I slam my free boot into its binding and kick off toward where Dad and the Everwater reps are waiting. I expect to be able to push the fight with Bay aside, but with every nasty stab of pain through my hip, they worm their way deeper.

Fraud.

I *am* a fraud. The only reason I'm on this mountain is because of Dad. How many snowboarders are out there who are more talented than I am, work harder than I do, and deserve it more than me? I told myself that it was okay that I took the drugs, that it was just to get through training, but *it wasn't okay.* I'm a spoiled rotten princess who doesn't know how to lose, and now I'm a cheat, too.

Fraud. Fraud. Fraud.

The word rings inside my head, so loud it's nearly deafening.

"DJ!" As I approach the halfpipe, I see Dad standing with a pair of men in bright blue jackets, embossed with the logo for Everwater. He waves me over, grinning, the tension I'd seen in his face this morning long forgotten.

My smile doesn't come as easily. "Hey, Dad." I skid smoothly to a stop beside them.

"DJ, this is Daryl and Lucas from Everwater."

They both ring my hand, smiling broadly. "Excited to get you on team Everwater, Delta," says the taller of the two; Lucas. "Everyone back at the office is so pumped, I had to fight off junior executives who wanted to come meet you."

This is the part where I'm supposed to laugh, saying something bright and sassy, like *"I don't blame them,"* but I can't. "Thanks," I mumble instead, offering a strained smile. Beside me, I feel Dad stiffen.

The second guy, Daryl, clears his throat. "Well, don't let us get in your way. I'm sure you've got training to do. We're just here to take some pictures for the Everwater social media page and have you sign those contracts. River here said you guys would join us for dinner at the Log Jam Steakhouse tonight to finalize?"

It's a testament to how shitty I feel right now that I'm not even slightly looking forward to eating at a place that sells baked potatoes covered in bacon and melted cheese. I smile weakly. "Sounds great."

Dad follows me up to the deck, which spans the length of the halfpipe, the silence growing heavier by the second. It's a beautiful day, the kind of conditions you live for, and yet I barely notice as I sit down on one of the benches to get my board on.

Fraud. Fraud. Fraud.

"What was that, DJ?" His voice is measured and low, calm even. He's standing beside me, surveying the pipe with his arms crossed. I'm not sure anyone who isn't related to him could see the frustration simmering just below the unaffected surface. "I would have killed for an opportunity like Everwater when I was your age."

Yeah, he probably would have. I turn my eyes back to my boots. My whole life is crumbling down around me, dismantling piece by piece while I stand there, unable to move one way or another.

Fraud. Fraud. Fraud.

"I'll put my game face on for dinner." Straightening up, I push over to the edge of the pipe, staring down the steep ramp. Off to the side, I can see the Everwater reps watching with their photographers and a handful of other random people. They're here for me, they're expecting me to be great, and like a child, I just want to run and hide.

Fraud.

"Dad." My voice cracks and my eyes burn. I turn, looking over my shoulder at him. "Dad, I can't do this. I can't. I'm sorry. I can't—"

"DJ." He steps forward, putting himself between me and the small group watching far below. "That asshole doctor got in your head. We'll discuss this later, but right now, you need to get your ass in gear." We stare at each other, and my tiny flair of defiance dies out almost as quickly as it was born. Dad's eyes flash furiously. "Do you want to be a goddamn failure, DJ? Is that what you want?"

The icy mountain wind rustles against my coat, biting at my exposed skin, but I barely feel it as I pull my goggles down.

I don't want him to see my face. Do I look scared? I think I'm scared.

"Wait a second, kid." My chest seems oddly hollow as I pause, waiting, but Dad doesn't speak right away. I'm not sure what I'm expecting him to say, something fatherly, or even commiserating. Lately, it's felt like there's so much unsaid between us, but maybe that's just on my side. He's the same as he's always been. I'm the one who's changing.

I'm the one who's failing.

Dad clears his throat. "You've been under-rotating on your second turn of the switch backside. Watch that."

Okay. I'll watch that.

He thumps my helmet and steps back.

Fraud. Fraud. Fraud.

I push myself over the edge.

How many unanswered texts does it take before I snap, drive across town to track down Delta Jacobs and drag her back to my office for medical treatment?

Brooks: I understand if you don't want to talk to me, but the possible infection needs to be checked immediately. I emailed your case to one of my partners, Jenna Walters. She can come in out of hours to see you today.

Brooks: I'm so sorry for everything. Please don't put this off because of me.

Brooks: Jenna said you never called. If you want to see someone else not associated with my practice, I understand, but at least let me know where, so I can at least look into them for you.

Brooks: Please talk to me. I'm going out of my mind, Delta. I'm sorry.

Brooks: Delta, you can't fuck around with this. If I don't hear from you by tonight, I'll see you at Blue Pike in the morning.

I stare down at the string of unanswered texts, dread, and regret twisting sickeningly inside me. I sent the last of them before I left for the hospital this morning after yet another restless night, and my day has been too busy to check for a response until now.

Mindlessly, I take a bite of the sandwich, setting it down on the cafeteria table. I hadn't been bluffing when I said I'd go, but despite not hearing a word from him in the wake of Delta's appointment, I have a feeling that River didn't take my perceived betrayal so placidly. There's a very good chance he's banned me from the property.

I even went so far as to look up Delta's home address in her chart, breaking about a dozen privacy laws in the process, and a quick internet search confirmed that it's located in one of the rich, gated neighborhoods at the edge of town. Another dead end.

"Paging Dr. Harrison to the E.R. Dr. Harrison to the E.R."

My shoulders sag as I gaze down at the single bite taken out of my turkey sandwich, mentally cursing myself for ever thinking medical school was a good idea.

It's been one of those days. As a private practice physician, I don't typically round at the local hospital. Unfortunately, one of my colleagues is out on maternity leave, and all the orthopedic surgeons in the area are pitching in to cover for her. The chaotic unpredictability of the hospital environment always grated on me, and returning to it after over three years of regular scheduling, a full staff to boss around, and a mini fridge in my office, hasn't been pleasant.

Now, fresh off a weekend where I did little more than stew in guilt and self-loathing while obsessively monitoring my phone for a message from Delta, this entire day has been bordering on unbearable.

Abandoning my sandwich, I start toward the other end of the hospital, my mood plummeting with every step. If I'm lucky, it'll be a simple fracture. I can ship the patient off for X-rays, steal a few minutes to eat, and make it down to the OR for the torn Achilles that came in this morning. Then, after work, I can try to think of a better way to intercept Delta.

It's a pretty feeble hope, and the moment I push open the door to the ER, I know I'm never going to see that sandwich again. The hall is a mess of harried doctors and nurses ducking in and out of doorways, patients being wheeled around, and a drunk guy in a hospital gown yelling for someone to bring him a beer.

A nerve in my eyelid spasms.

"You paged me?" I ask the charge nurse, who's sitting at the desk near the door, typing furiously with a stack of urine samples beside her keyboard.

She barely spares me a glance before continuing whatever she was doing. "We had a snowboarder airlifted in about half an hour ago, post-traumatic head injury. Pritchett is evaluating her, but your name is all over her chart, and he thought you'd like to know."

No.

It feels like my entire world has narrowed down to a single point. The chaos of the ER has died away, and all I can think about is finding a way around this horrible new reality. "Name?" I demand, my fingers biting into the edge of the countertop.

It's not Delta.

It's not.

The nurse frowns, her eyes darting over the screen rapidly. "They've got her in bay 12, let's see... Oh, here she is. Delta

Jacobs. Birthdate, December tenth—" but the rest of her words are lost to me, because I'm already running.

I thought I knew fear before this moment, but it was nothing compared to the visceral, overwhelming terror gripping me now. How many times have I laid awake at night, worrying I would get this call? I should be prepared for this, but I'm not.

Delta's hurt. The words are blaring through my mind like a fucking fire alarm, but I still can't quite believe they're true.

It has to be a mistake. It has to be someone else. *Anyone else.*

The doors to bay 12 are open, but when I skid to a halt in front of the room, the place where the bed should be is empty. Three grave-faced men in identical black snowboard jackets are clustered together, completely silent. All of them look up as I enter, and the worried, tense expression on River Jacob's face makes my whole soul plummet through the linoleum floor.

I've never seen him worried about her.

"What the hell happened?" I snarl, tearing my gaze from River to the two men by his side, each of them older, male versions of Delta—her brothers.

The younger of the two, Lake, I think, glances at his father and then back to me before responding in a low, strained voice. "She went in for a frontside 1080. It's nothing. She's done it a million times. She landed it fine, but then she just..." He looks at the floor, his chest heaving, and I can fill in what he's not saying on my own.

My girl went down. Hard.

I round on River, fury rising hot and fast inside me. I have never once told off the family member of a patient, even if they were the reason their loved one ended up on my operating table. I'm a surgeon. It's my job to fix their bodies, not whatever hurt them. This is different, though. *This is Delta,* and River has put his champion snowboarder's career before his daughter's health, over and over again.

He did this.

"I told you. *I fucking told you,*" I snarl, lunging forward to jab a finger into the center of his chest. I'm taller than him, but not by much, and I stumble when he shoves me back.

He's shaken, but his pride is obviously still intact because River's expression goes from worried to livid in seconds. "Get the *hell* out of this room. You're never treating my daughter again. DJ knows her limits. If she didn't respect them, *that's on her!*"

I lunge forward, but this time Lake is prepared and catches my chest, yanking me back. His distraction ends up costing River, though, when his eldest son delivers the blow I wanted to throw myself.

"Fuck you!" roars Bay, towering over his father as River clutches his bleeding nose against the wall. "*Bullshit,* she knows her limits. Bullshit, she knows when to stop. *She has no idea when to stop!* You never gave her a choice. You bullied and shamed and forced her into this, and *look where it's got her.*"

"Was she conscious? Talking?" I demand before River can recover enough to start throwing punches of his own, looking to Lake, who's watching his brother and father with a grave, set expression.

He turns to look at me, and my heart wrenches as I meet his eyes and see they're the precise shade of gray as Delta's. "She was in and out. Really confused." His expression crumples. "She'll be okay, right? People get into shit like this all the time—"

The room is spinning around me, and realize it's because I've forgotten to breathe. I don't have any information at all to base this crippling fear on, but every second that passes makes me more terrified. I didn't stop her, I didn't do enough, and now the woman I love is somewhere in this hospital.

What if I never see her again? What if I *knew* something like this could happen, and I didn't prevent her from walking out of my office by any means necessary?

What if she fucking dies?

Bay turns away from his bleeding father to look at me, and his eyes are narrowed on my hospital badge. "Wait— *Brooks? Brooks Harrison?*"

I blink at him, momentarily distracted. "*Yes?*"

There's something accusatory in Bay's stare. "She kept saying your name... When we got here, she kept *saying it.*"

My stomach rolls so violently that, for a moment, I'm positive that I'm going to vomit my single bite of sandwich all over the floor.

I need to see her. Now. "Where did they take her?"

Delta's brothers look at each other, communicating silently. Finally, Bay turns to me, his expression tight. "They took her down for a CT a few minutes ago. We haven't heard anything else yet."

Behind them, River gets unsteadily back to his feet, and I spare him one last furious, scathing look as I back toward the door. "You knew she was in pain, you knew this could happen, and you wanted her snowboarding more than you wanted her alive and healthy. If anything happens to her, I'll make sure the whole fucking world knows it. I'll burn your life down, River," I spit venomously, hating him more than I've ever hated anyone in my life.

There's a hell of a lot more I'd like to say, but right now, Delta is my priority.

CT and all the other imaging services are in the basement and I don't bother waiting for an elevator, vaulting down the stairs so quickly it's a miracle I don't end up back in the emergency room. The hall is empty except for a housekeeper wheeling a cart of laundry, and for lack of a better plan, I start yanking open doors, ignoring the startled looks from whoever was working inside.

I get lucky. Pritchett, the head of neurosurgery, is standing just inside the third door I try. The small, dark anti-chamber is crowded with two techs and one radiologist whom I've met in passing, Ferguson. They're all staring at me in surprise, but I ignore them, advancing to the window which looks out into the CT room. A slight female body is lying prone on the table, her head inside the massive machine.

She isn't moving.

"Harrison." Ferguson frowns at me. "Why did they page you? This isn't an ortho case, is it?"

"She's my patient." I tear my eyes away from Delta to look over his shoulder at the computer screen where the scan is still in progress. It's been a long time since my neuro rotation, and I have no idea what I'm looking at besides a brain. I turn desperately to my bemused colleague. "How is she?"

Pritchett hums thoughtfully and leans over Ferguson to tap the screen, staring at it appraisingly for a long moment. "Grade 3 concussion, and by the looks of it, a small subdural hematoma. Should resolve on its own. Her spine looks good, but they drew blood when she came in, and that came back positive for opioids. No prescription, obviously." He rolls his eyes like he's not even a little surprised that a snowboarder was doing drugs, but it feels like I've been plunged into ice water.

Opioids.

Fucking opioids?

She's been using highly addictive prescription painkillers that she got from god-knows-where to get through training, and I had no fucking idea. Drug abuse happens a lot. I see it almost every day, but I never imagined Delta would take things that far. How the hell did I not even consider it? Chronic pain patients are some of the most prone to addiction, and yet I never even thought to check? I bring a shaking hand to cover my mouth.

It never occurred to me because I was too blinded by my feelings for her. I was thinking like a man besotted, not a doctor, and because of that, I fucked up and missed something.

At her last appointment... the way I took away her medical clearance. I knew she'd be angry. *I wanted her to be* because it was easier to face her hurt and her anger than the fact I lost complete control of myself and did something I couldn't take back.

River did this, but so did I.

"Page me when the scans finish, Ferguson. I've got to be on this. We're going to have a lot of eyes on us." Pritchett looks at me accusingly, like I've been keeping secrets. "You must know she's an Olympian? River Jacobs' kid?"

I nod, my eyes on Delta's motionless feet as the hand pressed against my mouth falls back to my side. "Yeah."

Pritchett whistles. "Girl was probably born with a snowboard strapped to her feet." He leaves. I stand there for a moment, feeling lost and hollowed out by guilt and fear, before catching sight of a lead smock on the wall.

If Ferguson is wondering why I came running in here at top speed and am breaking hospital protocol to go into a room where an active CT is underway, he doesn't say anything. I don't look back as I push open the door to the room and duck around the lead wall. Delta is only a few feet away, still motionless beneath the blanket someone wrapped her in.

"Delta?" I say quietly, not sure if she's conscious and not wanting to startle her. Her foot twitches and my heart leaps. "It's me. Don't talk, okay? It will mess up the scans." I reach the side of the table and take her hand in mine, sagging with relief when she squeezes it.

My confrontation with River, the drugs, all of it fades away as I let that one, all-important truth sink in. She's alive.

The room is completely silent, apart from the low mechanical humming of the CT machine. "This is actually perfect," I joke dully. "You'll have to listen to me." Her hand grips mine a little tighter, and my eyes burn.

I know I should just be here for her, but *she could have died*. She could *still* die, and I feel so raw and terrified that the filters I usually use when I speak to her are nowhere to be found.

I bow my head and squeeze my eyes shut, letting the feeling of her warm skin against mine ground me. "I'm not sure if you've ever heard this before, but you're worth so much more as a person than you are as a snowboarder. You're excellent at what you do, sweetheart, the absolute best, but it's just *one thing*."

Inside the machine, Delta sniffs.

"You light up the whole room when you walk into it, Delta. You're funny and clever and strong. *So* damn strong. Anyone who tells you otherwise is fucking delusional. Every minute of the day, I wish like hell we'd met under different circumstances."

I'm edging perilously close to a confession. Any other time I'd be pulling back, trying to minimize my slip, but not now. Now, I'm so fucking terrified that something might still go terribly wrong. I'm a doctor. I *know* how quickly things can go from seemingly fine to critical. Just because she's conscious now doesn't mean she's okay, and it doesn't mean something else won't happen. I don't have it in me to worry about the consequences of my words.

What if she dies, and she doesn't know I'm in love with her?

What if she lives, and she does?

I look up at the graying ceiling tiles and take another long, steadying breath, trying to get my shit together.

"You have no idea what you mean to me, and I want you to have everything, but *it's time to stop,* baby. You can't keep going like this. I swear I'll guard the damn chair lift if that's what it takes. I'll throw you over my shoulder every time I see you trying to get back on that mountain. *Fuck* what River thinks, fuck what anyone thinks. This is about you, *your life.*" I lace my fingers through hers and lean forward to kiss the back of her hand. "I know you're afraid of walking away and what that would mean, but you'll never lose me. Do you hear me, Delta? Never. I'm here. I promise."

Suddenly, there's a long beep, and the machine quiets. For a moment, there's only the sound of our breathing.

"I'm going to pull you out now, Delta," comes Ferguson's voice through the intercom system, and the bed starts to move.

I don't let go of her hand. As she comes into view, I meet a pair of wide gray eyes and see they're full of tears.

Chapter 9

DELTA

I don't remember falling asleep, but the sky is dark outside the window of my hospital room when I open my eyes. My entire body aches horribly and in the dim light from the bathroom, I can see a nurse beside me, poking at the machines I'm hooked up to.

"How do you feel, honey?" she asks softly, giving me a sympathetic smile.

I try to talk, but my throat feels so dry, and she hurries to pour me a cup of water from the pitcher at the end of my bed. I gulp it down greedily, my eyes fluttering shut as I struggle to piece together what happened. I remember the fall, how badly it hurt, and my heart aches at the memory of Bay's panicked yells, the sound of a helicopter, and then... my eyes pop open, searching.

I don't have to look far.

Doctor Harrison is sleeping in a chair beside my bed, his head resting right on the hospital bed, one of his big hands wrapped around my ankle. He's here? He's *still* here? Swallowing the lump in my throat, I look past him and see my brothers on the couch against the wall, passed out as well.

Bay's head has dropped onto Lake's shoulder, and both of them are snoring quietly.

I expect to see Dad, but he's not here, and the tightness in my shoulders lessens a little with the knowledge I'll be able to put off facing his disappointment for a little while longer.

"You have quite the dedicated fan club," the nurse tells me mildly, lifting my arm to check the IV taped to my hand. "None of them would go home when visiting hours were over. The *doctor* made quite a fuss."

I squeeze my eyes closed, struggling to recall what Doctor Harrison was saying to me as I was getting my brain scan. Everything seems fuzzy and distant, and every time I try to reach for a memory, it only gets further away. It's maddening, because even though I can't remember what he said, I know it was important. Really important.

"Hey, now." The nurse pats my hand gently, still keeping her voice hushed. "Things are going to be a little confusing for a while. You had a pretty serious concussion and a brain bleed."

I open my eyes and blink up at her dimly. "But I was wearing my helmet." It's such a stupid thought. I know people can get head injuries even with protective gear, but in my concussed mind, nothing makes sense. "Wait, my brain is bleeding?"

She smiles sympathetically, reaching for a blood pressure cuff on her cart. "Doctor Pritchett will be in to talk to you in the morning, but you're not in any immediate danger. You just need to be monitored. Bleeds like these usually stop on their own."

I stare at Doctor Harrison as the nurse wraps the cuff around my arm and makes a note on her chart before leaving with a promise to come back and check on me soon. He's still completely passed out, his lips parted slightly and an angry red mark on the bridge of his nose from where he must have been pinching it. He looks so human, obscenely handsome, but just a man.

"Every minute of the day, I wish like hell we'd met under different circumstances."

The words float back to me, more substantial and real than anything else in the hours following my fall. Did he really say that? It seems a little suspicious that I sustained a head injury and now I'm "remembering" Doctor Harrison saying things like that to me. Especially considering the last time we saw each other, he watched me walk out of his office without a word, and the two days of silence that followed pretty much confirmed he was done with me.

He's *here*, though, sleeping with his head on the end of my bed, holding onto me like he needs to make sure I don't go anywhere.

My eyes burn. He wouldn't need to be here at all if it weren't for my own stupidity. I shouldn't have been on that mountain today. I should have known my limits and told Dad I couldn't do it. He's a hardass, he pushes me, but he's not completely unreasonable. I've had two concussions before, neither as bad as how I feel right now, and both in the off-season. It'll take weeks to heal, and that's not even touching the fact that *my brain is bleeding.*

It's over. I know it in my heart, but I don't understand why the feelings I have don't seem to be bad. I think I'm... relieved?

I must be shaking with the effort it takes not to cry because, although I haven't made a sound, Doctor Harrison jerks awake. He looks around wildly, still half asleep, and if I didn't feel this horrible, I'd laugh. It's not funny, though, not now, and especially not when his eyes find mine and his expression seems to crack.

"Delta." He's on his feet in an instant, hovering over me. "Can you tell me where you are?"

I nod, pressing my lips together to keep myself from sobbing. "The hospital," I gasp, tears finally beginning to fall.

He stares at me for a moment, his chest heaving, and then I *know* I must be having some sort of brain bleed hallucination because he sits down at the edge of the bed beside me and pulls me tightly into his arms.

I don't remember ever being held like this, as though I'm something precious. "You're okay," I hear him murmur against my temple, his voice breaking as I cling to him, burying my face in his chest. One of his hands weaves through the hair at the back of my neck, cradling my damaged head so tenderly it makes my heart ache.

"I'm sorry," I blubber, my tears soaking through his scrub shirt. Even dizzy, emotionally drained, and likely out of my mind, I still have the foresight to try to remember all the little details of how it feels for him to hold me like this. "I was so stupid—"

"Stop." He grips me tighter, and I swear I feel his lips press against my temple. "You're going to be okay. *You're okay.*" It's like he's reassuring himself just as much as he is me, but the sound of his deep, measured voice cuts through my panicked haze, anyway.

I don't know how long we stay that way, clinging to each other without saying a word, but eventually, my tears dry up and Doctor Harrison untangles himself from me, returning to the chair he was sleeping in. He looks so tired, and I feel another stab of guilt for putting him through this.

"We need to talk," he says quietly, glancing over his shoulder at where Lake and Bay are thankfully still asleep. His throat bobs. "Why didn't you tell me?"

I blink at him in confusion, my sluggish brain struggling to comprehend what he's talking about. "What—"

"The pills, Delta." He bows his head, pressing his face into his hands.

Oh.

I'd forgotten, but of course, they would have taken my blood when I came in. Everyone knows now. I thought I'd cried myself out, but tears sting my eyes all over again and I press my lips together to stop myself from sobbing out loud. Shame fills me like bitter bile, eating away at my already bruised heart.

So, this is what rock bottom feels like.

"I'm—I'm *so sorry.*"

Doctor Harrison shakes his head and finally looks back up at me. We stare at each other in silence for a moment, me with tears pouring silently over my cheeks, him with his palm pressed over his mouth like he doesn't trust himself not to call me an idiot. Maybe he should. I've been so, so stupid in so many ways. It seems pretty pointless to deny the obvious.

"How long?"

My bottom lip trembles. "Not long."

"Delta."

"Since training restarted," I confess in a rush. I wish he would look away again. It would be easier to say all this without those warm, familiar eyes on me. "It's not why I fell if that's what you're thinking. I started off okay, but then there was this pain. I might have passed out—"

Doctor Harrison hisses, his eyes flashing. "Do you think I give a shit *why* you fell, Delta? You shouldn't have been on that mountain to begin with. You put your life at risk and *you could have died.* Do you know how fucking insane that makes me?" And he does look a little crazed, his fists clenched and chest heaving.

I stare at my lap. Everything is ruined. My snowboarding career is finished, my body is broken, and the man I've been in love with for three years hates me. "I was trying to do the right thing," I bleat feebly, wrapping my arms around my shoulders in a vain attempt to keep myself together.

"For who?" Doctor Harrison demands, his voice a dark snap. "Who were you destroying yourself for, Delta? Because I don't buy for one second that you want another gold medal badly enough to tear your body apart, endanger your life and become a *fucking drug addict.*"

He's right. I still can't say it, though. Not when admitting it out loud, or even to myself, would mean the end of the mythological figure that is River Jacobs. I've spent my whole life looking up to him, propping him up as the gold standard I should strive to be, and the fact I'm lying in this hospital bed is incontrovertible proof that he's just a man. A man who cares more about what I do and how the world sees me, than who I am or what I want.

"He makes me feel like I'm weak. Every single day, *I feel like a failure.*" The truth sounds so much worse when I say it out loud. I want him to leave so I can curl up in a ball and sob into my pillow. "And I am! I'm not good at anything else. I was such a shitty student and now I can't even snowboard—"

A large, warm hand touches my cheek, and I start, looking up to meet Doctor Harrison's fierce gaze.

"Delta." His eyes search my face, and I expect him to draw back, but he still doesn't move his hand. "You're the strongest person I've ever met, and I can think of half a dozen things off the top of my head that you're incredible at, which have absolutely nothing to do with snowboarding."

I let out a hysterical little laugh. He's so sweet for saying it, but the hospital bed I'm lying in right now seems like pretty convincing evidence to the contrary. "I'm a mess. I'm *broken!*"

"*You're not,*" he snarls, so suddenly and furiously that my mouth snaps shut in shock. "River's version of you is broken. Personally, I'm excited to see more of your version."

"Doc—"

He shakes his head and interrupts me with a single word that makes me feel warm all over. "Brooks." My breath catches, and he seems to shake himself, shying away from the seriousness of the moment with a wry smile. "I think we're past the traditional doctor-patient relationship, don't you?"

"Brooks," I echo, testing it out. It feels good to say it, but not as good as the way *Brooks'* jaw tightens when I do.

"You'll never lose me. Do you hear me, Delta? Never. I'm here. I promise."

I blink, trying to cling to the words that just floated back to me, but it's no use. Holding on to them is like cupping water in my hands, and before long, I'm left with nothing but frustration and longing.

Doctor Harrison—*Brooks* suddenly looks grave again. "Will you tell me where you got them? The pills?"

"I had them," I blurt out automatically. "I had my wisdom teeth out over the summer."

"Don't lie." We both look around. My brothers are both awake, and Bay is getting to his feet, his expression murderous. "Stop protecting him, Delta. You know it's wrong. You know how fucked up this is."

My vision blurs with a fresh wave of tears. I do know it's wrong, I do, but admitting it out loud? Admitting that my father would rather me be a drug-addicted, broken champion than a happy, healthy failure?

"Bay—" Lake, forever the peacemaker, protests quietly, "She's messed up right now. She doesn't need to be thinking about this shit."

"Yes. She does," Bay argues, coming to stand beside Brooks' chair. "She knows, and she needs to admit it, other-wise she'll be back to buying every line of his bullshit this time next week." He plants his hands on the edge of my hospital bed and leans forward, staring me down. "Where did you get the drugs, Delta?"

I close my eyes, instinctively reaching for that piece of me that's always stood firmly in defense of my father, but it's gone. The piece that's yearned for nothing more than to be loved and cherished by River Jacobs has vanished, leaving a rough, gaping wound in its place. Like he knows I need it without me having to ask, a hand I know belongs to Brooks finds mine and squeezes it in silent reassurance.

I suck in a shallow breath, my chest shaking with the effort to not start sobbing, and I finally open my eyes to look at the three men clustered around my bed. "I had some. From my wisdom teeth," I admit, and my voice is tiny and full of shame. "They ran out last week. Dad could tell. He asked me if I was taking something and I admitted it and he—and he gave me more."

All three are silent, staring at me with varying shades of fury in their eyes, and I'm suddenly so tired. I'm tired of being in pain, I'm tired of feeling like a failure, of never being good enough and lying awake at night thinking of all the things I should do better.

Did Dad see that?

Did he keep me down so I would strive to be better?

Did he starve me so I would fight to survive?

"Delta," Bay begins again, but Brooks shakes his head vehemently.

"Don't." His voice is firm and leaves no room for debate. "It's enough, Bay. She knows. Why don't you guys go home for the night and get a few hours of sleep? I'll stay with her and call if anything changes, but she's stable."

"Probably not a good idea." Lake rubs the back of his neck wearily. "Dad is her emergency contact. I don't want him to turn up here and start calling the shots. He'll throw you out, Brooks. The only reason he's stayed away this long is because he had to deal with the media shit storm."

Apparently, while I was unconscious, a new alliance was formed.

Brooks doesn't look worried. He's staring at our hands,

still intertwined on the bed like he forgot he reached out to me, and again, I remember his voice.

"You have no idea what you mean to me."

I'm not imagining him saying those things.

I look past Bay and Brooks to Lake who is lingering just behind them, pale-faced and exhausted looking. Defiance is kindling deep inside me. I'm not a victim, I'm not a puppet, and I'm never going to let myself forget it again. "Can you get someone to bring me the forms I need to sign to change my emergency contact?"

Chapter 10

BROOKS

part from a very shitty week with the flu about two years ago and the morning I went to see Delta at Blue Pike, I haven't taken a day off work since the practice opened. I like my job, and my conspicuous lack of a personal life has lent itself to spending a lot of time in the office. Generally, mine is the first car in the staff parking lot every morning, and the last to leave at night.

So, when I call the front office to let them know I won't be in for the third consecutive day in a row, I'm not entirely surprised to encounter some questions.

"Give me the phone, Courtney," I hear my business partner, Caleb's, muffled voice. There's a clatter and then, "*Three days in a row? Got something to share with the class, Harrison?*"

"You take every Friday off to golf during the summer. I think I've earned some personal time," I bristle, leaning against the wall outside Delta's hospital room.

Caleb laughs. "I'm not giving you shit. I'm curious. Come on, I'm married with three kids. The most exciting thing that happened to me this week was my husband finally agreeing to let me get myself a zero-turn lawnmower for my birthday. Give me *something*."

I watch as the old man occupying the room next to Delta's inches into the hall, pushing his walker with a swarm of nurses hovering around him. "You're a gossip. If I tell you anything, the whole office will know by noon, and contrary to popular belief, personal lives should be *personal*."

"God, you're so boring. *Boooo*—" I hang up, striding back inside just in time to see Lake toss a cheese puff across the room to Delta, who leans over the side of her bed to catch it in her mouth. All three Jacobs siblings cheer and I grit my teeth, snatching the massive container away from him.

"Would you *stop that*? She just had a head injury!" Who the hell let him through hospital security with a five-gallon bucket of cheese puffs? Isn't that some kind of health code violation?

Despite having witnessed the entire accident, Lake and Bay had barely assured themselves that their sister would make a full recovery before teasing and joking with her about the whole thing. I wish I shared their resilience.

Delta's lips twitch, looking up at me like she knows exactly what I'm thinking. "Has anyone ever told you that you're overprotective?"

"I'm your doctor. It's my *job* to be overprotective."

From his perch on the AC unit by the window, Bay snorts, "I've seen no evidence of that. It's Thursday morning, and you haven't left this room to do more than change your clothes and brush your teeth for three days. Don't doctors, you know, *work*?"

I ignore him, focusing my attention on pouring Delta a glass of water, which she takes with a sweet smile.

Bay isn't wrong. I've been sleeping on the couch to "monitor" Delta even though Pritchett quickly concluded her brain bleed wasn't progressing and she'd likely be able to go home soon. The infection in her hip was thankfully mild and the last piece of the puzzle before her medical team clears her for discharge. If her blood work last night was any indication, that will be today.

It's all been good news. Things are looking up, and yet I'm not acting like it. The terror I felt those first hours after the accident seems to have burrowed under my skin, and I can't shake the fear that the moment I walk out of this hospital, something will happen to her.

"Miss. Jacobs?" A nurse edges into the room, wincing apologetically at Delta. "Your father is here. He, *um*, asked for a word alone with you. Again."

I bristle, prepared to remind the woman that we've already informed her several times that River isn't welcome, but Delta beats me to it. "Tell him to leave," she snaps, crossing her arms defensively. "I'm sure he's making a fuss, but I'm an adult and he has no right to be here if I don't want him. *Which I don't.* I would appreciate it if you stopped asking."

Bay grins as the nurse leaves, properly chastised. "Fuck yeah, DJ. When did you get that badass?"

I let myself smile, too. She *is* a fucking badass.

"Could you get my phone, Brooks?" asks Delta. "I think I left it in the bathroom."

I do as she asks, attempting not to feel too pleased by the sound of my first name on her lips. I'm still not used to it, and despite the blatantly unprofessional nature of our relationship now, I won't let myself forget that wanting more is still impossible. Neither of us has brought up the *moment* in the exam room before her accident, or the things I said to her afterward, and I don't know what I'm going to say when it inevitably comes up. How could I possibly deny I have feelings for her when my actions have proven the contrary over and over again?

When I pick up her phone, though, an incoming notification from a popular apartment search website adds yet another worry to the mounting list.

"Thanks." She yawns, reaching out to take it from me and I sit down mutely, watching her cross her legs and take a long sip from the orange soda one of her brothers must have slipped her while my back was turned.

"You're looking for an apartment?"

"Well, yeah." She wrinkles her nose. "I don't think it's a good idea for me to be living with Dad at the moment and, *no offense guys,* but I don't want to live with Lake, Bay and whoever they take home to their all-you-can-bang buffet."

Both of her brothers roar with laughter at this, but I frown. I hadn't considered where she would go when she was discharged, and the last thing Delta needs right now is to be alone. She's recovering from a major head injury, will probably need surgery on her hip sooner rather than later, and is headed for a massive lifestyle change as she leaves snowboarding behind. Then, there are the drugs. I failed her once and I know I'll never stop regretting it. I refuse to watch her slip away from me again.

"You just had a brain bleed, and the underlying issue with your hip is still unresolved. You'll need surgery soon, which is *another* recovery."

Delta rolls her eyes, exasperated. "What do you want me to do, Brooks? I'm not sure if you're aware, but *all I know how to do is snowboard.* I've never had a normal person job. I don't have friends or classmates, and even if I found a roommate, it's not their responsibility to look after me."

She suddenly looks so fucking sad, and the suggestions on the tip of my tongue die away. She doesn't want to hear it, and I can't say I blame her. I don't know what my life would be like if I could no longer operate, but I'm positive I wouldn't be handling it as gracefully as she is.

Automatically, I reach out and take her hand in mine, and

warmth spreads through me at the way her expression softens, and the tension bleeds from her shoulders, comforted by my touch.

I'm not used to that. Nearly always, my attempts to support or commiserate with the people I care about have ended in forced smiles and a swift change of subject. My family and friends know I love them, but I'm no one's first choice for comfort during tough times and god knows patients don't come to me for my bedside manner.

Delta is the only person in my life who makes me feel like who I am is enough.

Across the room, Bay clears his throat, and when I look up, he raises an eyebrow at me cooly.

Hint taken.

Giving Delta's hand one last gentle squeeze, I draw back and she sighs, "Sorry, I'm being a bummer. It really will be okay. I have money for now, and I can get a coaching job while I figure out what I want to do next. I love cooking. Maybe I'll start a blog or something."

"You'd be a terrible coach," Bay adds unhelpfully, taking a long slurp of his orange soda—I feel confident that we have identified the junk food smuggler. "You didn't even like talking to the other girls in the club. You'd be too chicken-shit to tell people when they're being assholes. You do cook like a boss, though. I say lean into that."

"Yeah, because the girls in the club either hate me or they're obsessed with you. *Or you.*" She makes a gagging noise, and I press my lips together to keep myself from laughing. I'd thought Phoebe and Elliot were just particularly meddlesome, but apparently, it is a universal truth that siblings can irritate each other as no one else can.

I've found myself liking Bay and Lake more and more. I was wary at first, but my respect for them doubled on the second night here when they announced to a tearful Delta that they'd signed on to finish their season with a competing club across the city. Like their sister, the Jacobs brothers want nothing to do with River in the wake of the accident.

Lake, whom I quickly deduced is the most peaceable of the three, glares at Bay. "You're being a dick. DJ, you'd be a great coach if it's what you wanted. Don't you want to chill for a while, though?"

"Sure." Delta lifts her shoulder in a shrug, fiddling with her phone to avoid looking at us. "Rent isn't cheap if I want to stay here, but I guess I could go stay with Granny and Gramps in Connecticut while I regroup—"

My heart stalls. "No."

Bay, Lake, and Delta all look over at me, their expressions ranging from bemused to annoyed.

"Do you have a better idea?" asks Delta waspishly. "Because I'm going to be discharged soon, and as it is, my choices are either Dad's house, staying in a hotel, or crashing on the couch in my brother's apartment. Did I mention they share it with four other guys, all of whom have made it clear they'd be down to sleep with me at one point or another?" There's a challenging glint in her eye, and *I know* what she's doing. Behind her, Lake and Bay exchange murderous looks.

It's a testament to how utterly gone for this woman I am, that even knowing that I'm being provoked, I still can't resist biting. "You're not staying there. Or in a fucking hotel."

This is a bad idea. A terrible, impulsive idea that is almost guaranteed to lead to me doing something I shouldn't. I shouldn't say it. I should let her go to Connecticut to stay with her grandparents. They'd look out for her and I could do my best to protect her from afar. It's the reasonable thing to do, the way to prove to myself once and for all that nothing will ever come of my feelings for her.

When she says the word "roommate", though, an idea

began to take shape in my mind, one that's equal parts mad and wonderful.

"Oh no," Bay suddenly groans like he knows exactly what is going on in my head.

I lean forward in my chair and know I must be grinning madly. "Delta, how do you feel about dogs?"

"She used to *beg* Dad for a puppy," Lake snickers, elbowing Bay. "Remember? She tied her stuffed animal to a rope and dragged it around the neighborhood every day for a month to prove she was responsible enough to walk it. The thing got so beat up—*oh fuck*—it's legs were hanging on by threads." They're both howling with laughter by the end of the story and even I have to chuckle.

Delta isn't laughing along. She's staring at me like she didn't hear a word of what Lake said. Slowly, she turns away to look at her brothers. "Hey guys, could you get me another milkshake?"

They head off immediately, pleased to have a mission, and the moment the door shuts behind them, I wince. "I'm sorry. I didn't mean to make you uncomfortable. I think it makes sense, though... I have room."

She lets out a long breath. "I'm not uncomfortable. I'm just confused. If it weren't for the accident, I'm not sure I would have even seen you again, and now you want me to live with you?"

I balk at her suggestion, "Of course you would have seen me again!" I was threatening to track her down for fuck's sake. Did she think I was bluffing?

"Really?" Her eyebrows lift challengingly. "We kissed, you practically threw yourself off me, pretended it didn't happen, put me on medical suspension and I—we're supposed to be friends and you didn't even check in with me after all that. You can see where I'm getting some mixed signals here, right?"

"What do you mean, I didn't even check in?" I demand,

feeling sick. Should I have gone to see her in person? Called? I'd assumed she was furious with me. I was sure as hell furious with myself. Texting had felt safer. Did I overlook some social technology etiquette? "You didn't respond to the texts, so I thought—"

But Delta looks as confused as I feel. "You texted me?"

Wordlessly, I reach into my pocket and pull out my phone. Unlocking it, I open the string of messages I'd sent her in the days preceding the accident and pass it over. As she reads them, her eyebrows knit together, and panic flairs in her eyes.

"I didn't get any of those." She passes it back, staring down at her own phone. "That's weird, right?"

I don't think it's weird at all. Especially if she's on the phone plan of a controlling, vindictive asshole like River Jacobs who must have realized he was losing his grasp on his favorite trophy. Delta must be thinking along the same lines because her expression freezes.

"We'll check," I assure her quickly. "We'll find out what's going on, and we'll get you your own phone, on your own plan. *Today.*"

Delta nods jerkily, but I can tell she's still in shock. "Wait." She turns abruptly to look at me, wide-eyed. "Do you really have a dog?"

Chapter 11

DELTA

I'm living with Doctor Brooks Harrison.

In separate bedrooms, which definitely wasn't part of the elaborate fantasy I've been concocting for the last three years, but still. I'll take the win.

My heart practically leaped out of my chest when he first suggested it.

I'd said no at first. Obviously. *I had to.* He's a single man in his late thirties and *surely*, he doesn't *actually* want a newly retired twenty-year-old with a brain injury crashing in his bachelor pad.

I was wrong. Apparently, having a newly retired twenty-year-old with a brain injury living with him is exactly what Brooks *does* want, because he wouldn't take no for an answer. He even managed to convince—a clearly skeptical—Lake and Bay of what a perfect and not-at-all weird arrangement this was, and then all three of them were on me to accept.

When I'd hesitantly asked how much rent would be, Brooks looked at me like I'd cursed at him and resolutely refused to discuss taking my money. He wouldn't budge on it,

114

but reluctantly agreed to let me take care of cooking and cleaning, and only because I enjoy it.

They didn't give me a chance to change my mind. Lake had taken off to get my things at the house boxed up while Dad was at the mountain and move them over to Brooks' place. Bay, who also isn't on speaking terms with Dad for reasons he still hasn't told me, went out to get me a new cell phone that isn't on Dad's plan, and Brooks called his housekeeper to make sure his spare room was ready.

By the time I was discharged a few hours ago, the three of them had me all moved into a house I'd never set foot in before.

Where I'll be living with my orthopedic surgeon.

I'm pretty sure that concussion was worse than I thought because my life has suddenly gotten super weird. At least, brain damage seems like a reasonable explanation for the three massive balls of fluff lying on top of Brooks in the entryway to his cozy, A-frame house when I walk inside for the first time.

He'd insisted on going in before me when we pulled up, and when I saw him taken down by what appeared to be three slightly undersized white bears through the crack in the door, I knew why.

"I feel like this is weird, Brooks," I call, lingering in the doorway while he coos and scratches the dogs from his place flat on the floor. One of them, the smallest of the three, catches sight of me and gets off Brooks' leg to trot over, fluffy tail wagging.

"That's Tibia," Brooks informs me, hauling himself up and brushing dog hair from his clothing. "This is Fibula, and that's Femur."

I giggle, squatting down to let the not-so-little pack sniff my hands. They're beautiful dogs, *enormous*, but beautiful. The largest of the three, Femur, must weigh as much as I do. "Really, Brooks? Tibia, Fibula and Femur?"

He's such a dork. I love it.

His answering, lopsided grin sends up an eruption of butterflies inside me. "What can I say? I like what I do. Come on. I'll give you the tour." We move deeper into the house, the dogs trotting along with us like fluffy, panting clouds.

Brooks must have taken the trouble to have the place professionally decorated because it's *cute*, a little outdoorsy, but still cozy and modern. I was braced for a slightly nicer version of the nightmare palace where my brothers live, but I should have known better. His office has never been less than impeccably clean, and I once saw this man fold a paper napkin before throwing it away. *Of course*, there wouldn't be piles of dirty laundry on the couch or beer bottles on the counter.

"I pay for all the streaming services. They're logged in on the big TV there, but if you want the password for your computer or whatever, I'll text it to you," he rattles off, leading me around to the sliding doors, which span the entire back of the house, overlooking a stunning view of forest and snowy mountains in the distance.

I immediately understand why he bought this place.

The house can't be more than fifteen minutes from his office, but it feels like we're in the middle of the woods. There are no neighbors in sight, and after so long in the spotlight, my heart lifts at the prospect of disappearing for a while.

I love it here.

Brooks pulls opens the door and the dogs and I follow him out onto the back deck. There's a grill and lounge chairs, but best of all is the hot tub situated beneath a wooden pergola at the furthest end of the house from us.

I'm not sure why, but I feel a sick little twist of jealousy at the sight of it. How is it just now occurring to me that I'm here as Brooks' *roommate*? Roommates who made out one time—and have yet to discuss it—don't get dibs on each other. He can date whomever he wants. *He can bring them home if he wants.* What if I have to lie in my bed listening to the man I've been in love with for years having sex with someone else in the next room?

He said he didn't date much. I'm not imagining that, right? Still, he can't be completely celibate. He's ridiculously hot, and super successful, and—

"Delta?"

I blink, turning to look at Brooks, whose brow is creased with worry. "Sorry. Spaced out."

"Are you in pain?" he demands, going into doctor mode immediately, eyes scanning my whole body, looking for symptoms of distress. "Should we call Dr. Pritchett?" He starts to take his phone out of his back pocket, but I wave him off.

"No. Seriously, I'm just tired. That hospital bed isn't exactly comfortable, and having someone come in every thirty minutes to shine a light in my eyes kind of interfered with my REM cycle."

Brooks doesn't look convinced. "Do you want to try out the hot tub? I thought the heat might be nice on your hip. I got the model with the steps so you wouldn't have to—"

"Wait," I interrupt, warmth spreading through me. "You got that for *me*?"

"I mean, I'll use it too, I'm sure," Brooks confirms, suddenly sheepish. "It's nothing, Delta. I've wanted one for ages."

I won't let him blow this off and pretend it's nothing. *It isn't nothing.* It's so incredibly sweet and considerate, and I can't believe he went out and bought a hot tub for me to soak my hip in. He must have paid a fortune to have it installed and delivered with less than a day's notice. "Brooks." My eyes burn, and I close the distance between us, wrapping my arms tightly around his waist.

When he hugs me back, tucking my head under his chin

and pulling me into his warm, hard, Brooks-smelling chest, I could die happy.

I want him to hold me like this every single day, not just for comfort, but because it feels good.

"Hey." I can feel the deep rumble of his voice from his chest and burrow closer as Brooks weaves a hand through my hair at the base of my skull, so careful and gentle it makes my heart ache with longing. "I just want you to be comfortable here. I didn't mean to overstep."

I laugh weakly—no chance of that. I'm worried I'll get *too* comfortable, and he'll end up needing to drag me out kicking and screaming when he inevitably gets tired of having me here.

This can't last forever, can it?

Like he knows that's what I'm thinking, Brooks pulls back just a little, staring down at me imploringly. "Look at me." I do, and I know the dizziness I'm feeling has absolutely nothing to do with my head injury. "You can stay as long as you want, Delta. Redecorate. Paint the whole house pink. I don't give a shit. This is your home now."

I'm barely breathing. All those words from when I was in the hospital and the weeks leading up to my accident, *the kiss*... I haven't dared think about it too much, firmly trying to shut my idiot heart up before we both end up in pieces. When he touches me like this, though, there it is. *Possibility.*

"Come on." Brooks lets his hands fall but presses one to the small of my back, leading me inside to where the dogs disperse to their huge, fluffy beds arranged along the living room wall, watching us curiously.

I've never had a pet before, and as I got older, I did understand why. We traveled a lot and were all on the mountain from dawn until dusk. It wouldn't have been fair, but that didn't stop me from wishing I could. "I have to admit, I didn't picture you as a dog person. Never mind a horse person," I muse, peaking a look at Brooks, who is watching me cautiously. "I feel like there's a story here."

He chuckles, surveying them with a kind of exasperated fondness. "There is. Somebody dumped a box of puppies by the front door of the clinic in the middle of the night, maybe two years ago. There used to be a vet in the building, so the theory is they didn't bother reading the sign or *didn't care.*" He sounds disgusted, and I feel my jaw drop.

"They just dumped them?" I hiss, automatically moving over to kneel beside the closest dog, Fibula, I think, and scratch behind his ears. They're all so sweet, and they must have been the most adorable puppies ever. How could someone leave them in front of a random doctor's office?

Brooks sighs. "Yup. We got them on the security cameras and sent the footage to the police, but I have no idea if anything came of it. I took three, Tibia, Fibula, and Femur. My partner Caleb and his husband Todd took two, Patella and Ulna, and one of our nurses, Sean, took another, Radius." He shrugs like all this is no big deal. "I'd just bought this house, and it has a lot of land, obviously, so it made sense."

Hands down, the dorkiest, cutest thing I've ever heard.

"You'll have to show me their routines, so I can take care of them while you're at work." I climb back to my feet, hissing at the familiar shooting pain through my hip. "I'm not going to miss that," I sigh, rubbing the joint wearily.

"There are no painkillers in the house."

Oh. Ouch.

I don't look at him. It's fair to be worried about that. I fucked up after all, but it still hurts. He must know I'm not a drug addict. I was in the hospital for three days and didn't take anything stronger than an ibuprofen. The pills were a means to an end, a way to get through the pain I can now recognize was my body screaming for help. I was stupid to ignore the signs, stupid to fight so hard for something I'm not sure I ever truly loved, but *it's over now.*

I remember the hushed conversations between Bay, Lake, and Brooks at the hospital when they thought I was sleeping, and a new, terrible suspicion sets in. "Is that why you wanted me to live here?" I ask quietly, keeping my eyes on the dogs. "So you could watch me?"

Brooks hesitates long enough for my heart to plummet. "Not entirely, but I'd be foolish not to take this seriously, Delta. I'm not sure you realize how many patients I've seen addicted to prescription painkillers, or how often those people turn to street drugs when the pills aren't an option anymore. I would never forgive myself if I watched you go down that path and didn't do everything in my power to stop it."

I should be happy he cares about me and wants me, but right now I just feel *small.*

"It's fine, I get it," I tell him out of habit. It's the truth, I do get it, but when I see his worried, frustrated look, my heart sinks. I take a deep breath. "I'm sorry, that wasn't true. I'm feeling—" It's a struggle to name the emotions intense swirling inside me, but I owe it to him to try. "I'm hurt you didn't tell me that, and guilty I put you in this position, and sad too, I guess. That I'm a burden."

Brooks stares at me for a long moment, silent and expressionless. "You're not a burden, Delta. Not in the least. You're a person I care about tremendously, and you've been through an incredibly difficult period of your life. I want to support you. I'm sorry I said what I did about the painkillers. It wasn't kind."

He's not lying. I know that because Brooks has *never* lied to me, and I wish I could hug him again without it being weird.

"Let's just forget it." I tug my sweater tighter around my

body, trying to protect myself against his effect on me. "Did Lake ever get the chance to drop off my stuff?"

Brooks seems relieved to have something to do. Gesturing toward a flight of polished wood stairs, he leads the way up onto a landing which overlooks the great room below. There's nothing up here but a little area rug and a lamp in the corner, and three doors leading off.

I hang back as he opens the closest and leads the way into my new room. There's a big window, partially obscured by boxes, and warm wood covering the slanted ceiling just like the rest of the house. It's not a huge space, but there's a cozy armchair and a comfy-looking bed that's piled high with blankets.

"It's small." Brooks clears his throat. "I'm sorry, nobody's ever lived in here. There's a half bathroom downstairs off the kitchen, but there's only one with a shower." He nods back toward the landing.

"It's beautiful," I reach out to squeeze his hand reassuringly and my stomach flips at the pleased, crooked smile he gives me in response. "Why are you smiling?"

He chuckles, eyes glinting in amusement. "Because *you* are, Delta."

I am?

Oh shit, I am.

My emotions lately have been wildly out of control, swinging between complete devastation, guilt, and joy every ten minutes. "I'm sorry. I don't know what's wrong with me right now."

I've been waiting for the longing for my destroyed career to hit me. I should be missing the mountain, the familiar strain of my muscles as the earth slides beneath my feet, the sun on my face, and the cold wind biting at my cheeks. *I should be missing my dad.* What does it say about me that I don't? What does it say about me that of all those feelings swirling inside me, the only one that's constant is *relief*?

"There's *nothing* wrong with you." He sounds so sure about that, even angry that I suggested it. "You've been through a lot. You need time to process and a professional to talk to if that's what you want."

I let out a hysterical little giggle. I'm not against starting therapy, but the idea of confronting all the shit I'm feeling is beyond daunting. I want to be okay, though. No, more than that, I want to be happy, and I've never been one to back down from a challenge. "I probably should." I finally concede. "I'll call some people on Monday to see if I can get an appointment. It might be hard with the holidays coming up."

Brooks opens his mouth to say something, but we both still when the sound of the front door opening comes from downstairs, along with the padding of paws and a single booming bark.

"Brooksie?" calls a man's voice, and Brooks' eyes widen comically. He looks horrified.

"Oh, Christ. I apologize in advance for this," he mutters, shaking his head, before calling out, "coming!"

I follow him back down the stairs but stop short on the last step when I see the man standing in the entryway, playfully ruffling Femur's fluffy ears. He's tall and *built*, with muscles straining behind a fitted black t-shirt and leather jacket. His dark hair is long enough to be pulled back into a bun and while I can't see most of his skin, the tattoos scattered over his neck and hands suggest they're everywhere.

The stranger turns when Brooks clears his throat, but his eyes move right past him to where I'm standing, his lips curling into a gleeful smile. "Well, well. Who do we have here?"

"Delta," Brooks grits out, looking severely annoyed. "This is my brother. Elliot."

Damn, how many other impossibly attractive Harrison siblings am I going to encounter?

"Eli works, gorgeous. That's what all the girls call me." Elliot grins, straightening up. He moves right past Brooks, unphased by the death glare, and holds out a hand for me to shake.

When I do, Brooks' eyes narrow.

"No. *Eli* doesn't work." My grumpy, brand-new roommate crosses to the front door and opens it. "You've come, you've antagonized, you can leave now."

I was thrown off by the tattoos, long hair, and leather jacket, but there's definitely a resemblance between the Harrison brothers. They have the same square jaw, the almost-black hair, and straight nose. Elliot looks like a blue-eyed, slightly shorter, delinquent version of Brooks. He's closer to the kind of man I should probably be interested in, but beyond the aesthetic appeal, he does absolutely nothing for me.

Apparently, my type is obsessive, overprotective, orthopedic surgeons.

Elliot ignores Brooks' not-so-subtle attempt to get him to go, taking his time to look me up and down, eyes gleaming with amusement. "I'm going to guess you're *the complication* my brother was talking about over drinks last week."

He was talking about me?

My heart flutters, and I pull my sweater tighter around me, trying unsuccessfully not to read into that. "I couldn't say."

"I could." His crooked grin slips away. "Wait a minute. I know you, don't I? Delta..." His eyes widen, and he looks over at Brooks with a look of dawning comprehension. "*The snowboarder?*"

Brooks closes the door with a snap, glaring at Elliot in a silent dare to continue that train of thought.

Not fazed by his brother's nonverbal threats, Elliot laughs

gleefully. "I didn't know you had it in you, Brooksie. *Damn*. Breaking lots of rules lately."

I bite my lip, watching Brooks' scowl deepen. "I'm just going to go unpack for a while. I was going to make dinner for us soon, if that's okay, Brooks?"

"Of course." He isn't looking at me, though, and I feel a pinch of self-consciousness. Is he angry someone knows I'm here?

"Um. Are you staying, Elliot?" I offer hesitantly.

The Harrison brothers reply at the same time. *"No!"* and *"Yes!"*

I'm starting to get why Brooks was unfazed by Bay and Lake. *"O-kay."* I take another step back, but Elliot isn't done with me yet.

"Unpacking, huh? Going to be here all weekend?" he asks casually, but there's a suggestive undertone to the question that makes my cheeks burn. Am I supposed to tell him I'm living here? Is it a secret? Surely if Brooks wants me here for a while, like he's said, he had to know his family would find out.

"Delta lives here now," Brooks spits with the furious, reluctant energy of a man confessing to a crime he was caught committing.

I frown at him. I won't be for long if he's going to shove me in the coat closet whenever someone rings the doorbell. We're not doing anything wrong. He's not even officially my doctor anymore.

Catching sight of my face, Brooks winces apologetically. "I mean, *I invited her*. We're friends, and I want her here." His words are stumbling and awkward, but *he's trying,* and I feel my tension ebb just a bit.

"Well," Elliot smirks, looking between us. "I'll leave you to get your *friend* settled in, brother."

I retreat back upstairs to give Brooks the chance to scold his brother in private, feeling flushed and off-kilter. My whole life is suddenly upside down, and I've fallen into a strange parallel universe where sexual tension is the currency.

I'm just starting to look around my new room when the space is filled with an unfamiliar ringing. Peering around, I spot Brooks' phone laying atop the dresser by the door and I'm about to call out to him when my mouth snaps shut. It's stopped ringing, but the screen is still lit up, and I can still clearly see his background.

It's the picture he took of us at Blue Pike.

Brooks is peering right into the camera, unsmiling and serious, but I'm looking at him. Every single thing I was feeling is on my face, longing and hope and admiration. Nobody could look at it and not see I'm in love with him.

He made it into his background.

Pressing my hand to my mouth, I take a long, shaky breath, heart thundering in my chest.

I'm coming for you, Brooks Harrison.

Apart from my mother and sister when I was a child, I've never lived with a woman before.

Asking her to move in wasn't exactly planned, and in the ensuing scramble to get it organized, I had a few moments of worry. My routines are well-cemented and haven't changed much in the two years since I got the dogs. I expected that having Delta in my space would mean becoming tolerant to a certain degree of disruption and I was determined to be accommodating to *her* living requirements. Just because it's my house doesn't mean she shouldn't feel at home, or comfortable, and I hated the thought of her walking on eggshells, afraid of upsetting me for using the wrong napkins.

I was wrong. Yes, things have changed, but somehow she *fits*. I'm not sure if it's because we were friends first, or simply compatible as roommates, but I find the first few days of sharing space with her surprisingly easy. She might be a walking, talking temptation that makes me hard as a rock just from breathing, but she also cleans up after herself, dotes on the dogs, and her cooking "experiments" are all incredible.

Within a week, we've fallen into a comfortable rhythm. I

strategically get up early to sneak in some time in the basement gym, a necessity considering I'm no longer exclusively subsisting on pre-made salads and leftover rotisserie chicken. When I'm done, showered, and ready for work, Delta is usually up feeding the dogs and making breakfast.

She sends me off with lunch in a brown paper bag, a thermos of coffee, and a kiss on the cheek that lingers on my skin for hours afterward.

Evenings are spent taking walks through the snowy woods with the dogs, finishing up work at the kitchen island while Delta cooks dinner, and sitting a careful distance away from her on the couch while we read or watch a movie. Then I made an excuse to go upstairs early and spend half an hour in the shower, viciously fisting my cock to the memory of her doing something completely innocent, like bending over to pick up the fork she dropped.

I can't stop thinking about *the incident* in the exam room.

So much has happened since that day that it feels like another lifetime, but in reality, it's been just over a week.

Things were so intense for so long. I was worried about her hip, then terrified I might lose her, and now everything is... *normal.* She's out from under River's thumb. She's healthy, she's safe, and she's *living in my house.* Just as suddenly as I realized my attraction to her months ago, it hit me her first night here, how utterly fucked I am.

I've backed myself into a corner, eliminating all my usual routes of escape, and I'd done it all with a smile on my face. Hell, *I'd pushed for it.*

She isn't my patient anymore, either. River saw to that in the aftermath of her medical suspension, and now I'm scrambling for new reasons why being with Delta Jacobs is impossible. The more, the better. At present, my defenses are looking staggeringly weak after the removal of the ethics code violation.

Then there's the touching.

I don't make it a habit to put my hands on anyone in an interpersonal setting. My lack of physical affection was a major issue in my few failed relationships, but making a conscious effort to do it felt forced and awkward. Touching Delta is almost unconscious. I find myself taking her hand to help her over fallen logs when we go for walks, brushing her back when I pass her in the kitchen, and wrapping my arms around her to hold her close on those rare instances when I see a shadow of sadness cross her face.

Aside from my brother, nobody knows she's living with me, though I doubt I'll be able to keep that up for long. Sure enough, I'm on my way home from work exactly one week after Delta moved in—pretending it's completely normal for me to be leaving thirty minutes before the office closes rather than staying two hours late—when the phone rings. I have no reason to be suspicious, my mother doesn't stick to a particular time or day to call me, and yet I'm prickling with unease as I hit 'accept' and Mom's voice fills the car.

"You need to bring your girlfriend to Christmas."

Fucking Elliot.

I pinch the bridge of my nose as I stop at a red light. I was foolish for not seeing this coming. My mother is the sweetest steamroller on the planet, and even after thirty-eight years, I'm completely helpless to derail her when she decides what she wants.

I'm desperately trying to maintain some control over this situation, and bringing Delta home to meet my family sounds like a recipe for further complications. I'm not worried they're going to dislike her, I'm worried they're going to love her, and the last thing I need is one more reason why Delta Jacobs is the most perfect woman on the face of the planet.

"Mom, she's not my girlfriend. We're just friends," I attempt to argue, not expecting it to work. To the best of my mother's knowledge, I'm a monk, and discovering I now live with a woman has undoubtedly reignited her long-dormant hopes for more grandchildren.

On the other end of the line, I hear a deep sigh. "Brooks, *sweetheart*. I promise we won't embarrass you in front of your new girlfriend—"

"She's not my girlfriend." I just communicated that, and I can't tell if she's ignoring me or somehow missed it. "Do you need your hearing checked, Mom? Jenna's brother is an audiologist. I can make a call."

Another sigh, this one longer and steeped with disappointment. "Your *friend* then. Phoebe told me she is absolutely lovely, and Elliot says she's very nice and *pretty*."

My brother noticing how *pretty* Delta is, puts my teeth on edge, and it's yet another reason to keep her well away from my family.

I don't for a second believe Elliot would try anything. He's a good brother, and he's pieced together enough of the situation to understand I have feelings for her. He must understand that I can't do anything about them. What if Delta likes *him,* though?

She asked him to stay for dinner the other night.

Was she disappointed when I practically shoved him out the door?

Elliot is single, he owns his own business, he has long hair and tattoos, and none of the complications that would come from her having feelings for me—a possibility that has been steadily growing in likelihood, even as I resolutely attempt to ignore it. How many times did I say the wrong thing at the wrong time and hurt her unintentionally with my bluntness? How many times have I shown I was interested, only to return to cold professionalism moments later? If I were her, I would probably prefer my brother.

A sour taste fills my mouth at the thought.

"Mom, please. You'll meet her another time." I grip the wheel tighter than is strictly necessary as I make the final turn into our driveway and park beside Delta's jeep. Apart from the windshield and hood which I cleaned off this morning, the car is still dusted with last night's snow and hasn't been moved all day.

"It's very hurtful, Brooks. I won't pretend it isn't. I can't *believe* I had to find out you're *finally* seeing someone through your brother, of all people, and I swear he only told me to take attention from that dreadful new mark he got on his neck—"

Elliot has a lot to answer for, but telling Mom about Delta to distract her from his neck tattoo is a new low.

"I'm not *seeing* anyone, Mom, and Christmas is... a lot. Delta was hospitalized for a head injury recently. Can you guarantee that the boys aren't going to knock her down a flight of stairs or something? Because I can't." Holidays in the Harrison household are chaotic at best and bedlam at worst. My nephews behave more like wolverines than children, my parents always fight over whether the turkey is done, and Elliot gets so drunk someone—me—needs to drive him home.

"Phoebe has promised to have words with them. They're *much* better now, and *Delta* can wear a bike helmet if it makes you happy. Brooks, sweetheart, you struggle with this kind of thing, but even if she's just your friend, it's polite to invite her."

I stare up at the warmly lit house, itching to open my car door and go inside, but I force myself to stay where I am. This isn't a conversation I want to have in front of Delta. "I understand manners, Mother. I'm autistic, not a child."

The way my mother gasps at this, anyone would think I just swore at her. Despite keeping it quiet, I'm not ashamed of my diagnosis. If anything, it was a relief to have an explanation for some of my more frustrating idiosyncrasies, but Mom has always tried to dismiss it as much as possible. She means well. She's trying to protect me from the stigma, but it's tiring.

"Brooks William Harrison, I don't appreciate the attitude. I'm only trying to include your *friend* and welcome her into our lives. However, if you're so embarrassed by us—"

God damnit. I knew I couldn't win this, yet I fought her on it, anyway. I can only imagine how much extra energy and free time I would have if I accepted my mother's will without argument. "I'll *ask*," I grit out, annoyed beyond belief. "That's it, Mom. *Ask*. I don't know what her plans are. Listen, I'm just getting home and I need to walk the dogs. I'll call you this week to discuss it."

I refuse to let her long, suffering sigh make me feel guilty as I hang up and step out onto the snowy driveway.

The driveway up to the house cuts through almost half a mile of dense forest, I have no neighbors in sight, and the large windows that see straight into the kitchen and great room have never worried me before. With Delta living here, though, maybe I should install some curtains or blinds. She's a public figure, and I don't like the idea of her wandering around her own home only for some creep to sneak pictures from the woods.

The moment I open the front door, all thoughts of window treatments vanish.

The great room is empty, no Delta, no dogs, but as I set down my backpack and make to shrug off my coat, movement catches my eye from the back deck. Almost instantly, arousal surges to life like a live wire beneath my skin. I stand there, staring, exactly like the hypothetical creeps I was concerned about a few seconds ago.

Delta obviously found the Christmas lights in the basement, because they're strung up over the pergola which covers the hot tub, casting a warm glow over the back deck. All three dogs are lying in the snow, accepting pets from Delta, who is dressed in nothing but winter boots and a tiny black bikini.

It's like all the air has been sucked out of the room and I can't move. *I can't even breathe.* All I can do is watch as she straightens up and crosses over to the hot tub, steam rising into the icy air around her.

I'm hypnotized as Delta toes off her boots and steps right onto the packed down snow around the hot tub. She looks like a goddess of winter, her skin shining gold in the glow cast by the Christmas lights, so mind-numbingly beautiful that I half expect to wake up and discover this has all been a dream.

Holy fuck.

I'm hard almost instantly, and my thoughts seem sluggish and muted as I grip my cock through my pants, gritting my teeth to keep myself from groaning out loud. No good can come from me going out there. I should go upstairs, jerk myself off to the memory of how her ass is hanging out of that fucking bikini, and consider myself lucky I got to see her in it at all.

I don't go upstairs.

Possessed by a reckless impulse fueled by something greater than attraction or desire, I find myself moving toward the back of the house. Like a moth to a flame, I'm drawn to her against reason. I can't stop myself and, as I pull open the sliding door and step out into the cold night air, I'm not sure I want to.

Delta looks around at the noise and watches silently as I close the door behind me, smiling gently in welcome. It's bitterly cold out here and she's half my size. It seems impossible that she isn't freezing, but her teeth aren't chattering, she doesn't seem to even have goosebumps.

Like my eyes are working independently of my brain, they rake greedily over her body. I've never seen her like this before, fucking on display for me, feminine and strong and so mind-numbingly sexy my erection is bordering on unbearable.

I take far too long to look away, my heart thundering as I kneel to pet the dogs.

What the hell am I doing?

"How was your day?" she asks, her sweet, carefree voice carrying back to me over the winter air. There's a little splash and a sigh as she steps over the edge, sliding into the water.

"Good. Long. I was—" My words falter and I clear my throat, trying again. "I was in surgery."

I avoid looking up as long as possible, hoping and praying she'll be up to her neck in water and I won't embarrass myself by ogling her all over again. When I've delayed the inevitable long enough, I raise my eyes to meet hers. She's thankfully covered by the churning water, but it doesn't help. Not at all. Just catching another glimpse of her bare shoulder makes my cock throb painfully.

Delta hums, skimming her hand over the surface. "You must be sore. Why don't you put on your suit and join me?"

A terrible idea if ever I heard one.

"Maybe later." I swallow, my brain too sluggish and lust-drunk to think of a reasonable excuse for why. "How are you feeling?"

She's fine. *I know* she's fine, but I need something to focus on other than my need to close the distance between us and take everything I've ever wanted from her. An ache, a pain, anything to dampen the lust raging inside me like wildfire.

Her lips curl into a self-satisfied little smile. "Great. Better than I have in ages."

I cast around for another subject, something safe and completely nonsexual. "My mother wanted me to ask if you'd like to join us for Christmas dinner. I told her you'd probably have plans with your brothers."

Delta shakes her head. "They'll be in Utah. The first qualifying event is a few days after, and they're going out early to train for a few weeks with their new club. Don't worry about me, I was just going to hang out here. I wouldn't want to impose."

My stomach sours at the idea of her spending Christmas alone in my living room while I'm across town with my family. No way. "Come with me. We don't need to stay long, and I'll make sure they're on their best behavior." I'll try, anyway. At the very least, I'll be sure to clear up the fact that Delta is most definitely not my girlfriend with Mom before the day comes.

"Okay." She dips lower so the water touches her chin and the loose strands of her hair that have escaped her bun float out around her. "Are you sure you don't want to get in? It feels amazing."

"No," I answer firmly, fighting the urge to adjust my throbbing erection. "No, I shouldn't."

Delta doesn't reply for a long time, and I'm about to say something, *anything,* to break the tense silence when suddenly she stands. Streams of water run down over her body, shining from the lights above.

The term *'mind-numbing'* never made sense to me until this moment, when every conscious thought in my head is wiped away by a rush of desperate, dumb lust. If things were different, *if she was mine,* I could pull those little strings holding her bikini together and have her naked in seconds. I could make sure she never wore the damn thing in front of other people and spank her ass red if she had. I could carry her inside where it's warm, bend her over the kitchen table and fuck her so hard she'd feel it for days.

Blowing out a ragged breath, I'm only dimly aware that I've been staring at her for far too long, my eyes raking over her every inch of exposed skin as she steps over the edge of the tub. When I make it to her eyes, they're blazing with triumph and in a horrible moment of clarity, I know I've just walked into a test.

She was worried the exam room was a fluke.

She wasn't sure, but now she is. She knows I want her.

Delta moves gracefully down onto the deck, only a few yards away from me. "Why shouldn't you, Brooks?"

Tension hums in the air between us, pulling tighter by the second, and I realize I don't have it in me to keep up the facade anymore. She suspected before, and now she has confirmation.

I swallow the tightness in my throat, forcing myself to look directly into her eyes and not flinch away like I ache to. She needs to know why, she needs to understand. "We can't." Two words to break my own heart. "What happened in the exam room was a mistake. Regardless of how I feel about you... We can't, Delta."

"Brooks—" Delta takes another step closer to me, and her face has been transformed with such obvious, incandescent joy. "Say it again. Please."

I don't understand why she's looking at me like that, why the words I just told her don't seem to be sinking in. "We can't?"

Her face splits into a radiant smile, and even through my inner turmoil and frustration, I'm in awe of her beauty. "The other part."

"I—" I squeeze my eyes shut for a second, trying to assemble my thoughts. When I open them again, I'm looking directly into stormy gray. "Regardless of how I feel about you?"

A watery, joyful little laugh falls from her lips. "How do you feel about me, Brooks?"

My jaw goes slack as realization hits me like a truck. *She's happy because I have feelings for her.* I hadn't known, not for sure. I'd surmised she was attracted to me, had a crush, but the look on her face suggests she's just as in this as I am. It says she's been waiting for me to say those words, and now—

"No." I step back, blood rushing in my ears, my skin crawling with panic. "It's not only that we can't, *I don't want to.*"

Her smile falls just a little, but something else in her expression flickers to life. *Fight.* For the first time since we've met, I can see the heart of a champion burning behind her eyes. Unwittingly, I've just handed Delta Jacobs her next goal and I'm positive I should be terrified right now.

"So, I should find someone else, then? If you're not interested," she asks, and without even raising her voice, it's like a punch to the gut.

"Do you want someone else?" I bite back, and Delta moves forward again. I'm paralyzed, glued to the spot as she crosses the distance between us, not stopping until the vapor from our breaths curl together in the winter air.

Her smile isn't soft anymore, it's dangerous. "Not at the moment. Someday, though. A girl has needs after all."

What I wouldn't give to know what her *needs* are.

She's trying to provoke me into action, but it won't work. I know her heart, who she is, and the fact she won't go off and sleep with another man when she has feelings for me. But, even knowing all that, I'm not immune to the suggestion making me fucking furious. I don't care if it's irrational or unfair, or if it makes me a possessive, alpha male asshole. If anyone else lays a finger on her, I'm prepared to rip it off.

Gritting my teeth, I glare back at her. "*Enough.*"

I once thought Delta was the only one of us who wore a mask, but I can see now that I do too. I hold myself with confidence, I direct operating rooms and obsessively manage every part of my life. When all that control is stripped away, when she looks at me and breaks down every single door I've spent years hiding behind, what's left that's worth having? There are a lot of reasons it would be wrong to give in to my feelings, but *this*... this is the biggest.

This woman, an actual gold medalist, will conquer the world if given the chance. What would she do trapped in her hometown with an old doctor? She deserves so much more.

She'd regret me, regret wasting her youth on a man who wants less than she's capable of, and it would break me.

I love her, and that means putting her first, even if I hurt myself in the process. Steeling myself, I stare down at her, hating that I can still see the hope in her expression. "I'm not interested, Delta. I'm sure there are lots of men who would be impressed by your little hot tub routine, but I'm not one of them. Put your clothes on and go inside. Don't try that shit on me again."

Like the coward I am, I turn, walking back toward the house before I can see the damage my words inflict.

I f there was an Olympic event for avoidance, Brooks Harrison would be a gold medalist many times over.

It's been a week since the night on the deck, seven days of conversations engineered to be as unarousing as possible—Friday night's dinner was accompanied by a lecture on compound fractures—and Brooks doing everything possible to not be left alone with me.

Yesterday, Saturday, would have been our first full day together since I was in the hospital. I'd practically skipped out of bed, brimming with ideas on how to break his avoidance streak and provoke him into action, only to discover Brooks had invited Lake and Bay over to help him install a doggy drinking fountain. The installation process took a turn for the worse—not surprising considering two professional snow-boarders plus one orthopedic surgeon do not equal one plumber—and I spent most of the day grooming the dogs while the men in my life pumped water out of Brooks' flooded basement.

I'm sure he expected me to be wounded and resentful, or maybe even avoid him right back. That's how most women would react to being flat-out rejected by the man they're in love with.

Don't get me wrong, it sucked. I was hurt.

Then, just like I've been doing my entire life, I dusted myself off and planned my next attack.

I might be young, but I'm not naïve. I'm not the same seventeen-year-old girl who took one look at Brooks Harrison and *knew* he was the only man for me. I know what I want, I know what I'm doing, and now I know for sure this connection isn't one-sided. I might have doubted before, so wrapped up in my shit that I missed what was right in front of me, but that night confirmed what I think I've known for a while.

He wants me, he might even love me as much as I love him, but Doctor Brooks Harrison is also a neurotic, type-A nutcase who can't stand stepping off the beaten trail even for a second. Falling for someone so much younger than him, *his patient,* must be eating him up inside. This is a man who wouldn't let me use the new toaster until he read the instruction booklet that came with it from cover to cover. I'm not sure what he's telling himself to justify pushing me away, or what it's going to take to show him how wrong it is, but suddenly I have nothing but time to figure it out.

The trouble for poor Brooks is that the *someone* he wants is me. I've spent my whole life falling and getting back up. I've battered my body, broken my own heart, and pieced it all back together again.

I can do anything.

Even convince the stubborn doctor we're meant to be together.

* * *

"Good morning!" Brooks stops short on the second to last stair, staring blankly at where I'm standing at the kitchen island, cracking eggs into a pan. It's only six. He didn't expect me to be up this early, and now his plan to avoid me is foiled.

Oops.

"Good morning." He starts moving again, carefully averting his gaze as he sorts through the pile of mail I left on the table.

I bite back a smile, taking the opportunity to appreciate how good he looks in gym shorts and a fitted white t-shirt. "Coffee's fresh."

Brooks makes a noncommittal noise, examining a pamphlet for driveway sealing a little too intensely.

"Want a breakfast burrito? I put kale in them. Super healthy, but it doesn't taste like it." Sticking to Dad's insane performance-enhancing diets was how I got into cooking. There's only so many times you can eat steamed veggies and dry chicken before you start actively hallucinating about cheeseburgers. Now, with more time on my hands, I've started inventing my own recipes. It's fun and I like the challenge, but more than that, I love that I'm taking care of him in some small way.

Brooks hesitates, and I keep my eyes on the pan, pretending I don't feel the weight of his gaze on me. "Sure. Thank you." He finally agrees, moving over to the kitchen counter to pour himself a cup of coffee. I choose that moment to "drop" a dish towel, and when I bend over to get it, I hear the distinct sound of liquid overflowing from a mug, followed by a low curse.

"What are you—*I mean*—where are you going?" he asks when I straighten up, mopping up the spill and obviously taking a stab at the same nonchalance I'm employing, as if everything is completely normal between us.

"Oh!" I glance down at myself like I'd forgotten what I was wearing. It's nothing over the top, just a pair of jeans that make my butt look fantastic—hence strategic towel-dropping

—and a soft white sweater, much nicer than the oversized t-shirt and leggings I usually wear in the morning. "I'm having coffee with my agent in an hour. She's been getting a lot of job offers for me and I figured I should hear them out. I can't be a stay-at-home dog mom forever." I reach down and scratch my always-present shadow, Tibia, behind her ear.

Brooks isn't amused. "Shouldn't you wait until after we figure out the next steps for your hip? Your appointment with Jenna isn't until after Christmas."

I wasn't excited about being treated by the guy my dad requested to reevaluate my medical suspension, and Brooks' less-than-approving scowl when I brought him up sealed the deal. My first choice in doctor is obviously the grumpy grunter himself, but the last thing I wanted was to hand Brooks his *legal objection* shield of power back.

He didn't suggest that either, but did mention bringing one of his partners up to date on my case. Hell yeah.

I shrug. "It couldn't hurt to find out what's out there. I need to get a job." I flip the eggs off the pan on the waiting tortilla. "Besides, retirement is boring. There is only so much cooking I can do before we both explode. That *would* be a pretty sweet way to go, though."

Brooks chuckles, and for the first time since the hot tub incident, he's suddenly looking at me directly. "I might have something for you. It's not snowboarding related."

I blink in surprise. "Oh?" Something not snowboarding-related sounds ideal. I still haven't spoken to my father, and there's nowhere in the industry where he doesn't have pull.

It's been weird being removed from that world. On my second day here, Brooks showed me the shelves in the garage where Lake had stashed all my snowboarding stuff. It was all there, my boards, my favorite pair of neon-pink goggles that an equipment company designed just for me, three full bins of snow pants, jackets, helmets and gloves, and every award I'd ever won. My gold medal is in there somewhere, but I've made no effort to dig it out.

I wish he'd left it all at Dad's. God knows it all means more to him than it ever did to me.

"Delta?"

I smile apologetically, turning my eyes to the burritos. "Sorry. Go on, you were saying something about a job?"

"My sister, Phoebe? She manages a spa downtown. I was speaking to her yesterday, and she told me their after-school babysitter fell through unexpectedly. She's been setting the boys up in her office. Not ideal, believe it or not. It's only for a few hours every night during the week, more over winter break."

"Oh." I bite my lip, buying myself time to think about it as I slide Brooks' breakfast onto a plate and pass it over to him. "I'm not sure she'd want me for that."

I don't have a ton of experience with kids, but if I'm honest with myself, my biggest hold-up is the fact that Phoebe kind of intimidates me. She's gorgeous and perfect, and she makes other women look gorgeous and perfect for a living. Meanwhile, I gave myself my last haircut in the bathroom mirror, and wearing jeans that fit correctly is my version of making an effort. I was raised by a single father and I have two older brothers. I wasn't exactly getting lessons on how to get my eyeliner to do that fancy swoop thing.

I've heard myself called beautiful, and I can see my attractiveness in an objective, matter-of-fact kind of way, but I'm not sure I've ever *felt it*. Except maybe those few minutes when I was sitting on that exam table, and my orthopedic surgeon looked like he wanted to eat me alive. Admittedly, the subsequent rejections might be playing into my sudden body image issues.

Brooks makes no move to start eating. "If you're not interested, that's fine, but the boys would love you. They're wild, but I suspect you can handle it."

I turn to put the pan in the sink, all the triumph I'd gained from successfully disarming Brooks, draining away. I can feel him looking at me, knowing he's struggling to understand my obvious mood shift.

A babysitting gig doesn't sound bad. Playing games and doing arts and crafts sounds like exactly the kind of low-stress job I need, but I still hesitate.

"I might be a little intimidated by your sister," I admit, heat crawling up my neck and cheeks. "I'm sure she's nice, but would she? I don't know…" My words trail away as I play self-consciously with the ends of my hair. Admitting insecurity isn't something I have a lot of experience in. Twenty years of being trained to show no weakness has made expressing how I feel about as easy as pulling teeth. Brooks told me to be direct, though, if I want him to understand how I'm feeling, I have to say it.

He doesn't move, waiting patiently for me to gather my thoughts, and my heart squeezes with affection for him.

"My mom was a bikini model," I tell him, a little sheepishly. "The whole world knows that. I don't think I'm ugly or anything, but she was beautiful, you know? Like, *stunning*. There have been… comments. Online mostly."

"Comments?" Brooks demands, and despite his cool, controlled tone, I can sense an underlying fury.

My heart drops. He's been careful not to touch me this week, and I've never missed it more than I do right now. Feeling his arms around me had quickly become the best part of my day, and the absence of that connection aches worse than ever now.

I shake my head, grimacing. "It doesn't matter. I have a social media manager. I don't even check it anymore. Now that I'm not working, I'll probably delete all my accounts." That doesn't mean I'll forget the things I used to read daily, mostly from men, crudely wondering how the apple fell so far from the tree. "I really try not to be insecure, and I swear I like myself, but sometimes it hits me how little I know about girl stuff. It's not like I have a sister, or girlfriends, or—or a mom." My voice cracks on the last word, and I can't look at him. I'm too embarrassed.

For god's sake. I wanted to seduce the hell out of this man, not make him feel sorry for me.

Barely five seconds pass before warm hands wrap loosely around my arms, and Brooks pulls me into a tight hug. My eyes burn, but almost immediately, the tension drains from my body. I needed this so badly. I bury my face in his neck, greedily inhaling his woodsy, masculine Brooks scent and when his lips press against my temple, I could swear he trembles.

"Come on," he mumbles, drawing away from me just as quickly. "Let me take you to meet Phoebe. I promise you'll like her. Just trust me, okay?"

While she and Brooks are so different that it's hard to believe they're from the same family, Phoebe Harrison-Nichols quickly proves herself to be just as awesome as her brother. Where Brooks is reserved and quiet, Phoebe is outgoing and charming. She has a kind word for every single person and makes you feel like you're her best friend within the first five minutes of meeting her. It should seem fake or forced, but it doesn't.

Brooks clearly tipped her off we were coming because Phoebe didn't seem the least bit surprised to see us at her workplace, just greets me with a warm hug and a flurry of questions about my new retirement. The salon, which I learn she's working towards buying—though she glares at Brooks when he mildly suggests giving her a loan to help—is trendy and bustling with activity.

We end up sitting in her office for over an hour talking, but the day takes a turn when I mention scheduling an appointment for a haircut on my way out. Before I know it, I'm being shepherded into a salon chair and Brooks—who had long since stopped contributing to the conversation and was clearly tired of us—mumbles something about the bookstore before disappearing.

Phoebe, to her credit, waits for her brother to be gone before leaning in to ask conspiratorially, "So, what's going on there? Elliot told me you're *living with him?*"

I wince. "We're just friends. Kind of. It's... complicated."

"I'll say." Phoebe laughs, standing behind me to fiddle with my hair, and our eyes meet in the mirror. "So, are you *just friends* because my brother doesn't know what's good for him or because you're not interested?"

I've never talked to anyone about this, and I hadn't realized how badly I needed to until I'm spilling everything to Phoebe as she cuts my hair. She's his sister. I expect her to be on his side, but that's not the case. On the contrary, there are a lot of outraged gasps and disapproving head shakes as the conversation progresses.

"He's crazy about you, Delta," Phoebe concludes as she sets down her hairdryer. "I could tell the other day when we met at his office, and it's still there today. I've never seen Brooks look at *anyone* like that," she sighs, a little misty-eyed. "You're probably thinking of packing it in because he's impossible and probably a bit of a clueless asshole, but hang in there. He can only keep this up for so long. Brooks is the best person in the world, but you have to get through about twenty levels of ironclad defenses before he lets you see it."

She's not wrong. I *know* he's the best person in the world.

I stare at my reflection. I told Phoebe to use her best judgement, and she did. My light brown hair now hangs in neat layers, somehow effortless and put together at the same time. I feel so pretty. "Thank you so much, Phoebe. I love it." I smile at her in the mirror, my heart lighter from the talk and mini makeover.

"Has he already blown it?" she asks, worry coloring her tone.

Has he? I'm not sure. It occurs to me, though, that this time I might not be bouncing back as effortlessly as I usually do from a setback. Apparently, my threshold for emotional pain isn't quite as high as it is for physical. "I'm not sure," I admit, fingering the ends of my new haircut. "I think I might be a little scared to push it. He made it clear he doesn't want me. I don't know if I can stand hearing it again."

Phoebe undoes the snaps holding together the hairdressing smock, and when I get to my feet, she pulls me into a tight hug. "Why don't you come see me on Friday? I'll take you to lunch," she suggests when we break apart. "I swear it's only thirty percent a bribe to get you to watch the boys after school for me."

We both laugh, just as a cool, gruff voice cuts through the chatter of the salon. "Ready to go?" Turning, I find Brooks standing off to the side, snow dusting the shoulders of his wool coat, watching the pair of us with as inscrutable an expression as ever.

I nod, moving toward him, but Phoebe calls out, "What do you think, Brooks? Doesn't she look great?"

My steps falter, and I'm struck by the same sensation that always seems to grip me in the seconds before a fall. My body locks up, bracing for impact.

Judging by the flash of regret across his handsome face, Brooks didn't miss it.

"I'll see you Friday, Phoebe! Thank you!" I call over my

shoulder, moving past him to the door before he can answer his sister's question, hating that he can shatter the way I feel about myself with a single dismissive word.

Outside, snow is swirling, and Christmas lights sparkle from every store window. It's my favorite time of year, but I don't stop to admire any of it as I march down the sidewalk to where the car is parked, pulling my coat tighter against the cold. Brooks was right. I did like Phoebe, but the last hour I spent with her made me realize how much I ached for someone I can talk to, someone I can *really* talk to. Stopping at the car, I lean against the passenger door, staring down at the sidewalk. I only realize Brooks has followed when a pair of black boots stop right in front of me.

I let out a long breath, steeling myself.

"Delta." His voice is quiet and strained. "You look so beautiful. You always are, but right now especially." My eyes burn, but still, I keep them glued to the ground, not daring to meet his gaze. "I'm so sorry, Delta. I've been such an asshole, I'm so fucking terrible at this. I never meant—the other night, and in the exam room. You have to know you take my breath away on an hourly basis. I can't—I can't get through two minutes without thinking about you. I'm the problem here, not you, and *not* what I feel for you."

My answering laugh is short and humorless. "I know I'm younger than you, but I have heard the 'it's not you, it's me' cliché before, Brooks."

Slowly, like he's giving me every opportunity to make a run for it, the boots step closer to me and a warm hand nudges my chin up to meet his warm, blazing eyes. "I don't want you to resent me for not being able to give you the life you want," he whispers, voice rough with emotion. "It would kill me, Delta. Please understand."

That's why he won't let himself do this? Not because of

how we met or my age, but because he believes I would resent him?

My head spins. "Brooks, why would you think that?"

His throat bobs. "Look at the snowboarding. You did it, *you were the best at it*, even though it was hurting you. You damaged your body, you took drugs, you would have done *anything* because you thought it was right. I'm not the best thing for you, and someday you'd realize that. I won't be the next thing you tear yourself apart for."

Sleep doesn't come easily for me tonight.

After a silent drive home from Phoebe's salon, Delta left almost immediately to see Lake and Bay before their trip to Utah. The moment her headlights disappear down the drive, I want to call her to come back.

I pace the house for hours, replaying the events of the day. Whenever I remember the way her expression shuttered when Phoebe asked my opinion about her haircut, I'm gutted all over again. She was happy when I came in, so fucking beautiful she lit up the whole room, and she expected me to take that away from her. I tried to make it right, tried to apologize and explain, but nothing seemed to help.

All this time I've felt so *sure* I was doing the right thing by keeping her at arm's length. It might hurt, it might be fucking torture, but *it was right*. Now... Now, no matter how many times I tell myself it's for her own good, I can't dismiss the gnawing fear that I'm just a coward.

When Delta finally comes home, it's nearly ten, and I barely have time to scramble off the couch before she's wishing me goodnight and hurrying upstairs with all three dogs on her heels.

I'm trying not to take their obvious preference for her too personally. If I were them, I'd like her better, too.

Left alone beside the dying fire, my heart in my stomach, I'm so lost in my miserable spiral it might be minutes or hours before I finally trudge up to bed. I pause on the landing, hovering outside her door, warring with the impulse to knock. I don't, and my last thought before I fall asleep is that I have to fix this. There has to be a way to keep her here with me, happy and safe, without *more*.

* * *

It's still dark outside when I wake, blinking at the ceiling. The house is silent around me, and I'm groggily scrolling through a list of explanations for why I'm no longer asleep when I hear it. Across the hall, through two closed doors, a muffled cry.

As suddenly as if someone had doused me in ice water, I'm on my feet. Wrenching open my door, I cross the landing in three strides to Delta's just as another sob shatters the house's silence. I don't hesitate before pushing it open. Inside, the room is lit only by the first traces of hazy, early morning sunlight filtering through the blinds and I blink, struggling to make sense of what I'm seeing.

On the bed, Delta thrashes, her legs tangled in the sheets, her chest rising in falling in ragged pants. She isn't sick, or being attacked, or any of the hundred other horrible possibilities that flashed through my mind when I realized what woke me. She's having a nightmare.

"Delta." I sink down at the edge of the bed, my heart still thundering in my chest. Her skin is clammy as I smooth back her hair from her damp forehead, trying to wake her gently. "Delta—"

Almost instantly, she curls closer to me, one hand fisting the hem of my t-shirt. The blueish light gives everything an oddly surreal feeling, and it's like I'm watching from outside my own body as I swing my legs up onto the bed, and gather Delta in my arms. She comes easily too, murmuring incoherently as her hand slips beneath my shirt, spreading flat over the skin beneath my bellybutton, her warm touch searing me.

Her heart is still beating wildly and the occasional tremor wracks her body as the nightmare slips away. Does this happen often? For months, long before the accident, I thought she looked tired. I'd put it down to too much training, but could it have been this too? How many nights have I laid across the hall sleeping while she suffers through this?

The possibility makes me a little insane.

After a few long minutes pass and her breathing has become deep and slow, I begin to ease away. I can talk to her about it tomorrow and find a specialist who can help—

"Brooks," she mumbles, and the room tilts when one bare, toned leg slips from beneath the blanket to hitch over mine, effectively stopping me from moving an inch. She's not wearing shorts, just a pair of polka-dotted purple panties, and I'm hard almost instantly, my cock obscenely tenting the black boxer briefs I wore to bed, inches from where Delta's hand is settled.

Holy fuck. I need to leave. *Now.*

"Delta." I nudge her weakly, trying to wake her up without any real conviction. She only sighs, nestling closer to me, her toes skimming over the top of my foot. I squeeze my eyes closed, determined not to look. "Delta," I say a little more insistently, and this time, her body tenses.

Slowly, she lifts her head to look at me, blinking in sleepy surprise. "Brooks?"

"Hi." I grimace, glad she's looking at me and not down at my fucking cock. "I'm sorry, you were having a nightmare—"

"Oh!" she starts, as though just realizing that she's draped herself all over me. Scrambling back to sit on her knees, I take the opportunity to swing my legs back over the edge of the bed, my mouth dry. "I'm so sorry I woke you up."

I swallow thickly, remembering the fear in her sleeping face when I first came in. "Do you get them a lot?"

Delta's lips quirk into the usual sheepish half-smile she uses when she's embarrassed about something. "Sometimes. I've been better lately since I stopped snowboarding. I get them more when I'm stressed."

My heart wrenches and for a long moment, we're both quiet. My reason for being here is gone, and it's not even five in the morning. I should say goodnight and go back to my room, but as I begin to move, Delta's hand shoots out to touch mine.

"Brooks." I pause, waiting, and see the briefest flicker of apprehension cross her face. "I threw the pills out."

My breath catches. *"What?"* It was the very last thing I expected her to say, and I lean forward.

Delta speaks in a quiet rush, as though she's been thinking about this a long time and wants to tell me before she loses her nerve. "The morning of my accident, I flushed them. I couldn't do it anymore. I know it doesn't excuse taking them in the first place or being dumb enough to get back on that mountain when I so clearly shouldn't have been there." She looks down at her hands in her lap, and I see a slight tremble in her shoulders. "I just wanted you to know, because snowboarding is not the same thing as you and me. It's not even close."

I have to close my eyes for a second, processing this piece of information that's completely shifted the way I see her and our situation. "How can you be sure?" I barely recognize my voice, and I realize as I open my eyes to look into the beautiful face of the woman I'm in love with, the woman I thought I would never have, that it's because I'm begging.

Please, let her be sure.

Delta doesn't answer right away, and I can tell by the bold, defiant squaring of her jaw that she's mustering her courage for what she has to say next. "I didn't love it." Her words falter and I ache to go to her but force myself to remain still, heart hammering as she gathers her thoughts. "It's all I knew for *so long*. I clung to it because it was familiar and because I wasn't sure I could do or be anything else. I know now that isn't true. I want to surround myself with people who love me and love them back. I want to be a wife, a mom… I know those aren't big, exceptional things, but I'm so sick of not being happy, Brooks."

She didn't love snowboarding, but she loves me. She doesn't say the words, but I know it's what she means, and something slots into place inside me. I'm filled with fierce pride and joy, so powerful and all-consuming I'm positive I'll never recover from it. *She loves me* and I've been such a coward, pushing her away again and again, making up excuse after excuse to deny what has been right in front of me for months. Did I think she wanted an all-star career or to see the world? She could have done that. She could have left Colorado after her accident and never looked back, but she's been here. Fighting for *me*.

She loves me.

She loves me.

She loves me…. and I'm done not loving her back the way she deserves.

I thought I was strong, I thought I was resolute, but I was never enough to resist the storm that is Delta Jacobs.

Our first kiss was an explosion, the culmination of weeks of tension, and I barely slowed down for long enough to make sure she was enjoying it. This is so much more than that was, and—*fuck me*—I want to take her goddamn breath away. Delta makes a tiny noise of surprise as I swing my legs back over onto the bed, curling an arm around her waist to pull her flat onto the tangled sheets.

In seconds, I've covered her body with my own, pressing her into the mattress and I barely give myself time to appreciate how fucking beautiful she looks right now before I'm kissing her so fiercely I feel it through my whole body. She's right there with me, her legs parting, dragging me closer like she needs this as badly as I do.

We're doing this.

I have things I need to say, though, and before I lose myself in her completely, I pull back, staring down into her wide gray eyes. "I love you." My voice is raw and desperate. "*I'm fucking in love with you, Delta.*" I don't want any more misunderstandings, nothing else left unsaid between us.

Ours is insane and messy and unlike any love story I've ever heard. I was so sure I would be alone, and now a whole world of possibilities is blooming in front of me, in front of *us*.

Like she's seeing the same things I am, tears are shining in Delta's eyes now. A joyful little laugh bubbles from her lips, quickly silenced when I lean down to kiss her again, hot and hungry. Her legs hook behind my waist, and I groan into her mouth as my throbbing erection presses against that narrow strip of fabric covering her hot cunt, feeling the wetness she's already made for me. I let her take the lead, loving the way she keeps trying to get closer, rolling her hips against mine, clutching my shoulders, my hair, my arms, and my face.

"Brooks!" Delta's hands on my face pull me back from her, even as she keeps up her teasing little grinds, driving me crazy with how good this is. She smiles, and it's so radiant my heart seems to stall. "*I fucking love you too.*"

I know she does.

I bow my head to suck on her pulse point, hard enough to

leave a bruise. "Can I eat your pussy?" I mumble, still kissing her neck. It's all I've thought about for weeks. What would have happened if I hooked the fabric of her panties aside that day in the exam room? What noises she would have made? What her face would look like when she came undone?

Delta whimpers, still grinding her hot little cunt over my shaft. "Yes, please—"

Thank fuck.

I sit back on my heels and tug the bottom of her tank top up. She lets me, and we laugh when the clingy material gets caught around her head. Finally free, Delta sprawls back on the bed, naked apart from the utterly soaked panties molded to her sex. I take my time with those, peeling them as I shower her breasts with kisses that make her squirm and sigh.

"You're so sexy, baby." I curse quietly when she's finally naked, her legs spread wide on either side of my hips.

I'm going to eat her alive.

Delta whimpers when my hands skim over her bare legs and I lean down, kissing the skin of her sternum. "I love it when you call me that."

"Baby?" She nods wordlessly and I grin up at her, already moving back on the bed, getting ready to devour her. I keep my eyes on her face to make sure she's watching, and her lips part in a silent moan as I push two fingers through the shining, wet lips of her pussy. "*Fuck*, you're soaked."

There's a wet spot on my boxers over the head of my dick, and as I lower my head to taste her for the first time, my cock is leaking so much pre-cum that it's probably soaking her sheets. I don't care. My only concern right now is the sound of Delta's ragged breathing above me and the musky, feminine taste of her on my tongue. "*Brooks*," she whines as I lap greedily at her swollen clit, warm thighs pressing on either side of my head.

She's so fucking responsive. Every little flick of my tongue makes her twitch, but when I begin circling her entrance, Delta's hands in my hair stop me. "I've never...." She trails off, cheeks flushed with embarrassment.

"Never done this before?" I lift my head to see her properly. I'd guessed as much. Not because she seems inexperienced or I don't think I'm going to have to deal with half the men in the country wanting what's mine, but because *I know her*.

Delta Jacobs doesn't like to be vulnerable and doesn't give away pieces of herself so easily. She would never be sprawled naked across her bed with a man between her legs unless she trusted him completely, and I'm going to spend my entire life striving to be worthy of this honor.

I don't give her the chance to respond, ducking down to pull her clit between my lips, suckling and batting it with my tongue. I don't care if nobody has touched her. No, fuck that, I'm ecstatic. Every moan, every shudder, every time I have to press my eager girl's hips back down, it's all mine. Nobody else will ever see her like I do.

"I'm going to finger you." I sound like a caveman, growling and grunting at her, but one look up at her is enough to confirm that Delta isn't bothered. Keeping my gaze trained on her wide-eyed face, I push a single finger slowly into her little hole, and we both moan. She's tight, her walls gripping me like a warm glove, and I grow painfully hard at the thought of how good it will feel to shove my cock inside her for the first time.

Soon.

Delta whimpers, drawing her knees up instinctively, opening herself up for more. "I—I like it," she sighs, and sucks in an unsteady breath as I pull back and re-enter her with a second finger, giving her a good stretch. "*Oh fuck*, Brooks!"

"So goddamn tight." I think I could come just from dry-humping the bed I'm so turned on, but I keep my attention on her. I fuck her slowly with my fingers, occasionally leaning down to lick or suck her throbbing clit, and when I add a third, Delta squeals in surprise. I'm a depraved asshole for liking that so much. "Too much, baby?"

She shakes her head as her hands find her own tits, squeezing and teasing those tight little nipples. The sight is so hot, I can barely stand it. "I'm so close—"

Yeah, I bet she is. Every time I push this further, giving her a chance to slow it down, she gets wetter and her moans get louder. I'm nearly out of my mind with lust and excitement, but my mind is still scrolling through an erotic slideshow of a million filthy ways to push her comfort zone. Not tonight. It doesn't have to be tonight. This won't just happen once and then never again. We have time now. All the time in the world.

"Come on," I grit out, the sloppy, wet sounds of the cream she's been making filling the room as I fuck her roughly. "Give it to me."

I want to see this, *need to*, and when Delta's back arches off the bed and the walls of her pussy clamp down on my fingers, it's all I can do to keep from coming in my shorts. It's the most erotic sight of my life, watching every muscle in her body convulse and her hands claw at the sheets beneath us. We're both panting by the time her orgasm fades away, and in a flash she's sitting up, pulling me into a fierce kiss.

"Your turn." Her eyes are sparkling with desire when we break apart, already tugging at the hem of my t-shirt.

I let her strip me naked and push me back into the pillows, kneeling between my thighs in a reversal of our positions a minute ago. "You work out a lot," she murmurs, running her hands over my biceps and pecs, eyes gleaming with approval.

I've never considered myself a vain man until this moment, but fuck me if Delta's praise doesn't make me want to preen. "I've had some frustration to work off lately."

She smirks but doesn't comment further, continuing her exploration down my chest and abs before finally wrapping a small hand tentatively around the base of my cock. It twitches in her palm and I'm instantly transfixed, unable to do more than watch as she strokes me slowly up and down.

"Will you teach me how to give a blow job?" The question isn't coy or flirty, and that makes it so much hotter.

Yes. *Fuck, yes.* Not tonight, though. "Another time." Sitting up, I pull her into my chest and roll us as one, pressing her down into the mattress again.

Her eyes are wide, staring between our bodies at where my fat cock has settled right against her sloppy wet slit. "Are we going to have sex?" There's a slight tremor in her voice that sends a hot thrill of desire up my spine.

I curse, shaking off the impulse to do just that. We're so close, it would be so fucking easy—"*No.* Not tonight, baby. I'm just going to do this." I roll my hips back and forth, sawing my cock through her seam. She's so wet I go easily, both of us groaning at the brand new sensation, but it doesn't take long before Delta's hand snakes between us, wrapping around my shaft.

"I want to." She strokes me up and down, using her wetness to ease the way. Her touch feels so fucking good. "I need you inside me," she pleads, and my heart stalls as she fits the head of my cock to her entrance, rolling her hips, trying to get me inside her.

I'm almost shaking, unable to tear my eyes away from the sight of us like this. I want to push forward, want to claim her completely, but she deserves her first time to be mind-blowing, and as it is, I'll probably spill before I'm even balls deep. It almost kills me, but I shake my head. "I'm hanging on by a thread here, Delta," I groan. "I'd like to make this memorable for you. Soon, *fuck*, I swear it will be soon, but not now."

I don't move though. We're both staring at the place we're almost connected, my dick obscenely large against her smaller body. "Just a little?" She half laughs, half begs, and... fuck it. Yeah. That can work.

"Hold still," I growl, nudging her hand out of the way. "I'm going to fuck you with the tip, okay, baby? Just the tip."

Even after fingering her, it's still a tight fit. Gripping my shaft in one hand and pushing Delta's lower belly down with the other, I roll my hips forward, both of us watching her slick, pink hole stretch around the head of my cock until I'm just barely inside her. It's torture, erotic, exquisite torture, and I should have known this wouldn't be enough. The temptation to keep going is burning under my skin, but I manage to keep ahold of myself, fucking her with just the head.

Beneath me, Delta is writhing, her body trembling right alongside mine, and I groan when her fingers drop to her clit, rubbing circles frantically as I start to get into it, my balls tightening already.

"Come with me," I grunt, hypnotized by the sight of what we're doing. Heat is building at the base of my spine. I'm more turned on than I thought possible, and when Delta's back bows off the bed, her entire body shaking from the force of her orgasm, I can't hold it back anymore.

I come with a long, low groan, watching my cock twitch, the head still lodged inside her pussy, filling her.

Not pulling out was a reckless fucking thing to do. I was her doctor, and I know what medications she *isn't* on, but as she reaches for me and I fall forward to kiss her, not a single part of me regrets it. How often in one lifetime do you find someone who sees you and wants you, just as you are? How often do you find your best friend and the love of your life in one person?

She loves me.

Me.

This is my chance to be happy, to be part of something greater than myself, and I'm not wasting any more time.

"I'm sorry it took me so long," I tell her when we break apart, curling into each other's arms like we've done it a thousand times before.

Delta kisses my chest, her fingers floating back and forth over a little patch of skin on my arm. "I don't mind," she murmurs sleepily, and my eyelids begin to grow heavy, too. "I'm not the same person I was before the accident. I know it seems weird, considering I'll probably never snowboard again, but I think I'm stronger now."

"You are." My eyes burn, and I stare at the ceiling, listening to Delta's breathing grow slow and deep as warm light creeps in through the blinds. I have to go to work soon, and it seems so strange to go about my normal routine when everything is different.

As I close my eyes, I decide that I'll let myself be late. Just this once.

Chapter 15

DELTA

I've gotten accustomed to not making a big fuss out of my birthday.

My brothers are always sweet, bringing me some ungodly baked monstrosity from whichever local bakery I'm currently worshiping at the altar of and being their usual obnoxious, loving selves. Lake and Bay are driving to Utah right now, though, and since Brooks didn't mention anything when he gave me one last lingering kiss before leaving for work this morning—a full hour late—I kind of expected that my twenty-first birthday would be just as uneventful as all the other ones.

I don't mind. Even if not a single person remembers, I'm going to walk around with a big, cheesy smile on my face all day because *Brooks loves me.*

We still have things to work out. I'm sure there will be bumps in the road, but *this is it.* I'm not going anywhere, and neither is he. No more running, no more hiding, no more pretending. I've felt so unsettled since my accident, like my whole life was up in the air, but now... now all I can think about is that conversation we had weeks ago where I laid in my old bedroom and stared out at the night sky, wishing everything was different.

We'd talked about family, and my heart had ached that Brooks thought he would be alone. Now, I can't wipe the smile off my face because he was wrong. He has me now and I — "Am I being weird?" I ask Fibula distractedly, looking over my cup of coffee at the giant, fluffy baby, who is watching me closely through concerned brown eyes.

I probably am. It's only noon, Brooks won't be home for hours, and I'm still debating whether I should tell him it's my birthday or not. It's day one of our relationship, and big emotional confessions aside, I'd hate for him to feel bad about not doing anything. I don't care, I didn't expect it, and I've just resolved to let my twenty-first pass unnoticed when the doorbell rings.

The courier is already halfway back to his truck by the time I open the door, and waves at me over his shoulder as I kneel, my heart suddenly fluttering. Sitting on the doorstep is a big, light blue box, the kind you'd get in a high end department store. "Did you know about this?" I ask the dogs as I bring it inside and set it on the kitchen counter. There's no note, but when I lift the cover, my knees go weak.

Nestled in white tissue paper is a full outfit, and I take each piece out at a time, unsure if I want to cry or drive to his office to beg Brooks Harrison to marry me immediately. There's a dress that is the prettiest, classiest thing I've ever seen. A coat is tucked beneath it, with low ankle boots to match. He even thought to get a matching purse and a little pair of teardrop earrings that I really hope aren't real diamonds. At the very bottom, I find an envelope and open with trembling hands.

Happy Birthday, Delta.
I'm sorry I had to work today, but a car is coming at 1 p.m.

to take you to Phoebe's spa. I've booked what my sister—a notoriously excellent saleswoman—has assured me is the absolute best package they offer, and I'm absolutely not being up-charged for using her entire bottle of nail polish remover for a science experiment in 6th grade. Relax, enjoy, and I'll pick you up from there at five.

In case I didn't say it enough earlier, I am completely, madly, and obsessively in love with you.

—Brooks

It's a miracle I'm still able to stand. This is so much more than I could have ever expected. It's romantic and sweet and... *holy hell.* I'm so happy.

Trying to avoid squealing like a child, I pick up my phone and hit Brooks' contact. It's the middle of his work day and I don't expect him to answer, but he does on the second ring. He sounds like he's smiling when he asks, "You got it?"

"I got it," I confirm, running my hand over the dress which I've spread out on the kitchen counter after painstakingly checking for crumbs. "I can't believe you did all this, Brooks. You didn't have to."

He snorts, and I can picture his wry, exasperated expression. "I absolutely did. You've been responsible for all romantic progress in our relationship thus far. I need to catch up."

Butterflies erupt in my belly. "This should do it. I seriously don't know what to say. Nobody has ever done anything like this for me before. I can't stop smiling." Through the phone, I hear someone saying his name in the background. "I'm sorry for calling in the middle of the day, you're busy."

"*Always* call Delta. I won't pick up if I'm in surgery or with a patient, but I'll give you my assistant's number. You can text her if it's an emergency."

I bite my lip, flashes from early this morning coming back

to me yet again. "What constitutes an emergency situation, Doctor Harrison?" I ask coyly. Does horny count? If so, he needs to get home ASAP.

Hearing a change in my tone, Brooks groans quietly. "Fuck, baby. You're killing me. Later, okay?"

"More than before?" I know he was trying to be chivalrous, ensuring I have a first-time worth remembering, but it's only been six hours and I'm already sick of waiting. A super romantic birthday date seems like a good way to kick things off. "Because I really, *really* want to do more than before. A lot more."

He curses and I grin at the sound of more voices in the background. Something tells me I'll pay dearly for teasing him, and I can't wait. I want to undo every little bit of his restraint just to see what happens. "We'll, *ah*, talk about it."

"*Hmm*, sounds like fun. I love you." That last bit is thrown in with a smile because now that it's out there, I'm not taking it back. I don't expect him to return the sentiment so readily, not in the middle of a bunch of people at work, but the eternally professional Doctor Harrison doesn't even hesitate.

"I love you too, Delta. Happy birthday."

* * *

I've never felt so beautiful.

The dress Brooks got me not only fits perfectly, but is also completely *me*. Pale blue and made of a crinkly, lightweight material that floats around me when I walk, it elicits groans of longing from the other women in the salon when Phoebe sends me off to change at the end of my afternoon of being aggressively pampered. The little white boots he got have the lowest possible heels—undoubtedly out of concern for my hip

—and are bedecked with silver studs that match the buttons on my coat.

"You didn't help him with this?" I ask Phoebe yet again, who has been almost unbearably smug from the moment I walked in here, practically bursting to say "I told you so" while her staff whisked me around the salon for my massage, facial, manicure, pedicure, and generally pamper me to within an inch of my life.

"Nope," she sighs longingly, helping me into the long, dark blue coat that came with the rest of my gifts. "Talk about setting the bar high, though, *wow*. For my birthday last year, Josh got me a teapot."

I giggle, turning to admire myself one more time in the mirror by the door. My hair is arranged in loose curls and my eyes look huge, their lids dusted with silvery shadow. "Do you drink a lot of tea?"

Phoebe snorts. "No, but I mentioned replacing the old kettle because it was rusty." She looks past me to the dark street and sniffs. "I can't believe *that* is the little boy who once gave Mom a diagram of a dissected worm for Mother's Day."

I follow her gaze, and my heart skips a beat. Brooks is getting out of his car across the road from the salon, dressed in a black suit, a bouquet of flowers in hand.

Wow. I thought he was the hottest man on Earth in scrubs, but I stand corrected.

"Go," Phoebe nudges me, her eyes a little watery. "I'll only kill the mood being a sappy big sister."

There is a chorus of goodbye's and good luck's from all the other women in the salon, and I wave to them, beaming as I step outside into the cold night air. Brooks is just stepping up onto the curb when he spots me, and the flowers fall limply to his side as I descend the steps. He looks *so hot* in black, and even though he's made an effort to get his hair under control, I can't wait to make it messy again.

We meet in the middle of the sidewalk and he leans down to kiss me deeply, one hand curling around the back of my neck. How much romancing can a girl take before she just dissolves into a puddle on the ground? I'm warm all over, and my heart had felt full enough to burst *before* he'd done all this.

"You look so handsome," I tell him when we break apart, swiping my thumb over his bottom lip to remove the glossy sheen left behind from my makeup.

Brooks' eyes haven't moved from my face for a second, and he looks dazed, as though he can't quite believe what he's seeing. *"Me?"* he huffs, with a hint of his usual, bossy, impatient tone. "You look so beautiful, Delta. Beautiful doesn't seem like a good enough word. I'm sure there's a better one, but my brain doesn't seem to be functioning at optimal capacity right now."

My answering smile is huge. A hook low in my belly seems to pull me forward into him, and I'm helpless to resist. As soon as I lean forward, Brooks curls an arm around my waist, ducking down to claim my lips with a kiss far less sweet than the last. It's edged in hunger, and when I press myself closer to him, I can feel the ridge of his erection pressing into my stomach.

Yes, please.

"Come on," he groans, sinking his teeth playfully into my bottom lip, hard enough to make my breath hitch. "We have a reservation."

I'm definitely less romantic than he is because I would happily abandon our first date in favor of fondling him in the back seat of his car, but I keep my mouth shut, allowing myself to be marched across the street. Brooks opens the passenger side door for me and waits until I've arranged my fluffy skirts before shutting it and striding around to the driver's side.

"You did all this today?" I ask as he pulls out into traffic, lacing our fingers together atop the center console.

Brooks smiles, clearly pleased with himself. "I might have called in a few favors. I'd already known it was your birthday, obviously, but my original gift was *not* romantic. Adjustments needed to be made."

Now I'm curious. "What was it?"

"A cooking class, with the owners of China Village. They agreed to part with their bacon garlic bread recipe."

He says it so nonchalantly, as though anyone else could have thought of it, but my jaw drops. "Brooks! That's crazy romantic! Bacon garlic bread is like, *our thing*!" I love that even when he was trying to be platonic, this man is still so incredibly sweet and thoughtful.

"Christ, is it?" he winces and I smack his chest playfully, my cheeks aching from smiling so much. I've had moments before where I felt happy, but it wasn't like this, and it wasn't an entire day of *can't stop smiling, heart might explode, the man I love loves me back,* happy. Glancing at me as he turns onto a side street, Brooks squeezes my hand. "I'll remember for next year. I'm afraid you're stuck with an intimate candle-lit dinner with your boyfriend at a place that does *not* sell any such monstrosities."

I drop my head onto his shoulder, my heart doing flip-flops at how easily he called himself my boyfriend. "Sounds lame. I'll try it, though."

"You'll enjoy yourself. I checked that they had at least one cheese-stuffed entrée before bribing Jenna for her reservation."

This guy loves the crap out of me. It's the best.

The restaurant turns out to be a brand new, trendy steakhouse downtown with a line of fancy cars waiting at the valet stand. There are tiny fairy lights strung through the trees lining the sidewalk, and I feel like I'm glowing when Brooks smoothly cuts off the valet, who attempts to help me out.

I'd been wondering if he would want to take it slow, or if there would be a period where we kept our relationship quiet for the sake of his career. Apparently, discretion isn't a concern to Brooks, because he walks into the restaurant with his hand pressed firmly against the small of my back and helps me with my coat in front of all the people waiting in the lobby. We look like a couple, and when the hostess welcomes us as "Doctor and Mrs. Harrison," his fingers dig possessively into my waist. He likes the sound of that.

Then again, so do I.

My buoyant mood lasts until we get into the dining room. At first, I don't notice him, too preoccupied with listening to Brooks murmur in my ear how unbelievably stunning I look, but then I turn slightly to avoid knocking into a table, and my steps falter because *there he is.*

My father.

Until now, it's felt a bit like I've shoved River Jacobs away in the boxes with all my snowboarding stuff, out of the way and contained. I didn't think about it, didn't *want* to think about it, and the ups and downs of my relationship with Brooks were consuming enough to let me avoid facing it for the time being. A part of me expected I would have to see him again someday, but I pictured it being on my terms, not randomly bumping into him at a steakhouse on my birthday.

He's sitting at a table across from a tall, beautiful woman with dark hair and skin. She's talking animatedly about something, but he isn't listening, staring over her shoulder right at me. Every muscle in my body tenses like I'm ready for a fight, the sounds around us seem to have died away, and for a moment we just stare at each other. Brooks leans down to speak into my ear, his voice a quiet rush. "Let's go home, Delta. Or to another restaurant."

I shake my head. "No. We're here. It's okay, Brooks. I had to see him sometime."

The hostess has halted a few yards ahead of us, bemused. "Is everything alright?"

I nod, hitching my trusty PR smile on my face, and it feels rusty and awkward after so long. We follow her past where my father and his date are sitting, right to the furthest corner of the restaurant where we're almost hidden behind a massive metal sculpture.

The moment we sit down and the hostess has gone, we stare at each other in numb disbelief.

"Shit," Brooks curses under his breath, obviously furious. "I can't believe this. What are the chances?"

"It's okay," I repeat, trying to shake off the numb shock. "It's just… weird, you know? I walked away and never looked back. Apart from my brothers, my life is totally different now. I haven't even been keeping up on what's happened with the club after Bay, Lake and I left."

Brooks hesitates. "I might have read some stuff. I didn't want to mention it, while you were focusing on recovering." I raise my eyebrows expectantly and he sighs, running a hand through his hair, effectively ruining the attempt at tidiness. "Let's just say River is getting a lot of bad press right now, and rightfully so. I did some digging, after your accident. Athletes who train under your father statistically perform well but retire sooner, and have a considerably higher rate of career-ending injuries."

A gaping hole has opened up in my chest. "Like me."

"Yes," Brooks confirms, looking tortured. "Like you. Your accident got a lot of attention. Bay felt very strongly that you didn't need to be exposed to the media storm, and I agreed. You could have looked any of this up on your own—"

"I didn't want to."

He winces apologetically. "Needless to say, I'm glad. When it was made public that your brothers had left Blue Pike, people assumed that they felt River had caused your accident. The circumstances certainly don't look good for him. Nothing concrete has been published, though. It's mostly industry speculation, but his reputation isn't quite as shiny as it once was."

I don't reply. Since leaving the hospital, I've gone out of my way to not think about the accident a lot, but when have, it's been in the context of being *my fault*. I was the one on the snowboard. I was the one who had reservations and chose to push through.

Was it, though?

Dad didn't force me over the edge, but he wouldn't let me back down, either. Then there's that moment, right before my accident, when I didn't want to do it. I *told him* I didn't want to do it. The Everwater reps were watching. His reputation, mine, and a pile of money were on the line, and he cared more about all that than he did about me. If he'd told me to listen to my instincts, I'm not sure we would be here right now.

"I think maybe he *did* cause the accident," I admit, my throat tight, and Brooks reaches over the table to take my hand just as our server appears.

He orders us a bottle of wine, that I don't dare look at the price of, before dragging his chair to the side of the table closest to me and pressing a kiss to my temple. "I'm sorry this all came up tonight of all nights," he mumbles against my skin, and I lean into him, feeling the tension ebb from my body just from being close to him.

"I'm okay." Brooks raises his eyebrows skeptically, and I smile. "I am. Especially now." I reach up to play with his now-messy curls. "I love your hair, have I ever told you that? You're always so clean and put together, but your curls stick up all over the place."

"It's going gray." He looks embarrassed, as though the reminder he's so much older than me will suddenly be an issue.

I smile, tracing my fingers through the silver strands on his temples. "I know. I'm into it."

He takes my wandering hand in his, kissing the delicate skin of my inner wrist, when a nearby movement makes us both look up. My father is looking down at us, his expression grave.

"Happy birthday, DJ." He gestures to an empty chair at the table next to ours. "Do you mind if I sit?"

"Yes," Brooks snarls, not bothering with pleasantries. "*We* absolutely do mind."

Dad's eyes narrow on him. "This is unexpected, Doctor Harrison. Do you entertain all your patients like this?"

"*Dad.*" My voice cracks, and glare up at him. "If I wanted to speak to you, I would have reached out. You pushed too hard, and I think you know that. You don't get to ambush me today of all days. *I need some time.*"

I expect him to fight back. That was always what happened when I exerted the tiniest amount of pushback in our relationship, but he doesn't. We stare at each other for a long moment, then, slowly, nods. "Okay." Stepping away from the table, he gives me a quick, tight smile. "Happy birthday, kid."

The second he's vanished from sight, I feel my shoulders slump, and I look at Brooks. "Can we get cheeseburgers and eat them in bed?"

He immediately raises his hand to get our server's attention, looking relieved. "Yeah. That sounds great."

Chapter 16

BROOKS

I'm expecting the encounter with River to mean the end of the night, but it isn't.

It shouldn't surprise me, but by the time we pull into the driveway, Delta is laughing and feeding me French fries. "I swear, I'm okay. I'm glad I stood up to him," she insists as we get out of the car, walking hand in hand toward the dark house. I had Elliot take the dogs, and I'm especially grateful for it when I turn on the lights and I'm greeted by a sweet, lingering kiss from my girlfriend rather than three enormous balls of fur flying at me.

I groan, dropping the food onto the entryway table so I can pull her against me. "That certainly seemed okay."

Our lips meet again and I gather her face in my hands, letting the urgency build. I didn't want tonight to be about sex. After all the shit I put her through, Delta deserves to be romanced, damn it.

My girl doesn't seem to mind, though, because it's not long before our kisses have turned frantic and her hands are roaming over my chest and shoulders like she can't decide where to touch first.

"Do you need something, baby?" I mumble in between increasingly desperate kisses, loving the way she leans in after me whenever I pull away. A breathy moan is all the response I get, and I have to chuckle at her gasp when I turn us, pressing her into the nearest wall. My erection already throbbing and painfully hard against her stomach.

We're both panting when we break apart, Delta gazing up at me through hazy, hooded eyes. She snakes one hand between us, rubbing my cock through my pants. "I don't just want the tip this time."

Fuck, yes. Though god knows the image of Delta coming on just the head of my dick while begging me to fuck her all the way, will turn me on until I'm on my deathbed.

"You think you can take it all?" My hips jerk forward, grinding mindlessly into her touch. I've been throbbing with need from the moment I saw her standing on those steps in the pretty dress I bought for her. "It might hurt, baby."

She keeps stroking me, and I know I'm swimming directly into dangerous waters. The fantasies I've had about her aren't for a twenty-one-year-old virgin getting her first introduction to sex. She might not be interested in the same things I am, might not be turned on by the edge of pain or the possessive, primal impulses she brings out in me. I should be taking this slow.

As though she knows what I'm thinking, Delta trembles, her hot breath ghosting over my throat as her hands move to fumble with my belt. "I want it to. I don't—I don't want you to hold back. I need all of you."

I let out a long hiss, trying to keep a handle on the lust now searing through my veins. "You've thought this through."

A small, warm hand finds its way beneath the waistband of my boxers and wraps around my shaft, stroking tentatively up and down. "I have," she hums, and I see a flash of wickedness in those stormy eyes that makes pre-cum bead at the head of my cock. She swipes her thumb over it, and it's my turn to gasp. "I used to lie in bed at night and fuck myself with my vibrator, wishing it was you." Pre-cum is dripping freely from my slit now and I hiss when her grip tightens, my hips jerking forward. "I like it when I can feel the ache later."

It's almost too erotic to imagine Delta naked in her bed, a little toy clutched in her hand, working so hard to make it hurt the way she instinctively knows she needs it to. My poor girl, aching and empty for so long, needing me.

"Did you do that a lot?" I ask, keeping my voice flat, low, and unimpressed. She's trying to get a reaction out of me, and I won't let her have it. Not yet.

Her grip on my cock tightens, stroking me faster. She's getting the hang of it, and I'd love to push her to her knees and teach her how to suck me the way I like, but tonight I have other things on my mind. "Almost every night," she admits, her voice hitching. "I thought about how good it would feel for you to use me however you wanted, to be helpless and just —just having to take whatever you gave me. Even if it hurt. *Especially* if it hurt."

I reward her with a soft, almost chaste kiss, my entire body strumming with pent up need. It surges through my veins like electricity, growing stronger with every stroke of her hand over my length.

She has no idea, no way of knowing, that her words are fulfilling my fantasies, too. How many times have I imagined a scenario just like this one? Delta coming to me and begging for me to fuck her, telling me how badly she aches for it and that I can do anything I want if I only give her what she needs to feel better. My hand drifts up her side, almost casually, and wraps loosely around her throat. Against the wall like this, it's barely any effort at all to push forward and steal her breath.

She's not the only one who is capable of testing the waters. I have to see, *need to be sure*. I love her far more than my own dark impulses, and if this isn't what she wants, I'll drop my hand and never try it again.

Delta *does* want it, though. Her pupils are blown wide, her lips parted, and as I slip a hand beneath the ruffled hem of her dress, I find her so wet that she's soaked through the tiny pair of panties she's wearing. "You *do* like this, huh?" I barely recognize my voice. It's so rough. "Do you want me to bend you over my bed and fuck your virginity away, baby? Is that what you need?" I spank her pussy sharply, and she quivers against me, sucking in a ragged gasp as I let the hand holding her throat relax.

For a moment, we stare at each other in the darkened house, panting.

"Now," I growl, and Delta tears away from me in an instant, darting toward the staircase.

I give her a head start, shrugging out of my coat and hanging it in the entryway closet before strolling after her. The control I have over both of us is a heady rush, and despite wanting to take the steps two at a time, I force my pace to remain even. On the wood floors, I'm positive she can hear the echo of my measured steps growing nearer, and I stop on the landing to pick up her discarded boots.

My bedroom door is ajar, and my eager girl is standing by the bed, kicking her dress away across the floor. I let her finish stripping, watching from the doorway as she shimmies out of her lace panties and bra eagerly. "Last chance to change your mind," I offer mildly, unbuttoning the cuffs of my shirt and rolling them back with practiced ease. "I'm happy to fuck you like a gentleman. I can light candles. Go out to get some rose petals."

I don't expect her to accept, not with the way her thighs press together and nipples pebble under my gaze as I rake my eyes over her body.

Sure enough, Delta shakes her head. She watches through

hooded eyes as I move further into the room, a predator stalking his prey. When I reach her, I take her breasts in my hands, brushing my thumbs back and forth over her tight nipples. It's beyond sexy how she bows her back into my touch, needing more.

"I don't want a gentleman, I—*ah*." Her voice is barely more than a whisper and turns to a squeak when I pinch her savagely. Drawing a shaky breath, she runs her hands up my chest, fumbling with the buttons of my shirt. "I want to get lost in you."

The words hit me hard. They weren't what I was expecting, but, oh, I can make that happen.

"Whatever you want, birthday girl." I claim her lips with mine again, savoring the dark thrill of anticipation crawling up my spine. How long has it been since I wholly let myself go? Have I ever? There's just one more order of business. "I'm not going to come inside you again," I say it out loud to hold myself accountable. Who knows what kind of lust-drunk haze my mind will be in soon. This is too important to leave up to chance.

Delta pouts, her eyes on my chest as the last button of my shirt gives away and I allow her to slide it off my shoulders onto the floor. "I liked it."

My cock twitches. "Did you?"

She nods, kissing the place above my heart as her hands move to pull my belt from its loops and toss it to the floor with a clatter. "I woke up with my thighs all sticky. It felt like I was yours."

"You are mine," I growl, and she gasps as I fist her hair, pulling her head back so she's forced to look at me and not my fucking dick. "We need to wait until after your appointment next week, baby. Getting pregnant would be a bad idea if your hip is still as unhealthy as it was."

Her tongue darts out to wet her lips, and I can tell in her

eyes how badly she wants that. We're moving at warp speed, but I wouldn't have it any other way. We've wasted enough time. "It's not, I promise. I've felt great—"

I cut her off with a searing kiss, backing us toward the bed before she can start begging for me to come in her. She might already be pregnant. I got carried away, and we were careless last night. There's nothing I want more than to build a family together, but waiting is what's best for her and I will *always* do what's best for Delta.

"I'm going to fuck you now," I murmur against her lips and she gasps as I grip her waist, turning her around and pushing her roughly over the edge of the bed. She barely has time to lift her head before I've fallen to my knees, holding her beautiful ass open with both hands so I can see every inch of her. Leaning forward, I lick her decadently, my mind fogging at the taste of her and the sound of her breathy little whines.

"That's so good," she moans, lifting one leg onto the mattress, offering herself up for more.

Fuck.

I dive in again, pushing my tongue into her tight opening, fucking her wetly. All it takes is a minute of that and two fingers on her clit before she's coming, shuddering and moaning as a fresh wave of her sweet cream flows over my tongue. I drink it down greedily, licking every inch of her until she starts to shake all over again, her cries turning to nonsensical babbling. I free my cock, waiting until she's loose and relaxed from her second orgasm before rising to my feet and kicking away my pants.

Though I said I wanted her bent over, I need to see her when I do this, have to remember the look on her face as I fill her for the first time. I know I'm a large man, too big for her to take comfortably, but we're both too far gone to hold back. Delta squeals in surprise as my hands bite into her waist, flipping her over and dragging her ass to the edge of the bed.

"Such a needy girl," I grunt, hitching her knees over my arms so she's spread wide and open for me, defenseless against what's coming. "Do you need to get fucked, baby? You're dripping for me." Even the insides of her thighs are shining, and I grip my cock, drawing it through the mess she's made. Both of us shudder as my tip settles against her opening.

Delta's chest rises and falls rapidly. A beautiful flush is spread over her cheeks from the force of her orgasms, and I can't resist bending forward to kiss her again. My bare chest brushes over hers, and even after everything we've already done, the sensation is enough to make both of us moan.

I do it before she can tense up. Tilting my hips forward, I drive down, sinking into her in a single thrust that tears a yelp from her lips and a rough groan of pleasure from mine.

She feels incredible, her tight cunt gripping every inch of me as her nails bite painfully into my shoulders, holding on for dear life as I push her legs open a little further. I can't get deeper. She's taken all of me, and yet it's somehow not enough.

I need to move.

Delta's eyes are still wide with shock, her lips pursed into an 'o' as I pull back. Dragging my length from her wet warmth and, watching carefully for signs she doesn't like this, drive forward hard enough to make her tits bounce from the force of it.

I should wait, let her adjust, but the sight of her little hole stretched around the base of my shaft is enough to obliterate my last functioning brain cells. My dirty girl wasn't lying when she said she wanted it like this. She's wetter already, and as I thrust into her again, harder than before, Delta throws her head back and moans.

She's perfect. I want to ruin her.

I let loose. Planting my hands beside her on the mattress, I hunch forward, fucking her so hard that my thighs strain from the effort of it and sweat beads on my chest. My low noises of pleasure are lost in the crude sound of our bodies slapping together and Delta's loud cries. It's rough and primal. I'm making her mine, and she loves it.

"Going to do this to your ass someday. Would you like that?" I growl, reaching back and spanking her hard enough to leave a mark. "Such an eager little slut, barely had your first cock and you already want it in all your holes." My crude words make her quake beneath me, and I bring my hand down on her ass again, the walls of her cunt fluttering over my shaft.

Her lips part, "I'm so close, oh god—"

My head bows forward to suck one pert nipple between my teeth, and Delta comes with a loud cry. Wetness floods over my cock as her inner walls clutch greedily at my cock. I have to pause, gritting my teeth and panting, so she doesn't drag me over the edge too. I'm nowhere near ready for this to be over. We could keep going all night and it wouldn't be enough.

Not pulling out, I drag her into my arms, hauling us both upright. Walking with my dick inside her is easier said than done, and I have to pause a few times to fuck her against the dresser, then the wall beside the bedroom door as I try to get the handle open without both of us ending up on the floor.

Delta is completely unhelpful, grinding and writhing in my arms, giggling as I struggle. "Where are we going?" she asks breathlessly, raking her nails over my back as we make it onto the landing.

If someone were looking through the window, they'd see us clearly on the brightly lit second floor. Me, a grown man of almost forty, walking through the house with my gorgeous, barely twenty-one-year-old girlfriend wrapped around me, impaled on my cock.

It's a mind fuck, trying to separate the woman I love from the dirty little slut I want to ruin, but the knowledge she likes to be both sends a dark thrill through me.

I pause, pressing her against the wall beside her bedroom door to fuck her for a minute, hard enough to make her gasp, nails digging into my back. "Where's that vibrator you were talking about, baby?" I ask gruffly, fumbling for the handle behind her.

She exhales shakily, and I smirk at how her cheeks glow at the mention of it. As if I'm not currently balls deep inside her, seeing parts of her no one ever has before.

"Um, my dresser. Top drawer. On the right."

I hit the switch beside the door and stride inside, setting her down atop the long dresser across from her bed. I'm temporarily distracted from my mission when Delta starts to roll her hips. "I'm going to have my hands full with you," I growl, enjoying the hell out of watching her desperate little attempt to fuck herself on my cock.

I let her have her fun, pulling open the drawer in question. My face splits into a broad grin when I see what she's been hiding in it. Such a dirty girl. Beside a jumble of technicolor panties and bras, is a small plastic bin filled with at least six different vibrators. "Don't judge." She giggles, still rocking against me. "You made me wait *years* for this, *Doctor Harrison*."

Her calling me that when I'm inside her is just a little messed up, and I think I love it.

"You *obviously* found other ways to occupy yourself," I smirk, selecting one and pressing the button to turn it on. A quiet buzzing fills the room and Delta whimpers as I bring it between us, settling the device directly over her clit. "Hold it there," I order, wrapping an arm around her waist and bracing the other on the wall behind her.

I could do this for hours, play with her, tease her until she cries, but the impulse to claim is still burning in my veins. For months, this woman has been relentlessly whittling away at every last scrap of restraint I possess, reducing me to little more than a grunting, snarling caveman.

Now, she's going to pay for it.

The vibrations are strong enough to travel through her body into mine, and we groan in unison as I thrust into her roughly, making the dresser bang noisily against the wall. "Oh *fuck*, Brooks!" Delta's head falls back, clinging to me with one hand as the other presses the vibrator to her greedy clit.

"Does that hurt?" I grunt, doing it again. Her pussy is already pink and swollen, and I stare between us, hypnotized by the sight of her opening stretched around my too-thick cock. I'm too far gone to slow this down, and as I find a fierce rhythm, she clings to me, her lips parting in a silent cry.

Her body is confused by the sensations, pain on the inside, pleasure on the outside, and a fresh wave of her arousal coats my dick as I adjust the angle of my thrusts, the head of my cock pummeling her g-spot. "Is it too big for you, baby?"

She nods, almost sobbing as tremors wrack her body. "It's too big, *it hurts* Brooks—"

I go harder, my orgasm coming on so fast it's dizzying, and when Delta's walls clamp down on my cock, she comes so hard I bite my tongue until I taste blood to keep myself from spilling inside her. I fuck her through it. Every muscle in my body is strained, and when she slumps against me, sticky and panting, I finally allow myself to follow. Pulling out, I come with a guttural groan, pleasure burning through me as I coat her pussy in long stripes of my cum.

"Fuck." My head drops to her shoulder, both of us panting. "Are you okay?"

Delta nods against me, and she fumbles with the vibrator until the buzzing sound dies away. Her hands find my face a moment later, and, knowing what she wants, I lift my head to find her lips with mine. What we just did was, without a doubt, the absolute best sex of my life, but the intimacy of this is just as intense. "Love you," she mumbles sleepily, curling into my chest when we break apart. "Best birthday ever."

Chuckling, I lift her into my arms, bridal style, and carry her back across the landing to my bedroom. She waits patiently while I fetch a warm cloth from the bathroom and wipe away the cum on her skin, making sure to kiss every red mark I left on her body.

"Move your stuff in here tomorrow," I tell her as I pull down the covers for her to get in, and Delta's answering laugh is soft.

"Moving in together? Already?" She's happy, though, looking around at the bedroom like she's deciding the best place to store her vibrator collection.

I pause in the act of gathering up our discarded clothing from the floor. "Yes. Already. Will that be a problem?"

Delta settles back in the pillows, beaming at me. "Nope."

"Good." I toss the clothes onto the chair in the corner and lean over to kiss her quickly. "Wait here a minute. I have one more way to make this birthday great."

She does as she's told, and I walk downstairs completely naked. When I re-enter the bedroom, I'm holding the brown paper bag containing our bacon cheeseburgers and fries in front of my dick. Delta's absolute delight is contagious and I find myself laughing too as I get into bed beside her.

I wasn't even aware I had a carefree, ridiculous side until this woman came into my life.

"You're the perfect man," she moans rapturously a few minutes later when I feed her the last lukewarm fry from the bottom of the bag.

I snort, crumbling up the wrappers and lobbing them toward the waste bin in the corner. I miss, and normally the trash on the floor would irritate me until I got my ass up to correct it, but as Delta curls one bare leg over mine and settles her head against my chest, there's not a single part of me that wants to move. "I have some ex-girlfriends out there who would beg to differ."

Her eyes had just closed, but at my words, one cracks open to glare at me. "Nope. You definitely don't."

"Right. My mistake. No ex-girlfriends at all." I yawn, pulling her closer. "I'm old. I get confused sometimes."

Her body shakes with silent laughter and I close my eyes, my heart so full it could burst.

For as long as I can remember, I've felt like I was an outsider in my own life, an awkward, lingering shadow in my family and friend's happy moments. It's all I've known, but as I fall asleep, Delta's soft breath ghosting over my chest and our naked bodies tangled beneath the covers, it occurs to me that I don't feel alone anymore.

"You're definitely coming in too fast." I tilt my head, squinting at the grainy cell phone clip that Lake sent me. He's attempting to add a 180-degree rotation to a trick he's had down for over a year, only a week before one of the biggest competitions of his life. I switch my phone screen back to the video chat where Lake is frowning into the camera, snowy trees in the background.

"Bay said that too, but I swear it's so off when I slow it down, like I'm losing my momentum, you know?"

"Sure." I snuggle deeper into the couch, raking my hand through Tibia's soft fur.

It's the first day of my period, and after having a good cry that I'm not pregnant with my boyfriend of two weeks' baby, I curled up in front of a sappy movie with every bag of junk food in the house. My brother called not long after, ranting about his new coach and how Bay slept with a girl Lake had talked to at a party for ten whole minutes—evidently a major brotherly dibs violation.

"You're overthinking it. Focus on what you were doing. You have enough points to qualify without this, and it's a major risk. If you're still not landing it now...." I trail off, lifting my shoulder with a sympathetic wince.

If it weren't for my hip, I'd be on Blue Pike now, sweating it out alongside him, and not a single part of me misses it.

Lake groans, raking a hand through his hair. "Yeah, you're probably right. I should go. Thank Brooks for me, will you? I started taking that lactic acid thing he sent me, and it's a game changer."

We hang up, and I shove a handful of chocolate-covered pretzels in my mouth. I know my brain is marinating in a hormonal cocktail at the moment, but it's ridiculous to be upset I'm not pregnant, right?

For one thing, the appointment for my hip isn't for another week, a few days after the first-ever Christmas I'll be spending with Brooks' family. I've met everyone now. His parents came to dinner a few nights ago and were predictably lovely, Phoebe and I now meet every Friday for coffee, and I've started watching her boys after school.

They all like me, and it's so nice to be part of a traditional family rather than the competitive pressure cooker I was raised in. I'm still a relatively unknown entity, though, and I don't want to rock the boat so soon. Surely, they wouldn't be happy if they believed I was trying to trap Brooks with an unplanned pregnancy or something.

I giggle to myself at the idea. If anything, Brooks is trying to trap himself with a—mostly—unplanned pregnancy. The man is an award winning physician. He knows where babies come from. If he didn't want one, he would rethink our birth control methods.

Admittedly, our current methods are pretty hot. Not that I'll be enjoying any of them when I'm this bloated and gross.

My head drops back and I groan. Seriously, *fuck* periods.

I'm in the beginning stages of researching how to make chocolate-covered potato chips when the doorbell rings and all three dogs start barking. Shushing them, I get up and drag my feet to the door, flanked by my small army of four-legged clouds.

I'm expecting a package, or maybe Phoebe dropping by unannounced to return the stand mixer I lent her. What I don't expect is a stranger standing on the mat, smiling tentatively. She's not that much older than me and dressed in a pantsuit and the kind of fluffy, fashionable coat they sell to tourists at the airport.

"Uh, hi?" I tuck my hair behind my ear self-consciously, wishing I'd checked through the window before opening it.

"Delta." She holds out a hand, "I'm Annie Ferguson, Newsday Magazine—" I immediately go to shut the door, but she shoves her boot in the way, grimacing apologetically. "Listen, I'm sorry to show up at your home unannounced like this."

"So, why are you?" I bite back furiously. "I'm not interested in giving an interview or whatever."

Annie shakes her head hastily, "No! I was hoping to talk to you off the record. Zero pressure, just a chat."

I cross my arms defensively, glaring at her. "About?" If she's looking for the inside scoop on my retirement, she's going to be disappointed.

"Your father."

I pause, curious despite myself. "I'll listen, but that's it." I step back, and she follows me inside, closing the door behind her.

"Cute dogs." She scratches Femur tentatively. "And your home is gorgeous. I love the view." If she's found me here, she must know whose house it is, and I'm not going to offer up anything about Brooks. We've been lucky so far. Nobody seems to care about a former professional athlete dating her former doctor, but all it takes is one gossip journalist putting an ugly spin on it to destroy his professional reputation.

Wordlessly, I gesture to the stools on one side of the kitchen island and lean against the counter on the other, watching her every move as she sits down and puts her bag beside her.

Annie, thankfully, cuts right to the chase. "I don't want to take up a lot of your time, so I guess we'll dive in." She pulls a folder out of her bag and sets it in front of her. "I've been investigating River Jacobs for about six months now, since well before your accident, though admittedly, I wasn't getting very far until then."

My heart is suddenly beating wildly, and keeping my expression impassive is a struggle. Is this related to what Brooks and I were talking about on my birthday? I swallow, "And what has your investigation turned up?"

Annie flips open the folder and slides it over the counter toward me. "It's bigger than just River. Essentially, a lot of unsafe coaching practices and a governing body, the USSA, that turns the other way. I've been working with a source close to River for some time now. They tipped me off that prior to your accident, your physician put you on an involuntary medical suspension, but your father made some calls and had your case transferred to another doctor. One who is notoriously lax."

She's looking at me appraisingly, and I can tell she's trying to figure out if any of this is hitting a nerve.

I give her nothing, but my heart has dropped through the floor, because *it's all true.* What am I supposed to do with that? It sounds horrible to hear the situation spelled out in black and white, like she just did. I'd be furious if I read about this happening to someone else, so why do I feel so defensive?

Annie continues, "We've submitted a records request, which could take months and will probably be blocked in court under the grounds of doctor-patient confidentiality. There are a lot of people over there who would walk away from this looking very bad if any of this is true." She leans forward, and I can see now that she's nervous, too. This is important to her. "Yours is not the only incident by a·long shot, but it's the most newsworthy. You're a gold medalist *and* River's daughter. I'm not expecting you to talk on the record. I know that's a really big ask and would be complicated for you on a personal level. I just need proof."

Proof like the email the USSA sent me confirming my medical suspension was pending and that my case was being transferred away from Brooks. I could open my phone and show it to her right now.

I clutch the counter like a lifeline. "I'd need time to think about it," I say at last, swallowing the tightness in my throat. "And I'm not saying any of what you just said is what happened, or that I have any of this hypothetical proof, but *if I did*, I wouldn't just give it to you."

Annie gets to her feet at once, nodding. "*Of course.*" She reaches into her bag and pulls out a card, setting it between us. "Thank you for hearing me out, Delta. I know it's a lot to even consider this, but the system in place now is designed to create champions, not protect athletes. It's not right, and I'd like to see it end."

* * *

When Brooks gets home, he finds me in the garage, surrounded by boxes.

"Ah, tall man. Just in time." I grin, kissing him briefly before pointing to the last box, which is on the topmost shelf and just out of my reach.

He obliges me, setting it down on the floor and standing back as I rip it open. "What are we looking for, short woman?"

I've already found it though, and yank the velvet box out with a triumphant whoop of victory. "God, Lake packed this stuff, right? He has some serious issues. Who would pack someone's social security card in a bag of half-used hotel shampoo bottles?"

"That's fairly deranged," Brooks agrees stoically, following me back into the house. He left this morning in a shirt and tie, but now he's wearing scrubs, and I hum in appreciation of the view. Setting the box on the counter, I turn so I can give him a proper welcome home.

"I missed you," I murmur in between kisses, pressing the length of my body against his and twining my arms around his neck. "Was your day okay?"

He grunts in response, too busy backing me toward the couch.

One of the many things I've learned about Brooks over the last few weeks is that he always has a lot of *tension* to burn off after a day in surgery. I'm usually more than happy to let him work out his control issues on me, but I stop his hands as they reach the waistband of my yoga pants, pulling back to wince apologetically at him.

"I, *uh*, got my period. This morning."

Brooks is silent for a moment, his expression far too grave for a man who *doesn't* want to get me pregnant. "Are you okay?" he finally asks, brow furrowed in concern.

I give him a watery, reassuring smile, abruptly over-whelmed by how much I love this man. "I'm fine. It's not good timing. We haven't been together that long, and there's my hip... I'm feeling really silly for being disappointed. If that's something we want, there's plenty of time, right?"

He nods immediately. "Of course. It's a discussion we can have after your appointment next week." But there's a glint in his eye that tells me the "discussion" won't be a long one. We don't need it to be.

"Come here." I wrap my hand around his wrist to tug him toward the couch.

Brooks' throat bobs and I can see he's torn between the desire to protect and the need to claim. "You don't need to do that." It's a pretty feeble protest, and I ignore it completely, nudging him back into the cushions with a smirk.

"You've had a long day, Doctor Harrison. Let me take care of you." I drop to my knees, blinking innocently up at him as my fingers move to the drawstrings of his scrub pants. I haven't had a chance to do this properly yet. Brooks is borderline obsessed with my pussy, and my few attempts at giving him a blowjob ended in me being fucked enthusiastically for my efforts.

Yeah, my life is super tough.

I take my time, kissing the ridge of his erection through the flimsy material, heat coiling low in my belly. Long before I had even the faintest hope of Brooks returning my feelings, I used to fantasize about this. Just the slightest hint of a bulge behind his scrubs was just about the hottest thing I'd ever seen. It still is, though, admittedly, there's nothing slight about said bulge right now.

Brooks lifts his hips, allowing me to pull his scrubs and boxers down enough to free his cock. "Tell me what you want?" I plead, blinking up at him as I lean forward, licking the underside of his shaft. He tastes so good, masculine and salty.

I want to worship him, but more than that, I want him to tell me to.

Groaning, Brooks buries his hands in my hair, guiding my mouth over his tip. "Do you want me to use your mouth, baby?" I'm too busy swirling my tongue around him, licking and sucking the best I can with my mouth stretched wide over his thickness, but my moan must be answer enough. He lets me play for a while, leaving sloppy kisses up and down his length, enjoying the low grunts and growls coming from above me.

I can tell when he finally loses patience with my games.

Hands tightening in my hair, Brooks drags my head down roughly, the broad head of his cock hitting the back of my throat hard enough to make me gag. I've barely recovered before he's pulling me back, almost to the tip, and shoving my head back down.

I gaze up at him through watering eyes, and heat pools low in my belly. He's not even looking at me. Brooks' head has dropped back onto the couch, his eyes closed and jaw tight with pleasure as he continues to use me as his personal toy, fucking my mouth so hard I barely have time to breathe in between thrusts.

"*Fuck*, that's good. Play with my balls," he hisses, and I do as he says instantly, saliva trailing over my hand.

It's rough and primal and borderline degrading, but I don't feel degraded. I feel powerful, and turned on, and I could do this every day and never get sick of it. Tasting his salty pre-cum flowing over my tongue, feeling his balls tighten up close to his body just before he comes, the sounds he makes... all of it makes me even more eager to make this good for him. Using the saliva soaking my hand, I slip a single finger back, pushing it past his tight ring of muscle into his ass.

Almost instantly, Brooks comes with a low groan that I instantly file away as the hottest noise ever made. His release seems to go on and on, flooding down the back of my throat until it becomes too much and I choke, pulling back with spit and cum covering the bottom half of my face.

Brooks' eyes widen in apology. "Shit, baby, I'm sorry—" He reaches past me, snatching a box of tissues off the coffee table, and wipes my face, his chest still rising and falling heavily.

"Don't apologize, that was awesome." I giggle, allowing him to pull me into his lap, his softening cock between us.

Brooks shakes his head like he can't quite wrap his mind

around what just happened. "I wasn't too rough?" One of his big hands comes up to massage my jaw gently, and I lean back to give him a disbelieving look. He chuckles, letting me curl into his chest again. "Point taken."

"I should have probably discussed that other thing with you first."

"Sticking your finger in my ass?"

"Yes. That. Though, to be fair, you did it to me without asking."

His chest shakes with a silent laugh, and sigh happily, savoring the comfort of his body against mine after a day apart. It's Friday, thankfully, and his office will be closed for the holidays for a full week, starting Monday.

We have big plans to eat, sleep, have weird sex, and watch Christmas movies for seven days straight. My brothers will be back just before New Year's, and Brooks' mom insisted on inviting them to the luncheon at the Harrison's house, which is adorable and so sweet.

I'd more or less decided to let Annie the reporter wait until I've had a chance to talk the whole thing through with Bay and Lake, but for some reason, my thoughts snag on my eldest brother, and I'm filled with an uneasy prickle of suspicion.

"What's going on in that head of yours?" Brooks asks, kissing my temple, and I frown, reluctantly getting to my feet.

"A reporter came here today. Just stopped by out of nowhere. She said she was looking into my father."

Brooks stands, retying his pants, brow furrowed. "Why didn't you call me?"

I shrug, crossing to the kitchen counter to get Annie's card and handing it to him. "I was processing, I guess. She told me she wasn't after an interview with me, and I believed her, but I was still careful not to tell her anything." I recount the whole interaction to him, almost word for word, and by the end, the tiny ember of suspicion in my mind has grown into an inferno. "I was wondering... I mean, do you think it's possible?" Swallowing the tightness in my throat, I stare at him. "Bay?"

Brooks takes his time responding. He's been leaning against the back of the couch with his arms crossed since I started talking, and I can practically see the wheels turning in his head. "You think Bay is her source?"

"There's not exactly a long list of people who know you suspended me before the accident. The USSA, my brothers, and us. *That's it.* Annie specifically said it was someone close to Dad, and isn't it a bit weird she found me here? I mean, even my mail is being forwarded to my agent."

"We haven't been hiding our relationship," states Brooks fairly. "People must know we're together by now, and I've lived here for over two years. The house is in my name. It wouldn't be an incredible leap to find you through me. What does strike me as significant is her choice to come to *River's daughter* and divulge her suspicions. You might be incredibly close to your father for all she knows."

Neither of us has to say it. *Nobody* is privy to the complete lack of contact between me and Dad since the accident, apart from Brooks, Lake, and Bay.

I blow out a long, slow breath. "It doesn't make a difference, whether Bay's been the one giving her information or not. Not really. At the end of the day, I still need to decide if I want to give her that email. It would *ruin him*, Brooks. I'm not angry, I've moved on, and I'm happy. Would destroying my father's life be something I could live with?"

My voice breaks on the last word and Brooks pushes off the couch. He crosses the room to pull me tightly into his arms just as the tears begin to flow.

I hope I never take for granted how well we fit together, or how good it feels to be held by him while reality rages around us.

"You don't have to decide anything now." He kisses my hair. "Wait until after the holidays. Talk to your brother. I will say, though, that River shouldn't be coaching anyone. He's made poor judgement calls that have hurt people, and I doubt he'll ever learn that sometimes the ends do not justify the means."

I squeeze my eyes shut and hold him until my tears slow. "I'll think about it," I finally whisper, and Brooks nods approvingly, leaning back so he can wipe away the last of the wetness from my cheeks.

"Go watch that terrible TV show you like. I'll make dinner. Let me take care of you."

I smile in thanks, accepting a brief kiss before retreating to the couch. I've just settled down, dragging the best fluffy throw blanket over my legs, when Brooks calls over to me from the kitchen.

"Are you going to tell me what you were looking for?"

Oh right. *That.*

"You can open it." I pat the spot next to me, and Tibia hops up, putting her big head in my lap. When I first moved in, there was a strict no dogs on the furniture rule, but the fluffy babies and I won this round.

"*Holy shit,*" Brooks chokes and I can't help but laugh, looking over to where he's staring down at the contents of the box, his eyes huge. "This has been *in the garage*?"

"What else am I supposed to do with it?"

In his hands, my gold medal glints in the kitchen lights, as brilliant as it was the day I won it. The thing represents a lot for me, and not all of it is good. I haven't looked at it since I got home from the Olympics three years ago.

Brooks shakes his head mutely. "No idea," he eventually admits, snapping the box shut and setting it back on the counter. "They're worth a lot of money, aren't they? So, maybe a safe?"

"If it makes you feel better, Lake stuck it with all my running shoes. So unless the burglar has a very specific fetish, I doubt it would be stolen."

"Why did you go looking for it now?"

There isn't a good answer to that question, except that I thought a lot about the days after I won it after Annie left.

When I'd gotten my scores, and it became clear I was going to go home with a gold, the first person I looked for was my dad. This was what I'd worked for, right? What I'd been fighting for since almost before I could remember? Dad had been happy, of course, putting on a good show for the cameras and telling every reporter who would listen how proud he was of his kid. On the plane home, though, he'd started talking about *our* summer training schedule, what *we* could change, and what *we* could do better for next time.

The win hadn't felt like mine.

"I wanted to see if it made me feel differently than it did back then," I confess, staring over at the box where it's sitting benignly on the edge of the kitchen counter.

Brooks meets my eyes from across the room. "Does it?"

I consider for a moment, and it's like my whole chest is breaking open with relief when I finally respond. "Yeah. It does."

Chapter 18

BROOKS

I t's not even a little surprising that when my mother throws open the door to greet us on Christmas Eve, she rushes to hug my girlfriend first.

"Oh, you're such a darling." Mom beams as she takes the foil-covered casserole dish from Delta. "Did you style your hair differently? *I love it!* Robert! They're here! Look how lovely Delta looks!"

"Hello, Mom. Where is everyone?" I lean down to kiss her cheek as she ushers us into the warm entryway, which is so crammed in Christmas decorations it's faintly ridiculous. Everything in the house is now either blinking, pine-scented, or bedecked in red and white stripes.

I have a headache already.

Delta—who is still an easy, inexperienced target for Mom's guilt trips—was convinced how *special* it would be if everyone spent the night at my childhood home on Christmas Eve and opened gifts together first thing in the morning, so I'm laden with an overnight bag, two bags of gifts, and the three dog's leashes.

"Oh, you know your brother. He's always late. Phoebe

and the boys will be here shortly, though. They're just finishing a late lunch with Josh's family." She wipes her hands on her Santa's Helper apron before stooping to pet the dogs who are wearing matching green sweaters. "I'm just going to pop the ham in the oven. I'll let you two get settled up in your old room, Brooks."

I lead the way upstairs, showing Delta where the bathroom is on the landing, before opening the attic door with a sheepish grin. Elliot and I shared a bedroom for years, but a particularly bad fight about dirty socks—actual blood was spilled—when I was twelve led to me moving all my stuff to the completely unfinished attic. Our parents, exhausted by the fighting and trying to force their polar opposite sons to share a small space, had the room insulated for the sake of everyone's sanity. I stayed up here until I went to college.

Delta steps into the room ahead of me, her eyes roaming over the periodic table poster above the bed and models of molecules on every flat surface. "Admit it, you're intimidated." I chuckle, wrapping my arms around her from behind and bowing to nip at her jaw. "I was incredibly cool. Obviously."

Delta giggles, turning in my arms to kiss me sweetly. She's been understandably out of sorts since the reporter's visit, but woke up today determined to set it aside. "I like it," she declares when she pulls away, moving further into the room. "Yet another piece of the Brooks Harrison origin story."

"Yes, this one is entitled 'lonely nerd who lost his virginity at twenty-two'." My heart seems to have lodged in my throat as she nudges the air mattress my mother not-so-subtly made up beside my old twin-sized bed, smirking over her shoulder at me.

"Should we mess up the sheets on it so she thinks I slept here?"

She's so fucking cute.

"Absolutely." Unable to stop touching her for even a

minute, I follow her to the side of the bed, weaving my fingers through her soft hair to pull her into another long, playful kiss that turns heated in seconds. Delta whimpers, and I back her toward my childhood bed, my cock almost instantly rock hard and ready for her. "I can't get enough of you," I groan, teasing her breasts through her sweater. "You taste so good, baby."

We sway on the spot, making out, and I'm about to reach for the button of her jeans when there's an unmistakable commotion downstairs. Phoebe is here with the boys.

Cursing quietly, I let my head drop back, feeling the soft vibrations of her quiet laugh against me. "For the record," Delta kisses my throat, the highest part of me she can reach without my cooperation. "I can't get enough of you either."

I know she can't, and it turns me on to no end—she was made for me. "Come on." I lace my fingers through hers and tug her toward the stairs. "Let's get this over with."

* * *

It's the best Christmas I've ever had, without question.

There's nothing technically different about it, we do all the usual family traditions, and yet it's a special kind of magic, having a partner to share it with. Had I been lonely before her? I can't remember. I couldn't have dated, though, or tried to find anyone else because—as hard as my empirical side tries to poke holes in the logic of this—it was always supposed to be Delta.

I love having someone to fix a plate for at dinner, leaving out the green beans because she hates them, and how she kisses me gently in thanks in front of everyone.

I love the way she curls up next to me on the couch, her fuzzy-sock clad feet in my lap as we watch a cartoon Christmas movie with the boys.

I love seeing her playfully nudge my mother out of the way

of the kitchen sink, rolling up her sleeves to do the washing up, and how I get to stand next to her drying the plates she hands me.

I love how casually my sister mentions hosting Easter at her house and asks Delta if she could come early to help with the cooking, with no unspoken question of whether she'll still be in my life then.

Yeah, it was always supposed to be Delta.

"I'm going to head up," she murmurs in my ear at the end of the night when everyone has simmered down, slipping her arms around me from behind. I'm sitting at the kitchen table, doing one last puzzle with a bleary-eyed Beau.

When I turn my head, searching, and she rewards me with a gentle kiss. "I'll be up soon," I promise, chest expanding as I watch her wish everyone a goodnight, slipping off toward the stairs.

"Oh, Brooks." The moment we hear the attic door close, Mom beams at me, her eyes shining. "We're all so happy for you."

"I know, right?" Phoebe yawns from her place in the armchair beside the fireplace. "Not to brag, but he couldn't have done it without me. I'm his wing woman."

Eli snorts, swirling his drink with a candy cane. "So, have you bought a ring yet, brother?"

"They've been together less than a month." Phoebe squawks in alarm, then, after a moment of consideration, "Though, that would be *so romantic*."

Mom gasps. "I still have your Grandma Phylis's engagement ring, Brooks! I suppose you'll want to get her something a little fancier—"

"Leave him alone," Dad huffs, the lone voice of reason. "He'll do it in his own time."

Everyone ignores him.

"She's going to be pregnant next year, I'm calling it. Oh

my gosh, their kids are going to be so cute. His hair and her eyes? Smart *and* athletic?"

Mom titters. "You kept the boys' baby things, didn't you? We'll have to go through it."

They don't need me for this discussion.

Nobody cares as I slide the last puzzle piece over to Beau and rise from the table and head for the stairs, filled with fond exasperation for all of them. They're excited, and I can't fault them for it. I'm excited too.

The attic is warm and quiet when I close the door behind me, lit only by the soft light of my old moon globe, which casts gentle shadows over the familiar room. Delta is already dressed in her pair of matching candy cane Christmas pajamas that Mom bought everyone, sitting at the edge of the bed with a magazine in her hands.

"I hope you have no plans on leaving me because they're still going to expect you at all family events regardless of our relationship status," I inform her dryly, unbuttoning my shirt.

Delta smirks. "Nope, I think I'll keep you, but *this*," she holds up the magazine, "is very shocking, Doctor Harrison."

I squint, and when I make out the cover of what she's holding, my stomach drops. "*Where did you find that?*" I cross the room to snatch it away from her, my face heating with embarrassment.

I haven't seen this in at least twenty years, though I recognize it immediately for the sole reason that I jerked off to the woman on those faded pages about five times a day during my early teen years. Before I convinced my parents to let me have a computer in my room, anyway.

Leaning back on her elbows, Delta laughs. "I was looking for another pillow. Imagine my surprise when I pulled one down from the closet and your adolescent spank bank hit me in the face."

"I'm only grateful it was you and not my mother." I

shudder at the thought and move to toss it in the trash, but Delta calls after me.

"It looks like page six was your favorite." Pausing, and curious despite myself, I flip it open. I'd folded the pages before six back so many times they're nearly falling out, and I instantly remember why. The woman in the faded picture is sprawled out across black satin sheets, her hands tied together above her head, and her legs spread wide with each ankle bound by an artfully knotted rope. She's not wearing a stitch of clothing, and I remember all the air going out of me when I saw it for the first time.

My body warms when I glance over my shoulder and find that Delta's eyes are still fixed on me.

She's lounging back on my adolescent bed, hair loose and tumbling messily around her shoulders. The hollow between her breasts is visible between the garish printed flannel. This situation shouldn't be sexy, but my body heats anyway.

"She kind of looks like me." Delta's voice has gone breathy and soft. I see her breath catch as I drop the magazine into the trash bin and stroll back to her, my footsteps muffled on the wide beam floors. "Am I your type, Doctor Harrison?"

The familiar, heady thrill of control fills me, and I let my head fall to the side, studying her. I had no plans of fucking her tonight, the Harrison family Christmas celebration was engrained in my memory as a thoroughly exhausting affair, and I anticipated escaping up here much sooner to refresh the headache medicine and sleep. This is a welcome change of pace.

I smirk. "Take your clothes off for me, baby. Let me check."

Delta obeys without hesitation and I lean against the wall, pretending her hands fumbling with the buttons doesn't turn me on more than anything else about this.

When she finally shoves down her pants and panties as

one, kicking them into a corner, I allow myself to move forward, raking my eyes over her bare skin. The chilly room has nothing to do with how her nipples have grown tight and pebbled, and when she squirms, pressing her thighs together, I don't have to touch her to know she's wet for me.

Humming thoughtfully, I close the last bit of distance between us and cup her breasts in my hands, loving the way her back arches forward for more, a soft, breathy moan catching in her throat.

I let my hands fall. "Lay back on the bed." She does as she's told, but her eyes follow my hands as they drop to my belt, opening it and slipping it out of the loops with practiced ease. "Sex—*getting off*—seemed so urgent back then. I was horny all the time." I muse as she squirms atop my old blue bedspread. In the dim lighting, it looks black, and her skin seems to glow in contrast, just like I'd once thought the woman in the magazine did.

She does look a bit like Delta now that I stop to think about it, though even the mind-numbing lust I felt for my fantasy woman back then doesn't begin to compare to how I feel about my dream come true spread out and squirming for me.

I'm going to devour her.

"Hold out your hands." It's so quiet that all I can hear is the sound of our ragged breathing as I step forward to loop my belt around her wrists, securing them together. She gasps when I pull them up, securing the belt to the headboard. "Is it like that for you, baby?" I ask, smoothing my hand over her beautiful body to rest just below her belly button. "Do you need it so badly? Are you aching right now?"

Her body trembles as she nods. "Yes. Yes, I-" But when I push my hand between her thighs, cupping her sex, her words turn to a guttural moan.

"*Shhh.*" I draw one finger through her slit, and my cock

throbs painfully at how incredibly wet she already is. "I'd love to help you feel better, but I don't think I can trust you to keep quiet, baby." To illustrate the point, I press a single finger into her tight hole and Delta throws her head back, mewling.

I have to bite back my smug smile.

Keeping my eyes on hers to make sure she's looking, I pull my hand back and suck her wetness off my finger, groaning at how good she tastes. "Brooks," Delta whines impatiently, but I don't miss the way her pupils have dilated and those gorgeous thighs have snapped back together, trying to give herself a tiny taste of the friction she's craving.

I take my time strolling around the bed, staring shamelessly down at her body. She's writhing with need and I've barely touched her.

Without another word, I cross to the closet and open it, pulling two wrinkled ties off the rack inside. I remember them both, artifacts from the same period in my life when I jerked myself off twice a day to the woman in that picture.

I'm careful not to let her see how hot this has me. Calmly, I sink to my knees beside the bed, knotting the end of the tie around one ankle, then pull it to the corner post of the bed. The other side is her bad hip, and I take my time kissing each of the small surgical scars I left on her skin, massaging the muscle. I keep my eyes on her face to check for even the tiniest flicker of pain as I tie that ankle, too.

"I'm going to put something in your mouth to help you stay quiet." I reach into the bedside table and find an old metal tin that must have once held lip balm. "Here." I press it into one of her hands before taking a second item from the drawer and laying it beside the pillow where she can't see. "If you're uncomfortable with any of this, I want you to tap it twice on the bed frame. Show me."

Tap. Tap.

Somewhere below us in the house, I hear the sound of

voices as my family heads to bed and lean forward to steal one last searing kiss from her breathless lips. Her vulnerability is intoxicating, but I'll stop this right now if she shows even the faintest hint of hesitation.

As though she knows what's going on in my head, Delta pleads, "*Please*, Brooks—" I growl, ripping away from her to pace over to the corner and extract her panties from the discarded pajama pants.

"Open," I order when I return to the bedside, my chest heaving and my cock pressing so hard against the fly of my jeans there's going to be a fucking indent. Delta obeys, and I press the balled-up panties past her lips, growling with satisfaction at the sight. As I straighten up, all I can do for a moment is stare down at her, willing myself to remember every detail of how she looks right now.

My heart is hammering as I round the edge of the bed and brace myself over her, smirking at the mess she's already made of herself. Her cunt is glistening in the dim light, wetness shining down to her inner thighs, and a little dark spot forming on the covers beneath her.

Fuck me, that's sexy.

She's perfect, completely fucking perfect, and she's mine.

"Such a hot, horny little thing. You'd do anything to have me put my cock in here, wouldn't you?" My thumb finds her stiff little nub, and I watch with no small amount of satisfaction as her body goes taut, shaking from that tiny contact. "Such a good little slut, letting me use you however I want."

Delta's eyes flutter shut, her muffled groan coming from behind the panties, and I bring my hand down in a sharp slap to the delicate skin of her inner thigh. She gasps, her body jolting, but that hand clutching the little tin doesn't move.

Fuck. Yes.

"Eyes on me. If I see them closed again, I won't go so easy on you."

Every filthy fantasy I've ever had is jockeying for position at the forefront of my imagination, and I'm not fighting it. She wants me like this, needs it even, and I'm positive I've never been so hard in my life. Pre-cum is leaking steadily from the engorged head of my cock and, needing some goddamn relief, I straighten up to strip down to my boxers.

"We're going to take this nice and slow," I tell her as I sit at the edge of the bed, biting and sucking at her breasts in between words. "We can't have everyone hear what a depraved little thing you are, letting me tie to you the bed on Christmas Eve."

Beneath me, Delta is shaking, straining against the bindings as I bring my hand back to her sopping wet cunt. "I'm going to make it hurt," I coo as I push two fingers inside her and fuck her slowly. "Tomorrow morning, you're going to sit next to the Christmas tree with a swollen cunt."

I pull my fingers free. Reaching over her to the side of the pillow, my hand closes around the item I took from the drawer, and Delta's eyes widen when she sees what it is.

Slowly, keeping my eyes on hers, I drag the old wooden ruler down the hollow between her breasts and over her stomach, finally pressing it flat to her pussy. "I'm going to hit you with this, baby. Hard enough to leave a mark. If you can take it, then I'll fuck you. Would you like that?"

Delta nods unevenly, her chest rising and falling in ragged pants.

She's wound so tight, squirming at even the lightest brush of my fingers, and the first *thwack* of the ruler against the sensitive skin of her inner thigh makes her hips jolt off the mattress. The blow wasn't hard, barely strong enough to color her skin, but I still look up to check she's still on board with what's happening.

Her pupils are wide, her lips parted over the panties stuffed inside, the picture of lust. She looks more erotic than any fantasy I've ever had, and my hand drifts down to caress the burning skin. "We're going to do ten. Do you remember how to get me to stop?"

Tap. Tap.

The first three lashes come in quick succession, hard enough to leave long, angry red marks behind, lined up one after another. After the third, I pause, finding Delta's hooded eyes. She's shaking, but from my vantage point, I can clearly see the wetness leaking from her swollen cunt. She fucking loves this, maybe even as much as I do.

"You're so sexy, baby." I slide the ruler up her thigh, taking care to press harder on the areas I marked, loving how she tries to jerk away only to find there's nowhere to go. She's bound and gagged by her panties, completely at my mercy.

"I don't know if I've ever seen you so wet." Dragging two fingers though her wetness, I find her entrance and push inside her hot, slick cunt, fucking her teasingly.

My dirty girl wants more. She wants to come, but I'm not ready to let that happen yet. Still, it's arousing as hell to get her close, and adorable to see her outraged expression when I pull back at the last minute. "You come when I want you to, and not a moment before." I suck her cream from my fingers and pick up the ruler again.

For her fourth, I bring it down harder than any of the first three, and Delta jolts, letting out a muffled cry of surprise. She wasn't expecting that, even so, that little tin stays clenched in her first.

The next two fall over the same spot, and my cock twitches at the tears streaming down either side of her face. "You're doing so well, baby," I coo, rubbing soothing circles over the angry red lines, taking care to brush the side of my hand against her soaked pussy. "Only four more to go, and then you'll get fucked. Do you want it nice and rough?"

She nods shakily in response, and I reward her with two fingers pressed over her clit, circling it lazily.

It's hypnotizing to see her grind and buck into my touch, the way her muscles go taught and her eyes beg me for relief. She wants to come so badly, *needs it*, but again, I pull away at the last minute.

The only way she's coming tonight is with me deep inside her, and she still has a little more to take before that happens.

"Four more."

I switch to the other thigh, mastering my need and hers at once. Every harsh *thwack* of the ruler brings more tears, more squirming, and muffled whines, but she's close to the end now and she wants her prize.

When there's only one left, I meet her eyes, pressing the flat strip of wood to her swollen cunt. The flash of fear tells me she knows exactly what I have planned, but the room is silent apart from our ragged breathing.

The slap of the ruler meeting her wet pussy is the most erotic noise I've ever heard, but the muffled cry and shallow, panicked breaths from the gorgeous woman tied up for me are better. "I'm so proud of you, baby." My hands move to her ankles, releasing them from their bindings.

Without giving her time to recover, I flip her over onto her belly, effortlessly arranging her so her ass is in the air and her face is resting on the pillows. I can see the red marks on her thighs and pussy. Later I'll rub them, kiss them, and treat her like the treasure she is, but right now I'm going to give her what she needs.

I shove my boxers down and kick them across the floor, crawling onto the bed behind her. Gripping myself roughly, I slide the head of my cock through her wet heat, aligning it with her clenching entrance. She's only taken my full length with quite a bit more prep than this, but I'm too impatient to hold back anything.

Fisting her hair in one hand and holding her hip steady with another, I punch forward, biting my tongue to keep myself from groaning in pleasure as I sheath myself inside her.

Blood rushes in my ears as Delta bucks beneath me, instinctively trying to find more space for the too-big cock she was just impaled with. It has to be uncomfortable, but she still makes no move to end this.

My dirty girl is wetter than usual, dripping from two almost-orgasms and how turned on she got from being bound, gagged, and spanked with the ruler I once used for physics homework.

"You're not getting anything I don't give you," I remind her as she tries to rock herself over my length, reaching down to spank her striped inner thigh threateningly.

Her cunt tightens over my shaft at the unexpected flair of pain, but she stops moving, her legs trembling against mine as I stay lodged inside her.

"Such a good girl." My hands tighten on her hips, and I begin. My thrusts are deep and measured, aimed right at her g-spot. Within a minute she's shaking all over again, and when I gather more of her wetness on my thumb, smoothing it in circles over her asshole, her orgasm is so intense it seems to last twice as long as usual.

I'm ridiculously turned on. My balls throb with how full they are, but she's going to take more before this is over.

Pulling out, I flip her back over and fall over her, ripping the panties out of her mouth and muffling her cry with a hungry kiss as I re-enter her poor, abused cunt. "Too much?" I grunt, my thrusts losing their controlled, steady pace.

Delta shakes her head, panting. "No, oh my god, no. I'm gonna come—" Her words are slurred, and I get it. I'm drunk on this too, floating on the power I just yielded and the pleasure of her body taking mine.

Somewhere in the back of my mind, I know we're being

too loud. If anyone is walking by the attic door, they'll know what we're up to, but I can't bring myself to give a shit.

I'm getting close, my orgasm is burning hot and urgent at the base of my spine, and this time I won't stop. Shoving a hand between our bodies, I find her swollen clit, pinching it.

Her orgasm is instantaneous and powerful, her inner walls clamping down on my shaft, milking the cum right out of me.

I groan into her damp neck, unable to do more than pump into her in shallow, jerky thrusts. "Fuck, oh god baby, I'm coming—"

"Inside me," Delta rasps, trembling beneath me as she comes down. Her hands find my face, and she begs, "please come inside me, *oh my god*, please Brooks—"

Reaching back to grab her thigh, I pull it high, driving my length deeper for one last thrust before I rip myself free, spurting over her mound and belly.

Fuck.

It's all I can do to hold myself up and not crush her as the energy drains out of me. It's messed up, but I'm pissed I didn't finish in her. I'm not sure if I've ever wanted anything so badly.

"*Christ*," I croak, collapsing on the edge of the little bed. "Baby, that was so good. Are you okay?" I reach behind me and find a piece of discarded clothing, using it to wipe my release off her skin.

Delta nods, curling close to me with a happy sigh as soon as I have her cleaned up. "I'm perfect."

Fuck yes, she is.

"Let me look at you." I force myself to sit back up, running my hand over the angry red marks slashed over her inner thighs. Her pussy is pink and puffy too, and her ass has my handprint on it.

Delta hums sleepily, her eyes fluttering shut. "Will I

survive, Doctor Harrison? If so, when am I fit to do that all over again?"

I chuckle, heart so fucking full, as I unfold the quilt at the end of the bed and pull it over our naked bodies. "You might be fit, but I'm not. Ask me in the morning."

Exhaustion is blurring the edges of my vision and on the pillow beside me, Delta's breathing is already slowing. I don't want tonight to be over, though. I trace my thumb over her full bottom lip, gazing at her in unrestrained awe.

"Are you still awake?"

Her lips curl, but she doesn't open her eyes. "Mostly."

I swallow the tightness in my throat, unable to stop looking at her even for a moment. I want to remember how she looks right now for the rest of my life. "Do you want to get married?"

One eye cracks open to meet mine, and the soft, lazy smile widens. "Really?"

"Yeah," I nod, my chest tight with emotion. This is a terrible proposal. I don't have a ring or a speech memorized about how much she means to me, but apparently Delta doesn't need any of that.

She nods, and her fingers weave through my own on the pillow between us. "Okay. I want to do it soon, though. Before spring."

"Okay," I agree, because that seems right. "We'll get married before spring."

Chapter 19

DELTA

Despite his assurances that he trusts his partner Jenna completely, Brooks still hovers at the side of the exam table, supervising and double checking everything she does and reviewing my brand-new scans over her shoulder.

"She's *my* patient now, Harrison." Doctor Walters reminds him waspishly when Brooks makes his third noise of disapproval in about sixty seconds. Holding out her hand, she helps me sit up. "Well, Delta, apart from having a pain-in-the-ass fiancé, I'd say you're looking pretty good."

Brooks clears his throat. "*Pretty good* is subjective."

Obviously deciding not to engage, Doctor Walters leans casually against the counter in the corner. "So, your pain is manageable, and it's been how long since your last injection again?"

"About six weeks," Brooks replies before I can even open my mouth, and I share an exasperated look with Doctor Walters.

Looking back at the X-rays on the wall, my new doctor hums thoughtfully. "I think we're in the watch-and-wait stage, then. We'll continue with your inflammation management, which should keep you comfortable as long as you're not training full time. Any plans to return to snowboarding?"

My mind drifts to the boxes of my stuff in our garage and I shake my head. "Maybe for fun with my brothers, but no professional training, no."

Doctor Walters nods approvingly before turning to Brooks. "Thoughts, Harrison? Since I'm sure you have them."

Brooks sighs, his focused, clinical doctor frown in place. "I think she's right, Delta. Your pain is manageable, your condition isn't deteriorating. I do believe a hip replacement is inevitable, but if you keep up with your physical therapy, there's no reason we can't put it off for a few years at least."

My heart soars, and I reach out to take Brooks' hand, unable to contain my smile. "No surgery?"

The two surgeons in the room nod decisively, and Brooks smiles hugely, the corners of his eyes creasing. "No surgery."

* * *

We barely make it home.

The moment we get in the car outside his office, I squeal, lunging over the center console to shower kisses over Brooks' smiling cheek. "Are you happy?" he laughs as we pull out of the parking lot, reaching over to squeeze my thigh.

I nod, beaming. I'd been so nervous before this appointment, terrified Doctor Walters would tell me that surgery was the only option or that I would need to put everything on pause for a while longer. I *feel* great, but the possibility that my condition hasn't improved as much as I thought has been a dark cloud over my head for weeks.

No more.

My body, my life, they're all mine, and I know the first thing I want to do with them.

As usual, Brooks must be able to read my mind because his grip tightens on my leg. "Do you want to get lunch?" His voice is strained, like he's forcing himself to be a good fiancé and not pull over to the side of the road and give me what we've both wanted for weeks.

I shake my head, parting my thighs in wordless invitation. His hand moves between them, cupping my already-throbbing pussy through my leggings.

Brooks lets out his breath in a long hiss, rubbing me steadily. "Tell me what you want me to do to you when we get home."

Whimpering, I arch my back and spread my legs wider, even if in the back of my mind I know he won't allow it.

Sure enough, I gasp when Brooks' hand comes down to give my throbbing clit a firm spank. "Naughty girl." His free hand tightens on the steering wheel. "Tell me. Now."

His eyes are on the road, and I'd almost think he was unaffected if it weren't for the intimidating ridge of his cock pressing against his jeans.

Too busy perving on him, I squeal when he spanks my pussy again, sharper than before. "I asked you a question, Delta."

I shudder, wishing he would drive faster. "I want—I want you to fuck me. I want you to come inside me."

Brooks grunts his approval at this response and rewards me by resuming the slow, measured strokes over the seam of my leggings.

My head drops back against the headrest, and my eyes flutter shut, allowing myself to enjoy his touch. We're on a public street. Anyone who looked into the car for too long would notice Brooks' muscular arm stretched over into my lap and my lips parted in a moan. I can't bring myself to care.

"That's it. Don't be shy." His quiet praise makes me quake

in my seat, arching against the seatbelt desperately. "Let's get that tight little pussy ready for me."

My eyes snap open when Brooks pulls his hand away for a fraction of a second, my cry of protest turning to a moan of pleasure when he shoves it beneath my leggings and panties, coming in direct contact with my swollen sex. He already fucked me in the shower this morning, but despite me begging for it, he came all over my ass instead.

"Put your foot up on the dashboard, yeah, like that." I do as he says, opening myself up for him. Two long fingers shove deep inside me, hard enough to make me jerk back instinctively from the sharp stretch. There's nowhere to go, though, and all I can do is clutch the seat as he scissors his fingers, stretching me open from the inside out. The heel of his palm is grinding relentlessly over my clit, and faster than I would have thought possible, I find myself coming with a loud cry.

Brooks pulls his hand free just as he turns into the driveway, skidding to a halt and turning the keys with the same hand that's still shiny with my release.

The silence in the car is ringing in my ears as he looks over at me, jaw tight and eyes darker than I've ever seen them. "Get in the house, Delta."

I fumble with my seatbelt, and wrench the handle open in seconds. Brooks is striding around the car to my side before I've even gotten to my feet.

His arm wraps possessively around my waist as we rush toward the house. The dogs are thankfully at doggy daycare today, so there are no interruptions when we get inside, almost tripping over the mat in our haste.

Brooks kicks the door closed behind him and then we're on each other, kissing frantically in the center of the entryway, clawing at each other's clothes without making any real progress.

I love it like this, when I feel his tightly held control slip, and he's just as feral for me as I am for him.

"Off," he snarls, finally wrenching himself off me to yank my shirt over my head. My bra follows, and Brooks descends on my breasts, kissing, biting, and sucking right in the middle of the room while his hands fight to get my leggings and panties down my legs.

"Holy shit," I gasp, clutching his hair as he pushes two fingers roughly into me again, sending me to the tips of my toes. "I'm ready. I'm so ready, Brooks. I want you. *Please*!"

"Shhh." He stands, walking us back toward the nearest flat surface, which is the couch. "I'll give you what you need, baby. I need it too."

I fall back onto cushions, legs spread wantonly, and Brooks stares down at me as he unbuttons his jeans, shoving them down just enough to free his thick cock.

God, he's so hot.

I reach for him and he obliges, leaning over to kiss me hungrily.

"You're sure?" he asks again when we break apart, though his eyes don't move from my pussy, like he's transfixed by the effect he's had on me. We've been having sex every day, twice some days, and it sends a hot thrill through me that he still wants me so desperately.

"I'm sure," I whisper, suddenly mesmerized too as he grips his cock, stroking it up and down, the tendons in his arms straining.

I expect him to fuck me like this, but he surprises me. Straightening up, he turns, sinking onto the cushion next to me and I follow instantly, scrambling to swing a leg over his lap.

He smirks. "You want my cum, baby?" A hand comes down firmly on my ass. "Come and get it."

We've somehow never done it like this before, and my

stomach flips with nerves as I wrap my hand around the base of his cock. He's hot and throbbing in my hand, and I stare down between us as I guide his tip to my entrance.

My lips part in a silent cry as I push down, impaling myself on his length.

It doesn't seem to matter how often we're together, or how much time he spends getting me ready. There's always an edge of pain to Brooks filling me. On days like today, when he's already fucked me once and I haven't had time to recover, it hurts a little extra.

My inner walls are burning and it feels like he's pressing against the deepest part of me. For a moment, all I can do is pant and squirm, struggling to adjust.

"You're okay," Brooks coos, kissing me tenderly. His jaw is strained and I can tell he wants to take over, but he still doesn't move, waiting for me to get to work. "Is it too deep, baby?" One warm hand moves to rub comforting circles over my back when I nod shakily. "You want my cum there, don't you?"

He's said the magic words.

Another wave of arousal coats his length, and we both moan as, slowly, I rise onto my knees. When just the head of his cock is left inside me, I drop down again, sucking in an unsteady breath as he hits bottom all over again.

"There you go," Brooks murmurs approvingly when I find my rhythm, rolling my hips so my clit grinds against his pubic bone. His eyes are on the space between us, watching me fuck him. "Such a good girl, bouncing up and down on my cock. You took it so rough earlier, too."

I moan in response. Clutching his shoulders for leverage as I begin riding him faster.

I'm going to come soon. Pleasure and pain are burning me up from the inside out, coursing through my veins and amplifying our every movement. Brooks must be getting close too, because he's lifting his hips now, fucking me from below.

"Come in me," I plead. "Please—"

"I'm going to, fuck—" His arms lock around me, holding me in place as he loses the battle to let me do all the work. My legs are spread wide and open, unable to do more than take the frantic thrusts he drives up into my pussy.

We're both on the edge, and when I break, my inner walls clamping down on his shaft, Brooks follows. He pulls me down until my ass is in his lap and I'm filled completely, his cock twitching deep inside me.

Oh my god.

Holy crap.

The moment his body relaxes, the strain of pleasure gone from his face, Brooks pulls me close. "We're doing that again in about half an hour," he grunts as I curl into his warmth, his cock still inside me, half-hard.

No objections here.

"You're going to be stuck with me," I giggle, playing with his chest hair.

Brooks snorts. "I think I've made it clear I'm down for that. I do have a question, though, about something I've been wondering about for a while."

His tone is so serious that I sit back to look at him, instantly worried. "What is it?"

Running both hands up my legs to settle on my hips, Brooks smiles wryly. "Why did you tip me off about River the day we met? I'd barely said anything to you."

It's been three years since that day. He's literally inside me right now, possibly getting me pregnant as we speak. He asked me to marry him a few days ago, but I'm somehow still embarrassed. "Seriously? You're going to make me say it?"

"Spell it out for me." His eyebrows arch expectantly.

I press my lips together to keep myself from laughing. His ego will be unbearable after hearing this. "I thought you were really hot."

Brooks' expression flickers in genuine surprise. *"That's it?"*

"Yup." I twine my arms around his neck. *"Really, really* hot."

"But—" He splutters, looking outraged. "You were a professional athlete. You shouldn't have been making medical decisions based on being attracted to a doctor."

"Don't worry, I googled you first and knew you were competent, but I'll remember that for next time." I laugh, pulling off him and climbing unsteadily to my feet.

His cum is dripping down my inner thigh, but when I go to reach for a tissue, Brooks' hands clamp down on my hips. My stomach flips when he uses two fingers to gather it up, pushing it back inside me.

I tremble.

"Are you angry with me for objectifying you?"

In response, my former doctor tugs me back onto the couch. I let him move my body how he wants it, until I'm lying flat, my hips raised on his lap. *Oh.* So we're *really* trying to get me pregnant.

He smirks down at me, one big hand spread over my lower belly. "I'll get over it. We have something to do before I go back to work tomorrow."

* * *

Brooks seems to care a lot more about my engagement ring than I do. He gives me an absolutely disgusted look when I tell the bemused saleswoman we'll take the first one she shows us, and proceeds to begin an in-depth discussion with her on diamond cut and clarity.

I wander off, staring into the brightly lit cases. The store is empty except for us, as apparently not a lot of people go shopping for fine jewelry during their lunch break the Monday after Christmas.

A little TV on in the corner catches my eye for a second and I do a double take, pierced by a dull stab of shock as I realize what's playing.

Pre-game commentary for the Men's XT Games.

Brooks and I were planning to watch Lake and Bay compete later, and I'd called both of them this morning before my appointment to wish them luck, I'd obviously known it was today but it's jarring to observe from the outside for the first time.

The camera pans over the slopestyle course as the commentator explains some elements. Athletes are warming up in the background. When the shot changes to a reporter, a man at the edge of the screen catches my eye, and my stomach drops.

My father.

River is talking to a man on a snowboard at the bottom of the hill, his arms crossed and brow furrowed in concentration.

I know that face well, I saw it before every significant event of my life. I was determined to set aside my feelings about Dad, Bay and the reporter's request until after my brothers returned from Utah. I'm not sure what makes me do it, but as I watch Dad talk, I pull out my phone.

Running into him on my birthday is still the only time I've spoken to him since immediately before the accident. I changed my number after discovering Brooks had been not-so-mysteriously blocked, and it's been a savage little comfort to know that he couldn't get ahold of me.

I liked having that power over him. I liked being the one in control for once. When I pull my phone out and hit his contact, though, it's without hesitation.

When it rings once, it occurs to me he probably won't pick up for an unknown number, hours before a major competition. To my surprise, though, I watch as Dad pulls out his phone and frowns at the screen. After what feels like an age, he brings it to his ear.

"Hello?"

My hand presses over the brand-new ache in the center of my chest. "Hi, Dad."

On the TV, I see his face register shock. "DJ." He clears his throat, brow furrowed in confusion. "How, *ah*, how are you kid?" His snowboarder leaves, and then it's just him, standing in a line of other coaches and competitors, staring at the snow.

"Good. Amazing, actually." I glance over my shoulder to where Brooks is still absorbed in his conversation with the saleswoman. "I'm picking out my engagement ring."

River is quiet for a moment. "You're marrying the doctor, huh?" His tone isn't cold or disapproving, just tired.

I smile to myself. "Yeah. I'm marrying the doctor."

Neither of us speaks, and in the background I can hear the familiar sounds of a chaotic mountain. I would have been there right now, likely standing beside Dad to cheer on Lake and Bay. The women's competition isn't until next weekend, and I'd have been a ball of nerves, analyzing every inch of the course for when it was my turn.

I never thought I would be thankful for my fucked-up hip.

He's not going to break the silence, so I ask the question that's been on my mind for most of my life. "I wanted to know if you have any regrets."

Dad scrubs a hand over his beard, brow furrowed. "Regrets?"

"About me," I clarify, my throat tightening. "The way I was raised. *Trained.*" I'm not looking for an apology, or even an admission that he fucked up. It's too late for us. He wanted me to be a snowboarder before being his daughter, and now I can't be either.

I wouldn't even know how to begin having a relationship with my father outside that world, but I need to know if this man is capable of growth. I need to know if he learned from what happened to me.

Almost like he can sense my eyes on him from hundreds of miles away, Dad turns toward the camera. There are so many people milling around that I keep losing sight of him for seconds at a time, but then the crowd clears and there he is, silent and staring off into the distance.

"I'm sure you wish I was different. Hell, maybe I should have been, but go back and watch your old competitions, DJ. You were remarkable. That kind of talent doesn't happen every day." And even from this far away, I can see it, the wild, obsessive glint in his eyes that sends a bitter chill down my spine.

He doesn't answer the question, not really, but I realize I don't need him to. I know for sure now that I was never as valuable to him as all that talent.

"Okay," I reply, turning away from the TV. "Thanks, Dad. Good luck today."

"DJ—" He begins, then pauses, clearing his throat. "I could open a coaching job for you. If you wanted to come back."

I watch Brooks examine a tray of rings, his lips turned down in concentration like this is the most important decision of his life.

"No, thanks." I lean against the display counter, something settling inside me. "I've got to run. Bye, Dad."

I hang up before he can say another word.

The email from the USSA is still in my inbox, dated seven weeks ago. I screenshot it and open the contact I saved for Annie, the reporter.

My thumb hovers over the 'send' button for a full five seconds before I finally press it.

I didn't do it for me, nor did I expect it to bring me any

relief. Once I do, though, it's like a million pounds have been lifted from my shoulders all at once.

If I wanted to be free, I had to send that email, and now I have.

"Delta?" Brooks calls, and I shove my phone into my pocket, crossing the store to his side. The ring he's holding doesn't have a diamond at all. It's made of delicate, braided gold, and nestled in the tiny prongs is a dark blue sapphire the size of one of my nails. My breath hitches as he slips it onto my finger, and we stare down at it together. "What do you think?"

I nod, my eyes burning. "This one."

He chuckles, kissing my forehead and tucking me into his side while I admire it. "You're not just saying that so we can leave?"

"No." I look up at him, beaming. "It's perfect. Don't you think?"

"That one has a matching wedding band." The saleswoman chips in and hurries off to get it, leaving us alone.

"I called my dad," I tell Brooks under my breath, tilting my hand so the ring catches the light from the store windows. It's *so pretty*. "I needed to hear it from him, that he doesn't regret his actions."

Brooks' hand tightens on my waist, pulling me closer, as though he can protect me from the past. "And did you get your answer?"

Lifting my face to meet his eyes, I nod. I'm not mad at River. I'm sad for him, because I'm positive he's felt nothing close to what I do right now. The only thing my father has ever loved unconditionally is snowboarding, and a sport will never give him the things Brooks does just by looking at me.

Even when he thought there would be nothing more than friendship between us, even when he was sure the best thing for me wasn't him, there was never a time when he didn't put me first.

"I did." I smile, loving the unfamiliar weight of the ring on my finger. "Can we get this one?"

Brooks agrees instantly, slapping his credit card on the glass display case as soon as the saleswoman comes back.

"I thought you looked familiar," she tells me a few minutes later as she double checks the fit of the ring. "You're Delta Jacobs, right? The snowboarder?"

"Not so much, lately," I reply with a wry smile, and the woman's eyes widen in understanding.

"Oh, I heard about that! You got hurt, right? How are you doing?"

I have to smile. "Oh, great. I got really lucky. My doctor was super invested in my recovery. Incredibly attentive."

Brooks' chest shakes with silent laughter as she goes to charge his card and wrap up the matching wedding bands we picked out. "I'm glad to hear it worked out for you, considering you chose your doctor on looks alone."

"Are you complaining?"

He drags me into his chest, kissing me so deeply it makes my knees weak. Pulling back, I can tell he's holding back a smile as he leans down to murmur in my ear, "Never again."

Epilogue

BROOKS

5 YEARS LATER

"And that does it, folks, Bay Jacobs has officially taken the gold, a first for the oldest member of Team USA—"

A chorus of screaming and ecstatic laughter drowns the rest of the announcer's words out, and I turn to watch my wife and brother-in-law jump up and down, waving their little flags and screaming their support of their older brother. In my arms, my son covers his ears, wrinkling his nose at the enthusiastic display from his mother and uncle.

At just over four years old, Harbor Jacobs-Harrison is already proving to have inherited much more of Delta than me. Our son is cheeky and determined, with the same bright gray eyes and pouty lips as his mother. Our daughter, Spring, who is sound asleep in a sling on Delta's chest, completely unaffected by the commotion, clearly takes after me.

"Mama!" Harbor squawks his protest, looking at me with his little eyebrows raised in alarm.

"Mama is excited." I laugh, pulling him close and kissing his dark curls. "Uncle Bay is the winner!"

"Uncle Bay?" Harbor frowns, looking around the crowded section where the friends and family members of team members are gathered, scanning the crowd for his favorite uncle.

Conspicuously absent from our group is River. His relationship with my wife and her brothers hasn't improved over the years.

All three of them have their own resentments and trauma from their years as River's trophy children, and he's too wrapped up in his shit to put much effort into repairing the damage. None of them are holding their breath waiting for it.

A few months after Delta and I got married, a national magazine published a very well-read exposé about corruption in the USSA, using River as a case study for everything wrong with the system. The article was littered with stories of promising athletes who trained too hard, pushed through pain they should have been treating, and lost everything.

Notably among them was his own daughter.

Delta declined to comment. She was pregnant by then and working on publishing her first cookbook, too content in her life out of the spotlight to even consider stepping back into it.

Bay had no such qualms, and six months after the accident that ended his sister's career, he gave a sit-down interview that sent waves through the professional snowboarding community. If I'd known half of what he told the world when my wife was still training, I would have fought a hell of a lot harder to get her out, a hell of a lot sooner.

At the thought, I reach over and wrap an arm around Delta's shoulders, leaning down to kiss the top of her head. Even through several puffy winter jackets and a baby sling, the feeling of her beautiful curves is enough to send heat through my body.

"Have something on your mind, Doctor Harrison?" Delta asks, looking cute as hell as she smirks up at me.

A figure breaks away from the crowd of athletes a hundred yards away and jogs right for us, his smile visible even from here.

"Uncle Bay!" Harbor squeals, spotting him and stretching his arms over the metal partition as Bay approaches to take him from me.

"Congratulations!" I laugh, gripping his shoulder as Delta and Lake engulf Bay in a hug, Harbor's face sticking out of the mess of jacketed arms. I can see media cameras zooming in on the scene, eager for a clip of the legendary Jacobs siblings celebrating Bay's triumph.

"Can you believe it?" Delta cries, wiping her eyes when Bay hands back our son and heads off to the podium for his big moment.

She got back on a snowboard for the first time, since she retired, only a few months ago. Lake and Bay were over at our house, showing the kids a video of their mama's gold medal event and Harbor had excitedly asked Delta if he could do that too.

It was a tense moment, and Delta's eyes had flown to mine, glimmering with a hint of the old pain I once saw in them far too often.

The next day, when I got home from work, I found Lake standing on the deck with Spring in his arms, looking down at two figures wearing snowboards on the snow-covered back hill. I stood with them for a long time, my heart in my throat as Delta taught our son to snowboard. They were out there for over an hour, and when Harbor started sniffing that he'd had enough, Delta picked him up and headed right back to the house. No questions asked.

Whenever I've thought I couldn't possibly love her more, my wife finds a way to prove me wrong.

"What?" Delta elbows me, wiping her eyes again, "Don't laugh. I know I'm a sap, I'm just so proud of him."

I shake my head, chuckling. "I love you, that's all." She sighs, leaning her head against my shoulder as we watch Bay step up on the podium to accept his medal, the crowd roaring around us. It's a big moment for any athlete, but it might be especially big for my brother-in-law and I'm fucking proud of him too.

"You know, you were pregnant the last time you cried this much," I muse, leaning down so only Delta can hear. Her head whips back around to look at me, eyes huge. "Oh no. No way. Spring isn't even one!"

I chuckle. "Just pointing it out." But I can tell she's thinking over the last few weeks, trying to remember when her period is due.

Four days ago, but I'm going to let her realize that on her own.

It's been a chaotic week, traveling overseas with the kids to see Bay compete, and her being late could be put down to stress. It isn't, though. It's down to the first weekend we spent away from the kids, locked in a hotel room to celebrate our anniversary. Delta shakes her head in disbelief, but her eyes are sparkling and she's fighting a smile.

"We're insane. I can't believe this." I pull her close again, wishing there were words strong enough to tell her what she means to me, or how grateful I am for her. I was alone once, and there are days when I can't fight off the nagging worry that I will be again, that all the love and joy in my life will all turn out to be a dream. It isn't though, this is my life, my family, and I'll spend the rest of my life trying to be worthy of every gift Delta has given me.

"We are insane." I'm beaming, unable to wipe the grin off my face for even a second as I hold my family close. "There are only so many bodies of water that make appropriate baby names."

Want more of Brooks and Delta?

Check out this sweet & (very) spicy bonus epilogue, set 18 months after the end of this story.

Thank You

Thank you for reading In Pieces!

If you have a moment, *please* **consider leaving a rating or review for the book.** Feedback is so important to me and is vital in helping new readers find my work!

Want to stay updated on my releases, events, free book promos and what I'm working on?

- **Subscribe** to my newsletter @ www.authorcleowhite.com
- Buy **signed books** directly from me through Beventi
- **Follow me** *@authorcleowhite* on Instagram, Tiktok, Goodreads, Pinterest or Facebook
- Join my Facebook **reading group** to connect with me and make like-minded reader friends – Cleo's Cliterature Collective

Thank you again!
    xo,
    Cleo

Cleo White's affinity for all things dramatic, and hopelessly romantic began the day she was born, which happened to be in the middle of a record-breaking snowstorm on Valentine's Day. Her love of literature came soon after, and she spent the better part of her childhood with both a book and a notebook full of unfinished stories in hand. Later in life, she found a love of writing spicy books with complicated characters and dysfunctional family drama. Cleo currently lives in Vermont with her husband and two daughters. When not writing, she can be found hiking, gardening, painting, and consuming excessive quantities of caffeine.